MS. BITCH

FINDING HAPPINESS IS THE BEST REVENGE.

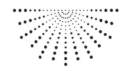

TRICIA O'MALLEY

LOVEWRITE PUBLISHING

Ms. Bitch

Editor(s):
Christina Boys
Elayne Morgan

TO ALAN – TOGETHER WE DIVE INTO LIFE, OUR PATHS FOREVER ENTWINED, MY HEART ALWAYS YOURS.

It's a semi-true story
Believe it or not
I made up a few things
And there's some I forgot
But the life and the telling
Are both real to me
And they run like the rain
All the way to the sea...
— Jimmy Buffett

CHAPTER ONE

"You quit your job?" Tess pushed back from her desk to see her husband, Gabe, beaming at her as though he'd just won the lottery.

"I did! You know I've been wanting to for a while now, babe." Gabe wrapped his arms around Tess, swinging her into a bouncy two-step.

"Um, not really, no. In the abstract, yes, for when we talked about moving to Colorado, but not like, you know, *now*." Tess's mind whirled as quickly as Gabe was moving her across the room. Their rescue bulldogs, Red and Ringo, joined in the dance at their feet.

"It just seemed like a good time," Gabe said. "Your books are doing so well, and I have a nice 401k. I think we'll be fine."

"But... why now? Wouldn't it have been better for you to leave once we actually decided to move? I mean, we haven't even explored any of the areas we think we might like to live, yet. What if we decide to stay here?" Tess asked, trying to slow Gabe down without dampening his exuberance.

She hadn't seen him this bubbly in a while – manic almost – and was trying to enjoy his mood while tamping down on the panic that threatened to choke her. Being thrust into the sole breadwinner position with zero discussion was not something she'd put on her agenda to contemplate this afternoon. Gabe danced her back over to her desk, leaning her back against it to kiss her deeply, and then peeked over her shoulder at her computer.

"Is that for our trip to New Orleans? You should definitely book those concert tickets. Now, we can go and be carefree and relax." Gabe nuzzled into her neck as he held her close.

Tess breathed in his familiar scent, letting him hold her there, and tried to relax into the moment. He'd been stressing over accounts at work, and putting in extra hours at the gym to deal with it for months now. When she'd tried to talk to him about it, he'd nearly bitten her head off more than a time or two. Maybe he did need this change—for both their sakes. At least he might be in a better mood for their trip next week to New Orleans. They'd planned it to celebrate their fifth anniversary, and she'd hoped it would bring him out of his funk and reconnect them.

Tess began calculating how much money they had in their bank accounts, and what would need to be set aside as a safety net now that they couldn't count on Gabe's salary.

"Okay, babe, I'll book the concert tickets. It'll be great. We could use some fun," Tess said, and watched as Gabe bounced away, pausing to tussle with the delighted dogs, before whistling his way downstairs.

The telltale clink of ice cubes hitting a glass and the squeak of the door on the liquor cabinet told Tess just how Gabe planned to celebrate. Turning, she stared out the window where they'd just had a brand-new cedar fence installed around their beautiful yard, a cost that she'd been willing to spend to keep her dogs safe. It had been her one condition about buying this house with Gabe, and though taking out a home equity loan had bothered her, she'd gone along with it to renovate the house.

Despite herself, she'd gotten caught up in the fun of it and they'd overhauled the kitchen, added a deck to the backyard, and made improvements to Gabe's man-room in the basement. All while they'd still talked about moving to Colorado. Tess shook her head and wondered at their decision-making, but a part of her never really thought they'd make the move out of Illinois. It had been somewhat of a pipe dream for so long, one of those 'what-ifs' they always talked about. She'd been shocked when Gabe had agreed to book a trip to Colorado that spring to explore neighborhoods. Now, she contemplated what her life would be like with Gabe at home every day, and her nails dug into her palms. She loved her husband, but she also loved being able to focus on her work at home uninterrupted.

"Tess, come have a drink with me," Gabe called up the stairs, and Tess glanced back to where she'd planned to work on a chapter for her next novel. "We should celebrate – this is the start of a new life for us."

A WEEK LATER, Tess stood beside Gabe in the sparkling marble foyer of their favorite hotel in New Orleans, admiring the graceful arches and high ceilings that added to the old-world charm.

"Welcome back, Mr. and Mrs. Campbell." The woman at the front desk beamed at them, sliding keys across the gleaming wood counter to Gabe. "And, may I say? Happy anniversary."

"Thank you," Tess said, smiling at the woman before following Gabe to the elevator. She loved coming here. There was nothing like escaping to another place, and the pulse of this city never ceased to excite her. Not to mention the location of the hotel was fantastic.

"Ta-da," Gabe proclaimed, coming to stop at the end of a long hallway, carpeted with the traditional fleur-de-lis pattern. He held his hands up to the door with a gilded sign proclaiming it to be the Tennessee Williams suite.

"Gabe! Did you upgrade us? I didn't reserve us a suite." Delighted at his forethought, she pulled out her phone to take a picture of the door. "Tennessee Williams! My readers are going to love this!"

"No," Gabe said, his tone sharp as he grabbed the phone from her hands. "I don't want you posting anything publicly about this trip."

"What... why? It's just a suite name. It's a famous author, I'm sure my readers would like it."

"I said no. You know I don't like it when you post about me on your author page. This trip is private. That's non-negotiable." Gabe pushed the door open to reveal a large suite, with floor-to-ceiling windows, a wrap-around balcony, and a huge seating area with a green velvet sofa and a bookcase packed with vintage books. "I want this to be just between us, Tess. This is our time."

Tess wanted to protest that she rarely posted anything about Gabe publicly, but he was already drawing her into the suite. She let the moment go to exclaim over the room as he threw the balcony doors open, letting in the full cacophony of New Orleans, and Tess joined him to look down at the people meandering the street below.

"Oh, look! A second-line." Tess smiled down at where a bride in a vintage-style gown and a groom with bright blue shoes paraded their way down the street behind a brass band.

The first time they'd visited New Orleans together, they'd jumped up from their meal and had run outside to see the parade dance by. Not only had it been exciting, but that moment turned out to be what inspired them to return to the French Quarter to get married. "Remember ours? It was so much fun!" She leaned into him, wishing he'd put his arm around her.

"Right? Time for drinks." Gabe barely glanced at the couple who pirouetted below them, lost in their bliss. Tess wondered if she'd looked that happy on their wedding day. She'd been so nervous that the day had flown by in a flash.

Reluctantly, she followed Gabe inside where he handed her a drink from the mini bar – the first of many they'd have that weekend. In New Orleans, cocktails were abundant.

The following day, they poked around the French Quarter, popping into antique jewelry shops until Gabe could find a necklace he liked for her as a memento of their anniversary. It was her credit card that paid for it, but Tess pushed the annoyance away, reminding herself that finances blend together after marriage. The biggest surprise came that evening when Gabe presented her with a private dinner on the balcony of their suite, complete with flowers and even more gifts – diamonds this time. Tess wanted to enjoy the romance, but she couldn't help desperately wondering who the person sitting across from her was. It was like watching someone tick off all the boxes on the checklist: flowers? Check. Diamonds? Check. Fancy surprise dinner on a private balcony? Check. Yet he hadn't touched her since they'd arrived.

Pasting a smile on her face, Tess chattered her way through dinner, and kept the conversation going on the walk to the Preservation Hall's famous jazz concert. As they stood in line to wait, a woman in front of them turned and glanced at Tess's sparkly dress, something she'd bought special for the occasion, hoping Gabe would think she looked sexy for their anniversary.

"Smashing dress, darling," the woman said, and Tess smiled her thanks before quickly glancing at Gabe to see if he would think the same. Instead, he downed the drink he'd brought on the walk with them and tossed the cup in a nearby garbage container. Ignoring her misgivings, Tess found their seats, and for the next hour, had the first moments of pure joy on this trip since they'd arrived. They sat on an unforgiving wooden school bench, a few feet from an old-timey jazz band, and listened as the band poured their souls into their music. Tess was delighted.

"What a great band! I'm so glad we went this time," Tess exclaimed after the concert while she waited at the bar for Gabe to order drinks for the walk home. She didn't even want a drink – she was riding high on the excitement of the show – but took the one he handed her nonetheless.

"They had such a funky vibe," Gabe agreed, as they wound their way back to the hotel. "I love how they all dressed the part too. It'd be cool to sit in a pub and hear their stories."

"Totally." Tess was already dreaming up characters around the musicians. "Their faces had so much personality, too. But the music... it really just kind of hit you in your soul."

Gabe let them into the suite and strode into the bedroom where he stripped and wrapped himself in a robe, before moving to the mini-fridge where he'd stored a bottle. Tess put her still-full drink on the table, and dug in her luggage before stepping to the bathroom.

"I'll just be a minute."

In the bathroom, Tess examined her hair and make-up as she slithered into a little red teddy she'd bought just for tonight, hoping that some hot anniversary sex would bring them closer again. Lately, she'd felt like the supporting role in Gabe's life, but never the leading.

"Hey," Tess said, standing in the doorway and posing for him. Gabe lay on the bed, wrapped in his robe, scrolling his phone.

"Oh, hey," Gabe said, and the look that crossed his face wasn't a particularly happy one – more like a grimace, if Tess was honest with herself. She knew what he was going to say before the words even came out of his mouth. "Babe, I can't tonight. I ate way too much food at dinner. Can we just chill instead?"

"Of course," Tess said lightly, so as not to cause a fight. She reached behind her to pull the fluffy white robe from the door. "I'm just going to sit on the balcony for a bit then."

"Sure." Gabe didn't look up as he typed on his phone. Tess picked up her Kindle and unhinged the swinging balcony door to sit where they'd had dinner earlier that evening. The melody of the city embraced her, and Tess glanced back over her shoulder, hoping Gabe would join her. Instead, she could just see his face, alight in the glow of his phone, a smug smile across his handsome features as he continued to type rapidly, a bottle of whiskey on the side table.

Tess blinked back tears as she turned away, burying herself in her book, forcing the questions down for another day.

CHAPTER TWO

He looked so happy in the photo. Tess sat, staring numbly at the computer screen in front of her where Gabe's Facebook Messenger sat wide open, the picture of her husband – naked in bed, his arms wrapped around a woman too young to know the difference between lust and love – searing into her retinas. Tess knew that look on his face – she'd seen it time and again after he'd satisfied himself with her body – a smile playing on his lips while she waited for him to come back from the bathroom with a tissue, stuck in the universally awkward situation that lovers often find themselves in.

Tess's hands trembled as she opened another browser window and slowly typed in the web address of their bank. The accounts popped onto the screen – at least the accounts they shared – and the tightness that had banded her chest eased a bit as she saw that all looked to be normal. The money in the shared account was mainly hers, as it had now been several months since Gabe had quit his job and embarked on a steady regimen of going to the gym twice a day and drinking too much.

Tess hesitated, her eyes flashing back to the picture on the screen in front of her, taking in the smug satisfaction on Gabe's handsome face, before calmly emptying their shared bank account and moving all the money to hers. She waited, taking one shuddering breath after another, to see if something would happen – anything – but only a blast of wind at the window and a silent house answered. What did she think would happen? Her phone would explode with angry texts or sirens would go off? It wasn't like she was doing anything illegal. Or immoral.

Her mind flashed to just days before, when she'd lain awake, watching the light from Gabe's phone blink, flashing repeatedly across the ceiling, incessantly pounding its message into Tess's brain. Gabe slept on, not a care in the world, while the blinking light refused to be ignored, his phone all but screaming at Tess.

Wake up, you fucking moron.

She'd slid from the covers, the air cool on her clammy skin, and padded around the bed. Tess had hesitated as she stood over Gabe, watching him sleep so peacefully, and wondered again if she was being paranoid. Perhaps she'd been imagining his distance from her lately. Her hand had hovered over the phone for a moment before she'd made up her mind and snatched it from the table. Racing around the bed, Tess had caught her toe on a nightstand as she headed for the bathroom, and unable to control the curse that shot from her mouth, she'd hobbled her way to the bathroom door.

But not in time.

Gabe had been on her in seconds, slamming her into the tiled wall of the bathroom as carelessly as if she were one of his sagging intramural football buddies, wrenching the phone from her hand before she'd had time to recover from the pain that still ratcheted up her leg from her stubbed toe. The crack of her head against the cold tile of the wall echoed the crack in her heart and she watched, astounded, as tears filled Gabe's eyes. He was crying?

"Oh, baby. Stop this. You know I don't want you on my phone. We've promised to trust each other. Don't do this."

He'd gone back to bed then, never asking her if she was okay, his phone tucked beneath his pillow. Asleep in moments, Gabe had acted like nothing had happened the next day.

Now Tess stared at the computer screen, her brain working in overdrive as she tried to process all the ways their lives were intertwined. Opening another browser, she systematically began to change the passwords to all her business accounts, a little zing of power zipping through her at each change she made. *Her* business email accounts. Zing! *Her* business vendors. Zing! *Her* business shared folders. Zing! *Her* mobile accounts. At that one, Tess paused. Curious, she clicked on Gabe's phone statement. It didn't take long to figure out the number that had been lighting up his line for so many months. Methodically, Tess screenshotted the number, as icily detached as she could be. Gathering information.

Building her walls.

She'd asked him, hadn't she? Repeatedly. Was something wrong? Was there something he'd wanted to tell her? She'd even asked him to his face – is there someone else? Gabe had assured her that he was just dealing with the stress of leaving his job – something that Tess had done everything in her power not to remind him he'd brought upon himself – and had brushed off her worried questions. She'd let it drop, knowing men tended to clam up when stressed.

Now she scanned the phone records, looking back for months as the text messages continued to that same number. Thousands of Facebook messages streamed before her, months of infidelity laid out in vivid, graphic detail, her future crumbling around her. Tess copied it all, saving the file to her password-protected shared drive. She nosed through any other important documentation she could find on Gabe's computer until there was nothing else to be found – nothing else she could do except confront her husband.

Tess sat still, frozen as the end of her marriage loomed. She waited in silence when the front door opened. She waited as Gabe greeted the dogs. She listened as he whistled down the hallway – cheerful, she imagined, from his most recent orgasm – until he rounded the corner into his office.

"Why are you on my computer?" Gabe's face contorted in rage.

Tess's hands clenched, and she shifted the chair, turning enough so he could see the picture on the screen behind her.

"It's over."

"Tess, that's not what you think," Gabe said, stepping forward to put his hands out, but dropping them at her look.

"I knew it. I *knew* it! I should've trusted my gut, but I let your voice drown out my own. It's over, Gabe. There's no way I – no, *we* – can come back from this," Tess said, her voice cold as betrayal sliced through her.

"Okay, let's just talk about this rationally. That woman means nothing," Gabe insisted, pacing in front of his desk, the dogs following his movement.

"Nothing? Really?" Tess turned to read some of the messages. "'I love you, Babers' — ick, *babers*? — 'I can't wait to have you in my arms again. We're meant to be together.' Really, Gabe?"

"That's just bullshit. You shouldn't be reading that crap. It means nothing," Gabe slammed his hand on the desk, causing the dogs to jump up and pace between them.

"Gag me, you're sending her Disney kissing emojis. What is this girl, fourteen?" Tess bit out, her heart pumping in her chest, sweat trickling at the back of her collar.

"She's in college, and I don't love her. It's not what you think."

She barked out a laugh, turning to look at the naked picture of them in bed together.

"I'm fairly certain I'm quite clear on what this is," Tess said, and raised an eyebrow at him. "A co-worker of yours, I see. I suppose this explains why you left work. Oh... were you fired? I bet you were fired." Tess slammed her own hand down on the desk. "That makes so much sense to me now."

"I was not fired." Gabe's face darkened, anger reaching his voice for the first time. "I chose to leave."

"I bet you were asked to leave, weren't you? For screwing your subordinate. Even for you – what a dipshit move," Tess said. She was so completely fed up with Gabe's lies.

"I said I wasn't fired," Gabe shouted.

Tess laughed at him, knowing it would antagonize him and not even caring.

"Oddly enough, Gabe? I'm having an incredibly hard time believing anything you tell me right now. I can't imagine why." Tess turned back to scan the messages on the computer screen.

"Stop reading those." Gabe tried to grab the computer's mouse, but Tess snatched it away from him, slapping his hand back.

"Hands off. As you'll remember, this is my company's computer and you're not allowed to touch it."

"That's such shit and you know it," Gabe seethed, continuing to pace.

"How could you, Gabe? Honestly? After everything I've done for you? You knew this was the one thing I'd never get over. You knew how important trust was to me – you *knew*. This is the way you treat me?" Tess searched his face, looking for any sign of remorse.

"It's just... I don't know. I screwed up. She was just there, and a distraction from everything, I guess." Gabe stopped to lean across the desk to Tess. "I swear to you, she means nothing. I love *you*, Tess, not her."

Tess wasn't buying it.

"I should've expected this, honestly, I really should have. It's not like you've been particularly trustworthy in the past, but I thought we'd moved past all that. I had hoped I wouldn't be another one of your casualties, and that you'd learn to love yourself enough to not do this to the person you're with, like so many times before." Tess crossed her arms as she leveled a glare at Gabe. "I guess I thought I'd be enough for you, Gabe. That I'd be the one to change you. My mistake."

"You are, Tess, I swear you are. You're more than enough for me. I don't deserve you." Gabe held his hands out to her. "Please, we can work through this."

Tess shook her head, ice flowing through her veins.

"You're right, Gabe. You don't deserve me."

He smiled. "Look, babe, you are making way too big a deal –"

She cut him off. "I've moved all the money and changed the passwords on all the accounts." She met his eyes dead-on. "Pack a bag and get out."

He stared at her, breathing through his nose, his chest rising and falling rapidly, rage clouding a face she'd once thought to be handsome.

"You don't have to be such a bitch about it," Gabe said

coldly. Then he smirked. There it was – just a glimmer of joy in taking his power back.

Tess was a contrary sort, however. And now seemed like the perfect time to stop listening to what people – most notably, Gabe – told her to do.

Bitch, she thought. Yeah, she could get behind that.

CHAPTER THREE

Tess lay awake that night, forcing herself to relive all the warning signs she'd ignored. Her heart raced as she rolled over repeatedly to lift the blinds and peek out at the driveway below, wondering if he'd come back. Tess wasn't even certain that she actually wanted Gabe to come back, or if she just wanted the validation of him begging for her. If she was honest with herself – and there really wasn't a more honest time than three a.m. on a cold spring night after kicking her cheating husband out – part of this was about her ego. Wasn't she worth fighting for? What did it say about Tess that the man couldn't even give it a try?

In the movies, the husband would stand in the yard and cry, pleading for forgiveness with flowers in hand – the grand gesture, so to speak. Tess wasn't sure that a grand gesture worked if you couldn't trust a single rotten word that poured from his mouth.

It hadn't been easy to get him out of the house. First came the lies, then the platitudes, then the finger-pointing. At that point, Tess had actually started laughing and retreated to another part of the house to call one of her best friends, Mae. She filled Mae in on every gruesome detail, knowing full well that Gabe could hear. Though she doubted he cared, as he was so busy trying to erase everything on his computer.

It was only when Gabe realized Mae had dropped everything to storm across the city in a blaze of righteous indignation that he jumped into action. Refusing to be concerned that Gabe was still home, Mae had banged right through the front door like an avenging angel of fury, and Gabe had fled, the back door slamming and tires squealing in his wake.

Mae and Tess had looked out the window in shock.

"Well, that was one way to get him out of the house," Tess quipped, laughing before the tears fell.

"That man is not worthy of you," Mae said, settling into the couch with a box of tissues, a bottle of vodka, and an open ear.

"I'm not sure what I did to deserve this," Tess whispered.

A tirade of curses fell from her normally docile friend's lips, her vehemence shocking Tess. "You did nothing to deserve this. How long have you been carrying this man for? How many times have you lifted him up? You bailed him out of jail for his DUI! Paid for a lawyer to reduce his sentence. Paid off his student loans. Bought him a new truck. Supported him when he randomly quit his job. Do you remember dropping him off at jail for his DUI sentence? You cried the whole way home."

"I did. A full three hours ride. And made his damn parents pick him up when he got out, as I was so angry with him."

"As you should have been. He put your life in jeopardy too. Honey...are you okay? Was he really upset, or did he apologize?"

"Oh, he was mad at me. Honestly, I'm not sure which he

was angrier about, getting caught or the fact that I'd moved all the money."

Mae refilled their glasses. "Do you know anything about her? Wait, do you think him quitting had to do with this girl?"

"He said it didn't, but he worked with her, so..." Tess shrugged.

"I bet we can find out."

An hour of internet sleuthing later, they had determined that indeed, the sudden quitting of his job had been in direct correlation with the fact that he'd been caught messing around at work with the new HR intern. Gabe had been kindly asked to leave.

"You'd think they'd teach them in Human Resources that nookie on the job is a no-no," Tess hiccupped, the vodka comfortably ensconcing her from feeling the pain too deeply.

"Well, she is just an intern."

"And not a very bright one at that." Tess laughed and then looked at Mae sadly. "Now what?"

"Now, you take it a day at a time and figure out what you want," Mae said, pulling Tess in for a hug. "I can't tell you what to do here. I hate him for hurting you, but this is your marriage and your choice. You have to decide what's right for you."

"I don't know what that is right now. It's so weird," Tess said, pulling back to meet Mae's eyes. "I just sat there at that computer and stared at it for the longest time. I already knew, I just *knew* what I'd find... and yet I hesitated. It was like a part of me just thought about the sheer exhaustion of going through the mechanics of a divorce. You know what I mean? It's like... just the *everything* of it all. Shit, I've changed my name for this asshole. We have bank accounts together. A mortgage. Everything is all tied together. We were going to move out of state. Do all these things... and now, it's just like... I just want to sleep. Thinking about the amount of effort and awfulness ahead of me is just not something I want to deal with."

"You didn't say anything about him... the loss of him," Mae said, gently running her hand over Tess's arm. "You've gone through really tough stuff before, hon. You know you can handle it when life throws bad shit at you. But what about Gabe? Can you live without him? Do you still love him?"

"I don't know," Tess whispered. "I honestly don't know. I... how many chances do you give a person? Is that what marriage is? Just forgiving and forgiving and moving forward as though you won't always be wondering where he is or what he's doing? I've already had my issues with him, as you well know. Our foundation of trust has been shaky for a while now."

"You have time," Mae said, stretching her long legs before her and propping her feet on the table. "You don't have to decide anything today except what you need in this moment."

"I just want to curl up in my bed with the dogs and tune the world out."

"Then do just that. Tomorrow is a new day. You can look at this with fresh eyes. I want you to know that I love you, sisterfriend of mine. I will support you no matter what you choose to do." Mae had hugged her and left shortly thereafter, motioning to the vodka bottle on the way out. "Not the whole thing, mmkay?"

"Roger that," Tess had said, though she did pour herself one more drink after Mae had left.

She'd walked the house aimlessly, unsure what her next step was. Room to room to room, sipping her vodka, the dogs following her curiously. They hadn't lived here long – just over two years – and the house had a load of problems. Tess loved the character of it, though: an old 1930s cream brick house with a real fireplace – a feature Tess had insisted upon. There was something so charming about having an actual fire during winter, while the snow fell outside, the crackling logs and scent of burning wood warming the living room, the dogs curled in their favorite spot in front of the hearth. It had been a good compromise for them – a house just outside of the city, with more space than the condo they'd been living in, but not so large that they couldn't manage the upkeep. Tess had stopped at one of the guest rooms, now her office, a room she'd once considered for a nursery.

It hadn't taken Gabe long to disabuse her of the notion of having children, and to her surprise, she'd found that she was just fine with the thought of being a childless couple. It wasn't like she'd spent her life yearning to have children, not in the way she craved the adventures of traveling. Tess did so love to travel.

Tess rolled in bed, punching her pillow as she thought about how much travel she'd put on hold through the years because of Gabe. Sure, they'd taken a yearly vacation when Gabe could use his time, but she'd never once taken a trip on her own since she'd married him. Not to do research for work or attend conferences that could help her build her career. Not to join any of the girls' trips she'd been invited on, no matter how much she wanted to go. Not even to visit her best friends. She couldn't. Not after she'd seen the true colors of the man she'd married.

He'd come home drunk from a friend's bachelor party. The drunkenness wasn't unusual, but he'd been surprisingly randy, all but jumping her and pushing her into sex she didn't particularly enjoy. Sloppy sex with a blind drunk man was not exactly the most seductive end to her night. He'd kept mumbling about his hat and his wallet, and Tess had tried to get answers about how he'd gotten home or where he'd been before he'd passed out on top of her.

The next morning, his wallet had been missing. Tess patiently tried to piece his night together for him, and he swore up and down that he had walked home from the bar, an easy five-minute walk from their house. Finding an ATM receipt in his pocket, they determined he'd gone to the gas station. He left for work, her questions unanswered, and Tess decided to go to the gas station to see if anyone had found his wallet. The clerk, a smiling elderly Indian man who'd always greeted her cheerfully, offered to review the security tape with her.

There she watched her freshly-minted husband get led to an ATM by a hooker, before being taken outside where he slid his hand up her skirt and had his way with her on camera. The pity in the gas station clerk's eyes as they watched the silent black-and-white scene play out before them on the small television was more than she could bear.

A part of her had died that day as she'd learned that she couldn't fully trust the man she'd just signed on to live her life with.

She never returned to that gas station. And she never left Gabe alone for a weekend again.

CHAPTER FOUR

"He did what?" Vicki's voice snapped through the phone. Tess felt her back go up, waiting for exactly what she knew was coming and the entire reason she'd avoided calling her sister the day before.

"Gabe's been having an affair."

"I told you he was trash," Vicki said, and Tess held the phone away from her face and gave her sister the middle finger.

"Yup, you sure did, Vicki. Repeatedly." Tess scratched Red's pointy ears. A French bulldog, Red easily fit into her lap and, sensing she was sad, had been glued to her side for days.

"Stop calling me Vicki; you know I hate that," Vicki griped, and Tess smiled, having scored a small point.

"Sorry, Victoria." Tess infused a snotty tone to her pronunciation, knowing it would annoy her sister but not really caring.

"Honestly, Tess, it's not like I didn't see something like this coming," Vicki said, "Gabe is as lazy as they come, not to mention his questionable intelligence. Frankly, I'm actually surprised he was even motivated enough to do something as interesting as have an affair."

Tess pressed her lips together and eyed the vodka bottle sitting on the kitchen counter from the night before, idly wondering if it was too early for a drink.

"Really? You find it 'interesting'? I'd say it's fairly trite and boring, no? Same old story. Middle-aged man has crisis of confidence and seeks out willing college intern to stroke his ego. And other parts of him," Tess bit back, annoyed that her sister couldn't just be there for her. Was it so hard to offer condolences instead of 'told-you-so'?

"Mmm. It is probably the most excitement he's had in years."

"Gee, thanks, Vicki. You know it wasn't for lack of trying on my part – I was the one who always wanted to book us vacations, go to concerts, or try new things. He didn't like doing things outside of his comfort zone."

"Yeah, which was mainly a barstool."

"Listen, I don't want to get into this right now. I just need a favor, okay?" Tess ran her hand through her long dark hair, wrapping it around her finger and tugging just until it hurt a bit. She needed to feel the pain – to not go totally numb.

"What do you need?"

"Can I bring his guns to your house? I know Chad has a gun safe." Tess held her breath to see if her sister would understand what she was asking.

"Do you honestly think he'll off himself because of this? You certainly think highly of yourself." Vicki chattered on about men and their need for constant validation, while Tess, stung by her words, held the phone away from her face and blinked tears back. She would not let her sister win this round.

"Listen, just take the guns, okay? I'd rather remove them

completely from the situation." Tess refrained from mentioning that perhaps Gabe would use them to threaten her. Her sister would have laughed, telling her not to flatter herself. "I also need to hang at your place for an hour, so Gabe can come pack a few bags."

"When?"

"Now? I want to get this over with."

"Well, we did have plans to—"

"Please," Tess interrupted. "I don't ask you for much, but I'm asking for this."

At that, Vicki paused. Then, the edge gone from her voice, she agreed.

Tess hung up before the conversation could become any more disastrous. She had a tumultuous relationship with her sister at best, but they were all each other had. They'd lost their parents in a freak plane accident when Tess was just starting college and Vicki was a few years into her sales job for a nationwide office supply chain. Her parents had been traveling to a small island in the South Pacific on a prop plane when they'd hit a tropical storm, and the plane had gone down. It had been a dark time for the sisters.

Tess stopped in front of the gun safe, her hand trembling as she keyed in the code. Swinging the door open, she gingerly retrieved the two handguns inside the safe, cringing as her body responded the same way it always did around guns. A cold, clammy sweat broke out across her brow, goosebumps running up her arms. Tess had never been able to explain her visceral response to guns, but she absolutely despised them. Gabe had ignored her protests about having guns in the house, citing the ridiculous argument that they'd be prepared during a home invasion. Maybe he would, Tess thought as she slowly walked downstairs as though she was carrying a bomb, but she was more likely to shoot herself in the foot than fend off a burglar with a gun.

One of the guns was technically hers. Even knowing how much she hated guns, Gabe had bought her one for her birthday, and then insisted she go to the gun range with him. She'd blinked back tears while she learned to use the gun, her stomach roiling at the thought of ever having to shoot someone. She hadn't touched the weapon again until now. It was just another example of many, where Tess had acquiesced to keep the peace.

Tess made sure both guns were unloaded, then grabbed a bag from the closet, zipped them inside, put them in the trunk of the car, and headed to Vicki's.

After their parents died, Tess had planned to honor their memory by trying to travel as much as she could – though some would call it running away. Vicki had gone the opposite route, assuming the parental role in Tess's life, and had spent her time trying to monitor Tess's every move, all while doing her best to put on a front and show the world that she had the perfect life.

Even though Vicki had sought to control Tess's life, which Tess inherently knew came from the need to protect her, they'd still managed to share some great sisterly moments. They'd hiked in the Rocky Mountains for a weekend, laughing until they cried when they thought a bear had wandered into their camp and was knocking over their trash, only to finally peek their heads from the tent to find a chubby raccoon enjoying the spoils of their dinner. Or the times that Vicki would video chat with Tess, helping her to pick outfits for dates, or consoling her when she got a bad grade during her master's program. Vicki had helped her choose her wedding dress, and though she'd expressed her concerns over Tess marrying Gabe, she'd still cried her way right through the ceremony and raised a glass of champagne to toast their happiness during dinner. However, over the years, they'd grown further apart than closer, as Vicki's need for controlling her own environment and trying to live an impeccable life had driven a wedge between the two of them.

Tess thought perfection was boring. What she craved, more than anything, was love and freedom to live her life on her terms. When she'd first met Gabe, she'd been enamored with his carefree attitude, talk of playing in a band, and the fact that he'd made her feel like she was the only one he wanted. If she was being honest with herself, the real reason she'd gotten hooked on Gabe was because she had desperately wanted to be loved. For a while, he made her feel like she was the center of his universe. Looking back now, Tess realized his incessant text messages and need to constantly be in contact with her had been his way of controlling her. She wondered if that was why her sister had never liked Gabe – because then Vicki couldn't control Tess anymore.

Tess's whole life had been about trying to exert her voice, only to find herself repeatedly in situations where people tried to silence her. Vicki had told her on more than one occasion to be less difficult – less combative – and to go along with the way people wanted her to be to keep the peace.

No more, Tess promised herself as she pulled to a stop in front of Vicki's immaculate house – too large, in Tess's opinion. Playing by everyone else's rules had only gotten her here – which was exactly where she didn't want to be.

Before she went in, she texted Gabe that he could go to the house and pack his bags.

Vicki met her at the door, taking the bag with a frown and handing it off to Chad to put away. At least David, her seven-year-old nephew, was happy to see her. He gave her a hug, and chatted at her until his dad returned, and the two of them headed out to the backyard.

Vicki disappeared into the kitchen, and Tess reluctantly joined her, settling on one of the pristine white barstools as Vicki poured a pair of drinks.

"You've always picked the worst men," Vicki said, gesturing across the counter with her wine glass. Tess's eyes slid to where Vicki's perfectly normal husband threw a football to their adorable son.

"Yep," Tess said, sipping her own glass of wine and glancing at her phone, counting down the time until she could leave. Though she'd just promised herself in the car to find her backbone, Tess was just too damn tired to argue with her sister right now. "Sure do."

"God, remember third grade? We even heard about it in middle school." Vicki shook her head, clucking softly in shame for her sister.

"How could I forget?" Tess grumbled into her wine.

Now, as an adult, the seemingly small thing of telling a cute guy she liked him wouldn't ruin her life. But in third grade? It had been her entire world. She'd had the biggest crush on Paul for the first half of the school year. The teacher, Mrs. Fischer – had repeatedly warned the students about passing notes in class. It just so happened that the day Tess had finally worked up the nerve to confess her love to Paul was the day that Mrs. Fischer had decided she'd had enough. Intercepting the note, she'd opened it, read it, and proceeded to paste it on the chalkboard for everyone to read. The note stayed up for the remainder of the week, causing Tess to cry tears of humiliation, and Paul as well, due to all the teasing the note incurred. Not only had Tess unsuccessfully declared her love, but her crush was wholly uninterested, and horribly embarrassed by her intentions. It had been quite the blow to her tender little heart, and Tess had retreated into a shell for the rest of the year, her distrust of the trappings of love strong.

"Oh, get over it. So he didn't like you." Vicki shrugged.

"It's not the point! That woman had no right to post something so private on the board. Could you imagine if that happened to David?"

"He'd be fine. Toughens kids up." Vicki tucked a strand of hair that had dared to come loose behind her ear. "It's not like you didn't do the exact same thing to that other poor boy who liked you a year or two later."

"He embarrassed me!" Tess protested, feeling anger bubble up at her perfect sister. She'd always been the golden girl – popular in school, great at sports, perfect in relationships. All while Tess had fumbled along, finding everything a constant challenge. It seemed no matter what she did or said, she was always the disruptive one. She'd fought constantly with her parents, who made Vicki's controlling tendencies look like air kisses. All of the most important people in her life had told her repeatedly to pipe down, when all Tess wanted was to find her voice.

"You didn't have to tear up his banner," Vicki said, and shame crept through Tess. The boy she spoke of, Adam, had printed a banner for her and brought it on the school bus. It had read "Puppy Love," and he'd unfurled it in front of all the other kids on their bus route. Instead of being pleased, Tess hadn't known how to handle the attention – when the whole bus laughed, she'd torn up the banner and ignored Adam. Thinking of Gabe's words, she supposed Adam had probably also called her a bitch a time or two after that.

"I panicked, okay?"

"And what about that guy in high school you were dating who lied about you two sleeping together? Landon? I had to have my friend's little sister fix that mess." Vicki sighed, shaking her head as though the burden of repairing Tess's life was all on her shoulders.

"You didn't have to do anything. I defended my reputation."

"Yeah, but Sheila was way more popular than you, so people actually believed what she said."

"Is there a point to all this?" Tess asked, refilling her glass. Vicki went on, tapping a finger against her lips as she mentally cataloged all of Tess's failings – a favorite pastime of hers.

"Oh, and there was that nice guy in college who wanted to take you home to meet his parents. He brought you flowers and everything. You shit all over him." Vicki shook her head sadly.

"I didn't shit all over him! I just told him that I couldn't be with him anymore. I… I don't know. He wasn't the guy for me. I wasn't mean to him, I just didn't want to keep dating him. I was straightforward with him about that."

"Well, you broke his heart."

Tess blew out a breath. "Thanks for the reminder."

"And then you end up with wonderboy, Gabe, of all people. I still don't know what you saw in him. Long hair, in a band… I mean, a low-level marketing job? How was he even going to take care of you?" Vicki pursed her lips again, raising a perfectly manicured eyebrow at Tess. Chad was an investment broker, as Vicki had reminded Tess repeatedly, and Vicki enjoyed showing off all the gifts he bestowed upon her.

"Vicki," Tess said, smiling at the wince that crossed her sister's face, "why in the world did I go to college and get a master's degree if I was looking for someone to 'take care of me'? Isn't the entire point of getting an education to be able to take care of myself?"

"It's not like you even use your degrees," Vicki said, gesturing with her wine glass, "what with those little books you write now."

"Writing is a noble profession." Tess's head began to pound. "I'm proud of what I've accomplished."

"If you were going to be a writer, you could have at least taken some classes about writing, don't you think? Instead of wasting all that money on degrees you don't use? At the very least, maybe you could write something a little bit more literary than those... smutty little books you write now."

"Romance is not smut. It's a very popular genre." Tess sighed inwardly, knowing her defense fell on deaf ears.

"Well, at some point, I hope you'll consider getting a real job, considering you're the only one employed in your relationship."

Tess thought of pointing out that she was about to end said "relationship." Instead, she said, "I have to go." She didn't care if the time for Gabe to be at her house wasn't up. She couldn't sit here and listen to Vicki pick her apart a minute longer without saying something she wouldn't be able to come back from. She set her glass down carefully and stood.

"Wait – what are you going to do?" Vicki said, trailing after Tess. "Are you going to see a lawyer? I mean, even though I think you can do better than Gabe, shouldn't you at least go to counseling? Divorce is a big deal, you know. It'd be so embarrassing to have to tell everyone you couldn't make the marriage work."

"I didn't make it work?" Tess whirled on Vicki and got in her flawless face. "I worked my ass off at this marriage. Do you know how many times I tried counseling with him? For the drinking? For our relationship? How many times I tried to work on our communication? And nothing. Nothing ever changed. Gabe does exactly what he wants. So don't you dare tell me I failed at this marriage."

"Oh, calm down, you don't have to be so dramatic."

"I wouldn't say being upset about my life falling apart is being dramatic," Tess bit out, her hand on the front door, keeping her voice low as David and Chad approached.

"This is so typical of you. I'm just calling it as I see it. If you divorce, technically, it's a failed marriage. Honestly, you've always been dramatic. It's why you struggle so much. Try being less combative. You know, maybe that's why your husband left," Vicki said, her eyes flashing with the smallest bit of glee, fully aware of the barb she'd made.

"He didn't leave me, I kicked him out," Tess hissed.

"Really? Seems to me he left you a long time ago."

CHAPTER FIVE

T*ess,*

I packed some clothes and some things. A lot is left behind because I don't know where I'm going. I'll most likely sleep in my truck or at a friend's house until I can figure something out. Maybe I can pick up some hours at the gym to make some extra cash. I'm not going back to work for the firm. For many reasons. That would be my last option other than moving away all together. I'd rather move away, to be honest. I'm honoring your request for space, but I hope you'll let me know when I can come home again. There's no doubt what I want in this world – I knew all along. In my moments of weakness, I felt nothing but shame and hatred for myself. You've always been more than good enough for me. I don't know why I couldn't believe in us. I know I can be strong enough to rebuild – that we can rebuild. I know you left your rings for me, and I'll keep them until I put them on your finger again. In the meantime, I just don't know what to do with myself now.

Love you forever,
Gabe

"Maybe you should have thought about that before you

stuck your dick in someone else," Tess spat out, little pops of rage beginning to bubble up as she read his note once more – searching for anything that would make her want to hold on to him, to save this marriage. "This note's all about you, Gabe. You didn't even say you were sorry."

Tess had half-expected Gabe to be waiting when she pulled up at the house, but he had respected her wishes for once and packed his bags – though not without texting some serious complaints about the fact she'd taken his guns. The house was empty but for her two dogs smiling at the front door for her.

Her phone buzzed with another text message, and Tess almost ignored it. She couldn't deal with another "woe is me" text from Gabe or more unasked-for advice from Vicki. She glanced at it anyway to see it was from her friend, Elizabeth.

Hey, call you in five.

Tess wandered back to Gabe's computer – the one thing he'd tried to take that she had refused to allow on the grounds that it was technically her company property – and sat down in his chair. Despite herself, she typed in the new password she'd made and opened the browser to see Gabe's Facebook account still active. Shocked, she watched as a message box popped up from the girl.

She knew she shouldn't look. Tess already had all the answers she needed. But just like it was almost impossible to look away from a car accident, Tess enlarged the box and read while her husband messaged his lover. And who was she kidding? It would take a crowbar to pry her away from the computer right now.

I can't believe she kicked you out. Don't you own half the house?

Yeah, but what am I supposed to do? I can't force her out. God, she's such a bitch. I can't believe she's moved the money.

Do you think she'll come after us?

Probably. Women get so crazy about this stuff. We'll have to be careful. I hate this. I feel sick to my stomach. What am I supposed to do? Where am I going to go?

Awww, babers, come be with me.

You know I can't, babers. She'll probably be driving by like crazy.

She knows where I live? Is that bitch going to come after me?

Shit, she probably knows everything by now. I hate this. What am I supposed to do?

Babers, I miss you. I can't believe you didn't come over last night.

She was probably stalking me, I couldn't let her know where I was. I stayed at Ryan's house, babers, you know that.

How long will he let you stay there?

He's got room for me for now, he said. But hopefully I won't have to be here long.

Is she still going to be away this Saturday?

Tess's eyebrows shot to her hairline at that. She had told Gabe a few weeks ago she was going to spend the day down in Indianapolis for a writer's conference. Then Elizabeth's name flashed on the phone screen.

"Hey, I'm sorry I missed your call yesterday. Getting the business off the ground has been crazy." A professional organizer, Elizabeth balanced building a new business with a busy social life out in Colorado. They'd been friends since they traveled on a semester abroad together in college.

"Uh, we've got a situation." Tess's voice cracked.

"Don't tell me you're canceling your trip to Colorado," Elizabeth said, her voice rushed as street sounds rang out in the background.

"Well... you see, Gabe's been having an affair. I kicked him out and I'm currently sitting at his computer reading the messages between him and his college lover."

Silence greeted her for long enough that Tess pulled the phone away to look to see if the call had dropped before Elizabeth shrieked her rage along with a slew of inventive curses that Tess gave her solid points for.

"What do you want to do? I was already planning to take a few days off to head down to Key West to treat myself. I can't leave work any earlier than planned this week, but I can change plane tickets and spend the weekend in Chicago with you instead. We can sit on the couch and drink too much and cry or go out... whatever you need," Elizabeth said, still cursing every other breath.

"I don't know what I need. I can't seem to look away from these messages," Tess breathed, still reading as her idiot husband messaged his love to this girl.

"You have to get the locks changed."

"I guess I can call someone. I've barely processed the fact that I kicked him out. I haven't even thought about what my next steps are. He kept saying he wanted a life with me away from here. Like, oh, let's move to Colorado and all our problems will go away. Of course" – Tess started giggling – "he left out the part about the other woman he was sleeping with the whole time. I don't even know if he was serious about Colorado, or what."

"There's a term for that."

"Denial?" Tess asked.

"No, like an actual term. I think it's used for addicts. Relocation sobriety or something like that. Where they think if they just move and start fresh all their problems go away."

"Yeah, this isn't going away," Tess said, half-listening, half-engrossed in the text conversation.

"What are they saying?" Elizabeth asked, just as curious.

"What... no! Uh-uh..." Tess shook her head.

"What! Speak! I can't read through the phone," Elizabeth complained.

"It looks like he had planned to have her come here while I was in Indianapolis on Saturday. I was only going to be gone for one day," Tess breathed, reading the messages. Her stomach roiled in disgust at the thought of this woman in her bed, looking through her things, trying on her jewelry.

"Shut up. That's a new level of ballsy. He was going to have her at your *house*?" Elizabeth's screech caused Tess to hold the phone away from her ear.

"She says, and I quote, 'Awww babers, you've never invited me to your place before. It will be a first for us. I'm going to be so nervous though.'"

"Damn right, she'd better be nervous! She's going to a married man's house," Elizabeth shouted.

"Oh. My. God."

"What?" Elizabeth breathed.

"He goes, 'Don't worry babers, my dogs will make you feel all better.'" Tess glanced down to her two dogs – her babies – sleeping at her feet.

"Oh, hell no," Elizabeth whispered, knowing Tess's deep love for her dogs.

"Bitch already pet my man – she's sure as hell not petting my dogs," Tess swore, her dogs popping up in shock as Tess dropped to the floor and wrapped her arms around them, tears of rage clouding her eyes.

"I'm coming there," Elizabeth decided.

"No way. Let's go to Key West together," Tess declared.

"Even better. Just change the locks before you leave."

"On it," Tess said, promising to call her later before immediately looking up a locksmith. Her phone buzzed with a text message.

Tess, please. Can we talk? I know we can work this out. We're meant to be together.

Tess glanced back at the computer screen to see what the lovers were messaging about now.

Babers, you'd better get some money off her. You have rights, you know.

I'll take care of it. I miss you.

Come see me later... I miss your body on mine.

Tess got up, refusing to read the rest, and stomped her way into the kitchen, grabbing the vase of flowers – red roses; how unimaginative could Gabe be? She slammed out the door, shivering in the sleeting grey rain that had just begun to fall, and tossed the vase of flowers into the garbage can, relishing the sound of shattering glass.

Wiping her hands, Tess indulged in a floor cuddle-fest with Red and Ringo before pulling out her phone and texting a contact at a law firm she used to work at.

Send me the info for the best divorce attorney you know.

CHAPTER SIX

Tess smoothed her skirt, her riot of curls pulled back demurely from her face, and tried not to fidget as she sat in the lush waiting area of one of the top divorce attorneys in Chicago. A line from a song kept repeating in her head: *Separated we stand, together we fall apart.*

Had she stood stronger before Gabe? She certainly knew she'd had a more individual voice. It was as though she'd lost herself for years; only now had she begun to find herself again. Her voice needed to be heard one way or the other, and if it fell on the deaf ears of her husband, then she'd show the world who she was.

It appeared that didn't sit well with Gabe.

Same old story... Tess switched to another song, humming away, briefly wondering if she was going mental, as she thought about all the people she'd have to tell. All the expressions of barely-concealed glee from those who loved a tasty tidbit of scandal. Not from her best friends, of course, but everyone knew people who secretly relished dirty gossip and would pick everything apart. Her story wouldn't even be that interesting, Tess mused, the author in her annoyed by it all. If anything, the mid-thirties man sleeping with a younger intern was about as trite as it could get.

"Tess? She's ready for you." A well-groomed younger man beamed at her, and Tess silently applauded her attorney's choice of a handsome male assistant. It was nice to see the status quo turned on its head every once in a while.

Tess was ushered into an office designed in muted shades of grey and lavender, where a sleek woman in an even sleeker suit sat behind a shining glass desk. Rising, she held out her hand and gripped Tess's firmly.

"I'd say welcome, but I understand you're here under trying circumstances. I'm sorry for that, but I'm here to help." Sandra Moriarty, the attorney who had come highly recommended, gestured for her to sit and then discreetly nudged a velvet-lined tissue box across the desk.

"Thank you," Tess said, unsure where to start. "I... well, I guess I'm just here to learn my options."

"Do you want to tell me what happened?" Sandra asked, clearly expecting Tess to launch into a tirade.

"Same shit, different day for you, I'm sure," Tess murmured and then smiled weakly at Sandra's raised eyebrow. "Sorry, I'm sure you've heard the likes of this story a million times. It's really very boring. He's mid-thirties and slept with a young girl interning at his office. He was asked to leave his job, but he told me that he quit. It's been going on for months now." Tess shrugged and looked out the window at Lake Michigan, the water gray and choppy on this blustery spring day.

"I'm sorry. Truly. I've been there and it's awful. You deserve to trust and rely upon the person you've promised your life to," Sandra said, sympathy lighting her pretty face.

"Yes, well." Tess, usually so articulate, didn't know what else to say under the circumstances. "What now?"

"Ultimately, it's up to you. I can't advise you on whether you should file for divorce or not, but I can certainly outline your options."

"Please do." Tess strongly believed that knowledge was power.

"We live in a community property state. It doesn't matter whose fault it is, because the judge won't listen. Assets acquired during marriage are meant to be split fifty-fifty unless a marriage settlement agreement is signed prior to going to court. And based on the information you've sent me, it seems you've accrued considerably more assets than he has." Sandra eyed her over the top of the paper she was reading.

"I have," Tess agreed.

"Congratulations. Let's protect them then, shall we?"

"I'd like to. How does... how does this all work? Run it down for me."

"It takes at least four months from filing before you can divorce. At any time, you can decide to pull the papers and it all goes away. Even six months after your divorce is final, you can annul it and go back. Otherwise, with no children, it will simply be a division of property and moving on with your life."

"So, in theory, I'd have at minimum four months or so to change my mind if I file for divorce today?"

"Yes," Sandra said.

"Okay," Tess breathed, and blinked back the tears that threatened. She'd promised herself she wouldn't cry, that this was just the smart thing to do, but in the actual moment, the decision felt like a three-hundred-pound weight on her shoulders.

"I know this is hard, and again, I'm so sorry for that. But you have a company to protect. Even if the marriage isn't worth fighting for, your business is."

"How do you know when a marriage is worth fighting for?" Tess asked, meeting Sandra's steady brown eyes across the desk.

"I don't think you'd be sitting here four days after you caught your husband cheating if you thought it was," Sandra said, her tone gentle but her words like a bucket of ice water dumped on Tess's head. The woman was absolutely right.

"File. Today," Tess said, sliding a retainer check across the desk and rising before the panic that clawed at her chest made her collapse on the pretty floral rug.

"Yes, ma'am. I'll have copies sent over to you once filed. Don't worry, Tess. I'll get you through this." Sandra led her out to where the handsome assistant gently walked her to the elevator.

In moments, Tess found herself on the sidewalk, the bracing wind off Lake Michigan all but barreling her over as she forced herself to plod back to the parking lot where she'd been lucky to find a space in the middle of the day. Numbly climbing into the car, she almost ordered her Bluetooth to call her sister and tell her the news before she realized she owed someone else a call first.

Better yet, she'd go there.

Twenty minutes later, Tess sat on the street and eyed the little brownstone house that she'd been to many times before for friendly cookouts and to pick Gabe up after a guys' day of drinking and sportsballing. Gabe's truck was at the curb. Steeling herself, she got out of the car and walked up the sidewalk, the wind still buffeting her, and rapped loudly on the door. Tess stepped back, and saw a curtain twitch, but nobody came to the door. She knocked several more times, but to no avail.

On the way home, Tess called Gabe and he answered just before it went to voicemail. She pulled into her driveway and sat in the car, looking at the house that had been meant to hold their future.

"Gabe, I just stopped by Ryan's, but you didn't answer the door."

"Oh, I just got home, I must have missed you, babe." Gabe's voice sounded as contrite as it could.

"Uh-huh. So, I wanted to tell you this in person as I felt it was important to do so as adults, but I'll have to do it this way. I've filed for divorce, Gabe."

"You... you did? Already?" Gabe's voice shot up an octave.

"I did." Tears were filling her eyes. "I... I don't know what to say. What you did was so wrong. I'm just... I'm just done, Gabe. I can't do this. I can't trust you."

"But I can change, Tess. I can build on this and change, and you can trust me again." Gabe was whispering now.

"I think you have some major things to learn about your-self... about life." Tess ran a hand over her face. "You can't live like this or be this type of person. Not if you want to get anywhere, Gabe. I tried so hard to be a good wife to you."

"You were... you were a great wife to me. I don't know why I was so weak. What am I going to do? I don't know where to start. I don't know what to do."

"I..." Tess almost leaped in with suggestions to help, as she'd done for years. She stopped herself. "I'm not sure what to say. Maybe you should ask your mistress."

"Tess," Gabe warned, an edge to his voice.

"You're not my problem anymore, Gabe." As Tess said it,

a weight seemed to release itself from her chest, those chains that had tied her down for years.

"Tess, please don't do this," Gabe begged. "I don't know why I do the things I do."

"If you had tried any therapy, you might have a better understanding of yourself. Now might be a good time to go."

"Like I can afford it," Gabe shot back, annoyance lashing his voice.

"Again, not my problem. You could go back to your job; I thought they loved you there?"

"I'm not going back. For many reasons," Gabe said, his voice haughty.

"Why not? Really? I'm curious." Tess wondered if he would admit the real reason he'd left work.

"It's not what I want for my future, okay? I'm not going back."

Tess felt the old frustration build up. Years of his half-lies and never getting a straight answer from him made her surly. "Well, it seems you've chosen someone else for your future. Perhaps she'll help you with getting a job. Though I'm not sure what pull she has as an intern," Tess mused.

"Knock it off, Tess. I don't want to be with her. I just want to work this out with you! Look, let's just... let's start over. We can move to Colorado like we planned. Everything will be different there."

"I'm sorry, Gabe. That option is no longer on the table." Tess nodded at the locksmith van that pulled in next to her car. "Oh, I'm having the locks changed, by the way. I'll let you know when you can come get the rest of your stuff, or if there's anything you need, just text me and I'll leave it in the garage."

"Wait, what? You're changing the locks? Can you even do that?"

"I am. Honestly, Gabe, I'm alone here. I really just want to feel safe, you know?" Tess smiled brightly at the locksmith who waited for her.

"How would you not feel safe? I'm not going to threaten you."

"How can I be sure of that? You slammed my head into the bathroom wall not so long ago."

Silence greeted Tess.

"That's what I thought. Listen. I don't really know this girl you're hooking up with and how do I know you won't bring her here while I was gone? Plus, it would just be awkward for our dog-sitter. So, just to be on the safe side, I'm having the locks changed. I'll let you know when you can come by. In the meantime, please respect my space."

"Tess... wait, I..."

"Yes, Gabe?" Tess paused, wondering if he would say or do anything that would actually make her consider going back to him.

"Can I get my computer?"

Tess closed her eyes, willing back the tears. She'd made the right choice in filing for divorce.

"No, Gabe. You'll have to use your laptop."

CHAPTER SEVEN

"Y ou did what?" Vicki's voice went cold – harsher than Tess had heard it in years.

"I filed for divorce," Tess said, smiling at the airport bartender on her layover in Atlanta. He winked and gave her a thumbs up when he overheard her conversation.

"But you just found out on Monday. Are you out of your mind?" Vicki asked.

"Maybe. What do you care? I thought you'd be happy I'm divorcing him. Didn't you call him incompetent and boring?" Tess sipped her bloody Mary and checked the time. Elizabeth should be arriving any moment now.

"Irrespective of such. You can't just file for divorce and fly to Key West. It doesn't work like that. You have responsibilities to deal with."

"Like what?"

"Like handling your marriage. Yes, you may have committed to not the best guy in the world, but it's still a commitment. Go to marriage counseling. Fix what's broken. You don't just go off on a girls' weekend when everything's falling apart. You stay and face the hard stuff. That's what marriage is about."

"Perhaps that's your definition, but I'm done fixing it, Vicki."

"You've barely tried."

"Bullshit. I've tried for years. Years, Vicki. I've supported him through everything – bailing him out of jail for drinking, paying for lawyers to protect his record, paying off his debt, helping him to advance in the career he threw away – and all for what? To be shit on while he plays with some intern. For years I've listened to him talk incessantly about all these things he wants to do with his life. But you know what? It's all talk. No action. And I'm so damn tired of carrying the burden of this relationship. I want a partner, Vicki. I'd think you could at least understand that." Tess bit vehemently into the pickle that came with her drink, idly pretending it was Gabe's member.

"All marriages have tough spots," Vicki said, her voice prim. "That doesn't mean you just give up on them."

"I'm done, Vicki."

"I have to say, I think this is too sudden. I think you'll regret this," Vicki insisted.

"I don't recall asking your advice." Tess heard the big intake of air that signaled Vicki was about to unleash a tirade on her. "Gotta go, Elizabeth's here. I'll call you when I'm back from Key West." Tess waved cheerfully to signal Elizabeth.

"Tess, wait. You'd better know what you're doing. The world isn't kind to divorced women. It's not as easy to find love at your age."

"I'm thirty-six, Vicki. If I'm lucky, I have a good sixty years to find love again. I'm not too fussed about that," Tess huffed.

"You will be when you're all alone."

"That's the difference between us. I don't mind being alone," Tess said. "I'm hanging up now. Bye."

Tess jumped off the barstool and into Elizabeth's hug. They rocked back and forth, just as happy to see each other as if no time had passed at all. Elizabeth pulled back to look at Tess. Blonde, blue-eyed, and quick to laugh, Elizabeth was light to Tess's dark, a cool breath of fresh air to Tess's stormy seas.

"Love the shirt," Elizabeth proclaimed.

"Thought you'd like that," Tess laughed. She'd taken a last-minute shopping trip the day before and had picked up a t-shirt that boldly proclaimed *It's not me, it's you.*

"Are you sure you want to go on this trip?" Elizabeth asked, studying Tess's face, concern in her pretty blue eyes.

"Yes. I filed for divorce."

"Ah, sweetie, I'm so sorry. I know that had to have been a tough choice." Elizabeth hugged her once more.

Tess leaned into the hug. This was the response she had been looking for from her sister, she realized. Not someone telling her what to do, or accusations that she hadn't worked hard on her marriage. All she'd wanted was for Vicki to acknowledge that Tess had the right to make her own choices in life. Mistakes or not, this was her life.

But then, you can't choose your family, Tess thought, and shrugged it away.

"It was a tough choice. It is. But it's the right one," Tess said as their flight was called.

"In that case – ready to go?"

"More than ready. Get me outta here!" Tess laughed. Deep down, that was the only thing she really wanted to do – run away and keep running.

"Care to share a taxi?"

Tess beamed at the cute guy with his arm in a sling who waited in the taxi line outside the Key West airport. It wasn't uncommon to share taxis here, and Tess was feeling a little carefree and loose from the rum punch they'd been greeted with upon arrival at the tiny airport.

"Sounds great," Tess said, smiling widely. She'd been smiling a lot lately, she realized. Elizabeth rolled her eyes.

"I like your shirt," Cute Guy said as the taxi driver loaded their bags, and Elizabeth climbed in the front seat, leaving Tess and Cute Guy in the back.

"Thanks. I just filed for divorce yesterday," Tess explained and then blinked when Elizabeth slapped her palm to her forehead. Both the taxi driver and the cute guy grinned at Tess.

"Did you now? Key West is the perfect place to come then," the taxi driver observed, eyeing Tess appraisingly in the rearview mirror.

"I certainly hope so," Tess said.

"You'd be surprised how many people come down here to reboot their lives. It's like someone pressing the do-over switch and then they leave here, ready to move forward. Or some stay... and this is their new life." The taxi driver chuckled. "I'm one of them myself. I used to work in the mailroom back in Pittsburgh. One too many winters and I'd had it. Hightailed it to the Keys and haven't left. Be careful, girly, or this place will suck you right in. Which is great if that's what you want. It's a different way of life... an island vibe, you know?"

"I do know. I lived on an island once," Tess said, smiling at the taxi driver. "I liked it. My family considered it a failure, but aside from having a horrific boss who tainted my experience there, I really liked the island vibe. I could see myself by the water."

"If you move to an island, you'd better have a room for me to come visit," Elizabeth said over her shoulder as they pulled up to their hotel.

"Here..." Cute Guy finally spoke up, handing Tess his card. "If you want to get drinks this weekend, I'm around. I'm here for work, but my evenings are free." The double entendre was not lost on Tess and she laughed at Cute Guy, enjoying someone flirting with her freely for the first time in years.

"Okay, let's go," Elizabeth ordered, waving at Cute Guy before slamming the door and whirling on Tess. "He's got a bum wing, Tess. What's he even going to do for you?"

Tess laughed so hard she cried, and was still laughing after they'd checked into their room, changed into their swimsuits, and settled by the pool.

"Afternoon, ladies." A grinning waiter – twenty-one years old at best – stopped by to chat with them.

"Jared? We'd like you to keep the drinks coming," Elizabeth ordered. "Rum punch, please. This one just filed for divorce."

"Is that so? Well, if there's anything I can do...." Jared's grin widened, and Tess laughed, but also squirmed a little under his frank appraisal of her body. Gabe had always been highly critical of her weight, and him cheating with a girl more than ten years younger than her certainly wasn't doing anything for her ego at the moment.

"Just the drinks for now, Jared." Elizabeth shooed him along and shook her head.

"I swear, the D-word really gets a reaction," Tess mused, stretching out on the lounge chair and looking out to the water, taking her first deep breaths of the week. "It's weird to say it out loud, you know. I'll get used to it. But it's weird right now."

"I'm sure that's normal," Elizabeth said. "And I think these guys just hear that you recently filed and are thinking about a quick fling. Because you aren't going to be in the place for attachments right now – you're in Key West for a weekend, and probably ripe for a romp. I suspect it will be an interesting weekend."

"I... I couldn't have a fling," Tess sputtered. "Could I? I mean, it would just be weird."

Elizabeth shrugged and nodded as Jared sauntered back over, all tanned muscle and gelled hair. "Just let me know if you need the room."

Jared's aftershave arrived before him, and Tess was brought back to her college days when guys hadn't yet learned that less is more when it came to cologne.

"I think I'll be taking a hard pass on that," Tess murmured, smiling her thanks at Jared as he deposited an extra-large rum punch in front of her.

"I had them make it a double." Jared winked.

"You're a doll, Jared, an absolute doll," Tess said, and Jared crouched by her chair.

"I have off tomorrow afternoon, if you want to go out on the sand bar – a whole crew of us goes. Just let me know." Tess saw Elizabeth mimicking spanking behind him.

"I'll be sure to do that." Tess nodded vigorously, at this point just needing him to go away. A man certainly didn't have the answers Tess was seeking on this trip. She needed some time with one of her best friends to decompress and try and take some shaky steps forward – not dive headfirst into a drunken fling with a college boy.

"He could be fun," Elizabeth said, sliding her sunglasses

down her nose as they watched him stroll away, all strength and cockiness.

"He's too young. I don't want to have to teach him."

"That could be fun for you, too."

"Who has the energy? I'd probably end up crying in his lap. No, thank you, I am so not ready for this," Tess said, firmly shutting the door on that thought.

"The attention is nice, though."

"It is. It's weird, I'll admit, but it's nice."

"Don't let that asshole take everything from you, Tess. You're awesome, and there is someone out there who will appreciate that."

"I can't even think that far ahead right now. I just have to get through this, somehow, someway. This isn't the future I had planned for myself." Tess stretched out and let the sun warm her limbs.

Elizabeth turned her head to look at Tess, the palm trees and ocean reflected in her sunglasses. "That's okay. We all get a do-over, like the taxi guy said, right?"

"Damn right, I get a do-over. And this time I'll do it my way," Tess said, clinking her glass with Elizabeth's. Now, she just had to believe it.

CHAPTER EIGHT

"What should we wear out? Something fun?" Elizabeth asked, pulling two different dresses from her bag.

They'd spent the afternoon drinking cocktails and napping by the pool, with no agenda other than hashing through the nasty details of Gabe's infidelity and planning Tess's future – much of which included retiring to an island where she could scuba dive her days away.

Comfortably buzzed, they'd decided it was time to seek out food and had stopped in the room for a quick change of clothes.

"Sure, I threw something sparkly in here," Tess said, pulling out a dress with some fun sequins on it. Slipping it over her head, she stood in front of the mirror and the memory of when she'd last worn it hit her. She'd loved this dress – had felt so confident in it – and now she stood in front of the mirror feeling fat, unattractive, and outdated. Tears filled her eyes.

"Oh, honey, what is it?" Elizabeth said, running over to put her arms around Tess.

"I wore this dress for our anniversary dinner in New Orleans this year. He never even said I looked pretty." Tess blinked, trying to stop the tears, but they fell of their own accord. "All night, he was pretty much checked out. On his phone, or quiet. He barely touched me – didn't hold my hand, nothing."

"Even after he gave you those diamonds? And the balcony dinner?"

"He just crawled into bed and was on his phone while I sat on the balcony and read a book. I'd even brought sexy stuff to wear and everything." Tess hiccupped. "I came in from the balcony and he was on his phone. I thought he'd gone to sleep, but I realize now he was just texting her." Tess wiped tears from her eyes, looking down at this dress she had so loved.

"Take it off," Elizabeth ordered.

"Jeez, Elizabeth, I didn't realize you liked me like that," Tess joked weakly, and Elizabeth smacked her bum.

"You're sexy, but not my type. Now, put something else on and we'll go out. You're a beautiful woman with a million great things to offer someone. Don't give him your power. It's just a dress, Tess."

Tess took a deep breath and sighed, eying the dress that she knew she'd never wear again, then dug in her bag for something else.

HOURS LATER, Tess found herself sitting on the front porch of a bar surrounded by a rugby team that Elizabeth had proudly procured – seemingly out of thin air – for Tess. The mood was festive, as it often was in Key West, and a band played swing versions of popular songs in the corner of the garden. A few people stood to dance, while others sang along with the music. One of the rugby players, Luciano, continued his quest to flirt with Tess. There was nothing overtly wrong with him, Tess thought, leaning back and running her eyes over his tattooed muscular arms and dancing eyes that promised a load of fun for the evening.

"We could get out of here, you know," Luciano said, gesturing to where the team all laughed at a rude joke. "Go for a stroll."

"A stroll." Tess laughed, leaning back to assess Luciano.

"Or whatever you'd like, pretty lady." Luciano ran a hand lightly down her thigh, testing the waters. His touch secured the answer for Tess.

"Listen, Luciano – you seem like a nice enough guy. Though I wouldn't recommend touching women without their permission," Tess said, taking his hand firmly off her thigh. "But I'm not ready for this."

"I'm under the impression that I know how to make a woman ready." Luciano flashed a cheeky grin at her and Tess laughed despite herself.

"Better luck next time," Tess said, and waved Luciano off after brushing a kiss to his cheek. She motioned for Elizabeth to join her at the bar.

"He was cute! What's the deal?"

"This is too much for me, Elizabeth. Last week I was married and lying next to my husband. I just… it's kind of a mindfuck," Tess admitted, finishing her gin and tonic and placing it on the bar while Elizabeth settled the check.

"I get that. But it's not like Gabe gave much thought to that when he was playing fast and loose with the intern," Elizabeth said.

Tess winced.

"Shit, I'm sorry, that was horrible of me." Elizabeth immediately put an arm around Tess.

"Nope, you're absolutely right. He wasn't thinking about me or about the fact he was married. He was thinking about himself and what he wanted. I just don't know if I'm built that way. I can't pretend that I wasn't in a marriage just days ago and have a casual roll in the sheets with some random rugby player. I... I need time. I'm not even sure I could take my clothes off in front of another man right now!"

Elizabeth patted her arm. "I've got just the solution. Come with me." Elizabeth dragged Tess past the complaints of the rugby team and out of the bar, then headed down the street. They turned the corner off of the busy drag, continuing until they ended up at a dark restaurant outfitted in lush velvet and candlelight.

"What is this place?" Tess asked, squinting in the darkness.

"Welcome to Better Than Sex." A waiter appeared and led them to two red velvet stools positioned at a sleek black mirrored bar.

"It's a dessert bar. All the desserts are named after sex acts and, well, if you're not having sex on this vacation then you'll get the next best thing," Elizabeth declared.

Chocolate? It was enough to defrost the numbness around her heart. She smiled in anticipation and she and Elizabeth howled their way through the menu.

"I'm ordering a three-way," Tess decided.

"Perfect. I'll get the morning after," Elizabeth exclaimed, pulling out her phone to text.

Tess looked around at the fun décor while Elizabeth kept typing away. She found herself becoming increasingly annoyed until it bubbled out.

"Could you put your phone away? *God,*" Tess said. Then she looked at Elizabeth in shock.

"Um... I just wanted to tell my boyfriend that if he saw a

charge for 'Better Than Sex' that it was a dessert bar," Elizabeth said, confusion lacing her pretty features.

"I... I'm so sorry. I have no idea where that came from." Tess felt tears well up out of nowhere. "I have to go to the bathroom."

Tess slipped away from Elizabeth and found the bathroom – empty, thank goodness. She stared at herself in the mirror. What was wrong with her that she was snapping at her friend like that?

There was a tentative knock at the door. "Honey? Are you okay?" Elizabeth asked.

"I'm so sorry," Tess said, pulling it open and hugging Elizabeth. "I just realized how much Gabe was constantly on his phone the last few months. No matter where we were or what we were doing, he was always typing away at his phone. I think I just flashed to it when you pulled your phone out. I shouldn't have snapped at you."

"It'll be okay, Tess. We'll get you through this," Elizabeth whispered.

"I don't know what to do. I can't flirt, I can barely think of being with another guy. I know I'm supposed to be all like, 'woohoo! Key West!' and sleeping my way through men and burning Gabe's stuff on the lawn, but I just feel numb. It's like I'm broken. I have no confidence, I don't feel comfortable in my own body, and here I am snapping at my friend for no bloody reason."

"You're being too hard on yourself." Elizabeth laughed consolingly, wiping Tess's tears. "It's been *one* day since you filed for divorce. Let's just take this in baby steps for now, okay? We'll eat those decadent desserts, go sing some karaoke or something, and go home. Tomorrow we can lie on the beach all day long and sleep. That's it. Nothing else is required of you for the rest of the weekend. You have nothing to prove to anyone other than taking one step forward at a time, understand? And maybe, we'll come up with a plan for your future while we're here."

"I think I just want to move to an island..." Tess trailed off and laughed at Elizabeth's look.

"What?"

"I one hundred percent can see you moving to an island and finding some cute scuba guy to spend your days with."

"One can only dream," Tess said. As they walked back to their seats, impulsively, she pressed a kiss to Elizabeth's cheek. "I really love you."

"You too. And now that guy thinks we're a couple." Elizabeth pointed to where another waiter openly appraised them.

Despite herself, Tess winked at him.

CHAPTER NINE

She'd taken to pacing the house since she'd come home from Key West. The days blended into each other in a sea of phone calls, avoidance, and a touch too much vodka, if Tess admitted it to herself. Circling back around the foyer and through the hallway that led to the backroom where Gabe's desk sat, Tess finished up another phone call with yet another friend, the answers coming automatically now.

Yes, Gabe had an affair.

Yes, with a young intern.

Yup, what an asshole.

I filed for divorce.

Of course, it's a shock.

I'm fine, I can handle this.

Over and over, she reassured friends that she could handle this, and of course she could, but something Mae had said to her the other night had become her mantra.

"I know this may be ridiculous," Mae had said, "but I keep thinking about something my doula told me when I was pregnant."

"You're comparing my divorce to your pregnancy, got it." Tess rolled her eyes, but Mae knew her well enough to know she was teasing.

"I am and if you'd shut your mouth, I think the example holds up," Mae insisted, and Tess had waved her on. "Okay, so my doula was counseling me on giving birth and something she said really stuck with me." Mae relaxed back into the cushions on the couch and put her dainty feet up in front of her. "She said you can't avoid the pain – that's what labor is. But, if you want the end result – which for me is a happy, healthy baby – you have to go through the pain to get it. So, basically, what I'm saying is that with your divorce, you can't avoid the pain. You have to go through it to get out of it. Does that make sense?"

"You know, Mae, if I didn't love you so much, it would annoy the shit out of me how on point and reasonable you can be with your advice sometimes," Tess had griped. "But you're right. I can't avoid this pain, so I just have to feel all the feels, and hopefully, there will be light on the other side of it."

"That's the hope, at least. I think everyone responds to trauma differently," Mae said, her tone gentle.

"I just want this to be over. I know it sounds awful, but I just want to be through with this and have it all behind me. I don't want to do all this." Tess had swiped her hand out to encompass the house. "I don't want to pack the house myself, and move, and change my name. I don't want to start all over and go out dating and just... do all the newly divorced things. I'm exhausted thinking about it and that doesn't even include the fact that I have to go to therapy to deal with the emotional fallout that I know for sure is going to explode at some point with me."

"I know." Mae paused. "Tess, are you sure this is what you want?"

"Yes," Tess sighed. "Even though I hate having to go through this. Yes, this is what I want."

"Then you have to do all the things."

"I know, but I just want to run away. Isn't that awful? I want to book trip after trip and just go."

"So, do just that. You can work from anywhere. Nothing wrong with taking some time to travel."

Tess nodded. "I just might," she had said.

Now she sat down in front of Gabe's computer in his darkened office, the glow of the screen the only light in the room. Red and Ringo, their cute ears cocked in question, had followed her. Sighing at her feet, they curled up beneath the desk. They'd gotten used to her new nightly ritual, and it wasn't writing her novels.

Why do you care what she's doing, Babers?

Because that's my life over there.

What the hell, Gabe? I thought I was your life... your future.

You don't understand. This is super stressful to deal with. You've never been married.

I'm trying to understand. I love you.

I don't know what I'm going to do. She hired a hot-shot attorney.

You should get an attorney.

I can't afford one.

What is she saying? Is she trying to take all your money?

No, she packed all my things up and labeled them and put them in the garage.

I'm surprised, I thought she'd burn them on the front lawn, since she's such a bitch.

She's not like that. You need to stop talking about her like that.

You don't have to defend her, Gabe. I'm the one who has been there for you through this.

I wouldn't be in this position if it wasn't for you.

Hey, it's not like I forced you to have sex with me. If you recall, you're the one that came to my apartment... slammed me against the wall... picked me up and carried me to the bedroom...

Mmmm, it was like I couldn't control myself.

Babers loves his little girl, doesn't he?

Tess rolled her eyes as she watched them send a slew of Disney cuddle emojis to each other and try to hold onto the thread of excitement that was barely keeping them together. She'd grown entranced with their text messages, recognizing the same patterns and frustrations she'd experienced with Gabe in her own arguments and discussions with him. The man talked in circles, incessantly hounding a point until she'd eventually just give up, wondering if he was too stupid to see what he was doing, or if he was just that self-absorbed. The more she observed, fascinated with how he spoke, the more she realized that Gabe truly was a narcissist. He needed constant attention and reassurance.

It had been something that had first sucked her in when she'd met him. His need for her attention. It had grown to be normal to have him text her through the day, even while at work, and it was only now, as she stepped back from everything, that she realized other couples didn't communicate like that. Her friends had no problem going out for the night without their significant other lighting up their phone with text messages all night. Tess now saw it for what it was – a desperate need for attention. The affair was starting to make sense, the more she mused over it. As she'd started to write her books and put more focus into the growth of her career, Gabe had wandered, seeking attention elsewhere.

Biting her lip, she clicked away from their messaging and

continued to pore through his emails, screenshotting relevant information to add to a folder she'd been building about Gabe. She supposed it was pointless. Sandra had already told her they lived in a no-fault state. But Tess couldn't stop herself from digging.

Once she'd pulled the thread, it had all unraveled.

Babers hadn't been the first woman. There had been another at work before that, Cherise, whom Babers claimed to have helped Gabe to get over. There were account sign-ins for an online marriage cheating site, and a slew of other things that had made her stomach turn. She should have trusted her gut years ago, Tess silently berated herself, as she clicked on an online invoice. Wincing, she closed her eyes and forced herself to breathe.

The bill was for STD testing, paid in cash, the receipt emailed directly to Gabe. Tess's stomach turned as she realized what he'd really exposed her to.

"I hate you," Tess spat out. "That's my life you're fucking playing with, you piece of shit!"

Furious, blinking back tears, Tess looked up a local lab and reserved an appointment for testing first thing in the morning, something she should have probably thought to do right away. Someone she loved had put her life on the line. *Again*. And that someone was her husband.

CHAPTER TEN

S HE STILL WENT to Colorado.

Perhaps it was because she was angry with Gabe for potentially exposing her to an STD, or perhaps she just wanted to see if she'd have the guts to move to Colorado on her own, like she'd wanted to all those years ago in college, but either way, Tess found herself sitting numbly on a flight out to the mountains.

Tess arrived at Denver International Airport, her stomach in knots as she picked up her rental car. This was the trip she was supposed to have gone on with her husband, to plan their future together. Now she sat in her rental car, her palms sweaty, as she punched in Elizabeth's address.

She hadn't expected the tears to come after she'd been so strong the last few weeks. Packing boxes, getting STD-tested while explaining to her kindly doctor of years what had happened, waiting anxiously for the all-clear results, reading Gabe's messages to Babers while he continued to text Tess constantly and beg forgiveness – it was building to an explosion inside of her. And it seemed like it was going to happen right here in the parking lot of the airport rental car store. Tess sat and ugly-cried it all out.

"Damn it, what am I doing? Why am I even here?" Tess said, frustrated with herself for crying over this man who had so totally eradicated her confidence.

Only when the parking lot attendant started making his way toward her car, a questioning look on his face, did Tess throw the car in drive, sending him a little wave to let him know she was fine.

Colorado had always been the carrot at the end of the stick for her. For years, she'd told herself "someday." Tess's eyes took in the Rocky Mountains, picturesque in the distance, their huge presence seeming to remind her that her problems were small in the course of nature. During her senior year of high school, she'd been accepted to the University of Boulder and had tried to convince her parents to let her attend school out of state. The resulting argument, which was the majority of their conversations at that time, had decided it. If Tess wanted any help from her parents with the tuition, she had to stay in-state for her freshman year. If, after her freshman year, they'd determined she was capable of handling herself in school, they'd let her transfer to Colorado and help her pay for tuition. Considering Tess had been working for minimum wage at the local bakery and had missed the cut-off to apply for any scholarships, she'd capitulated and let her Colorado dreams go.

They'd never made Vicki prove herself at an in-state school, Tess thought, annoyance lancing through her. Vicki, the golden child, had flown off to a private college on the West Coast where tuition had run something like fifty thousand dollars a year, and her parents hadn't blinked. Tess, on the other hand, ended up attending all four years at a state school to the tune of six thousand dollars a year and had worked full-time, funding the majority of her college years herself. A political disagreement and a boyfriend she had been dating had led her parents to cut her out of their lives during this time. They hadn't even spoken in months when she'd lost them. It was still a sensitive spot for Tess. Life didn't always have a happy ending like in the novels she now wrote.

When the call had come about her parents' accident, Tess should have just packed up and headed to Colorado. At the time, she'd had too much guilt and confusion over their deaths to do much more than hold her head above water and barely finish out her college degree. Years of therapy later, she now knew that her relationship with her parents was toxic, and that normal parents don't withhold their love from a child in order to get them to bend to their will and beliefs. Her anger with her parents and subsequent grief at their deaths had perpetuated a fairly dark time in Tess's life, which she had just been coming out of when she'd met Gabe.

It had seemed, at the time, like he was a savior. Totally into her, Gabe had been all-consuming and intensely charismatic. As she'd taken new steps forward in various careers after college, Gabe had seemed like the partner who would help her start a new life.

Now *that* life was tumbling down around her, Tess thought as she pulled to a stop in front of Elizabeth's darling house in an up-and-coming part of Denver. Her friend flew from the front door to gather Tess in a hug, and she knew what she should have accepted years before. Her family actually comprised the friends she surrounded herself with and the people she let into her life. It had been her choice to marry Gabe, and now it was her choice to walk away. Though he wouldn't be by her side like he'd promised, her friends would. And though almost all of the foundational relationships in her life had failed her, her closest friends had yet to do so. For that, she could be grateful.

"I'm so glad you're here," Elizabeth said, squeezing Tess tight.

"I just lost my shit in the parking lot of the rental car company," Tess admitted as Elizabeth grabbed her bag and tugged Tess inside, where her even more darling yellow lab bounded over for attention.

"Hey, buddy!" Tess said, bending down to cuddle Gusto.

"I ordered a pizza, I have wine, and all the time in the world for you to recommence losing your shit. Let's go out back." They tromped through the house to the backyard, where the spring sunshine kept the air warm enough to enjoy sitting outside.

"I'm not even sure why I still came out here," Tess admitted, taking a sip of wine and scratching Gusto's fat head.

"Because you had nonrefundable tickets, a nonrefundable hotel reservation in Boulder, and you needed to get out of the house where you were sitting on a computer torturing yourself by reading Dipshit's messages to Babers every night?" Elizabeth asked, pouring herself a glass and settling in.

"Yeah, that's not quite the healthiest thing to do, I suppose," Tess admitted.

"I would do the same. Though at some point, you know you have to sign out of that account, right?"

"I know, I know. It's just helping me right now. He texts me constantly, all these loving messages begging me to take him back. I don't know how strong I would be if I didn't see what he was saying to this girl at the same time. It's like I take some sort of glee in knowing that I have this one-up on him, you know? Like, ha-ha, you lied to me for months, but now I know all your dirty secrets." Tess crossed her legs and stared out at the mountains in the distance.

"For sure. It's totally about taking your power back. I so get that," Elizabeth said.

"I know you do," Tess sighed, remembering Elizabeth's divorce a few years back. Elizabeth had discovered not only all the sex sites her ex-husband had been on and that he was a narcissist, but also that he was borderline manic. The low point for Elizabeth had been barricading herself in the house while she'd watched him get tasered outside by the police in their driveway, all while on the phone with a hyperventilating Tess who hadn't rested until she'd known Elizabeth was safe.

"How do you get through this? I mean, look... he's blowing up my phone." Tess held her phone up to show the list of messages. "It drives me nuts. I try to ignore it, but he's saying he won't give my wedding rings back until he puts them on my finger again."

"All while telling Babers how much he loves her," Elizabeth reminded her.

"And that he won't sign an agreement and doesn't want to get divorced. He just wants us to move away."

"Where all of this would happen once again if you don't give him the attention he craves," Elizabeth said, tugging a stuffed carrot out of Gusto's mouth and throwing it across the yard. "Narcissists, man. They're the worst."

"It's exhausting. I honestly don't know how I didn't see this in him – this constant need for attention. I guess I was so wrapped up in him."

"Don't be so hard on yourself," Elizabeth said, and Tess wondered if she was. What was this need in her to apologize for her mistakes? Isn't that what life was about – making mistakes and learning from them?

"I loved him." Tess shrugged.

"You did, and he failed you. He wasn't the man you needed," Elizabeth said. "But I have just the thing for us to do."

"What's that?"

"Remember when we went diving in Australia?"

"Yeah, it was amazing," Tess said, thinking back to the semester abroad where she'd met Elizabeth. They'd taken a trip to the Great Barrier Reef to go scuba diving, and it was one of her favorite memories.

"Well, I know how much you love diving, and I also know you're dying to travel as much as possible right now. I follow this deals website and they just posted a crazy good five-day trip to Cozumel. I've heard they have good reefs there. Want to go?"

"What? Really? When?"

"Whenever? I mean, it depends on your schedule, and I only have clients booked out for the next couple weeks. I could block off a window after that?"

"I can't...I mean, I probably shouldn't, right? I should stay around and take care of things at home."

"Is Gabe staying around and taking care of things? Or are you taking care of everything? As in everything? Does he have a lawyer? Is he going to help you sell the house? I mean...if that's what you decide to do with the house and all."

"I...I don't know. No, I don't see him helping with anything. And, yeah, I guess I will sell the house? I don't know. We haven't even gotten that far yet."

"My vote is to sell the house and move out here anyway. It can still be your plan. Just do it without him."

"You know, I've always wanted to live out here," Tess said, looking around Elizabeth's yard and enjoying the warmth of the spring air. The weather was much milder in Denver, and Tess could comfortably sit outside in her t-shirt.

The dogs would love it. "I'll have to think more seriously about it."

"Fine, let's shelve that for now. Mexico?"

"How much did you say it was?"

"Three hundred and fifty dollars for five days and nights in an all-inclusive!"

"Wow, that's not bad at all," Tess closed her eyes and took a deep breath, feeling the call of the ocean deep in her gut. "Okay, screw it. I'm in."

"ENJOY YOUR STAY, MRS. CAMPBELL."

Tess blinked at the clerk for a moment as he beamed at her, her brain cycling in confusion as she realized that while she'd only recently gotten used to being called a Mrs., now she would be returning to the Miss. She supposed it was better than the dreaded ma'am, though that had been increasing in frequency over the years. She wondered if women ever got used to transitioning from Miss to Mrs. or to ma'am. Men didn't deal with these things. They kept their names and the biggest affront they dealt with when it came to aging was being called 'sir.' Guys even aged better than women.

Grumpy, Tess barely noticed the beautiful lobby of the Boulder Hotel as she navigated the way to her room. She'd been deliberately avoiding the mound of paperwork that she knew would face her after the divorce was final. It wasn't just changing her last name; it was all the accompanying documents that went with it. Passport, license, Social Security card, bank accounts, tax ID, business vendor accounts, and so on. It would be a nightmare. She should have stuck with her gut instinct and kept her name, Tess mused, as she let herself into the room. She sighed in delight at the dreamy bed piled high with pillows and the deep soaker tub she glimpsed in the bathroom.

Diving onto the bed, Tess let out a breath and stared at the ceiling, luxuriating in the fact that she had three whole days on her own – to do what, exactly, she didn't yet know. She hadn't traveled alone in over eight years. Before she could think about her next steps, her phone vibrated with an incoming text.

I can't believe you actually went to Colorado without me. Honestly? How is that even fair? It's such a bitch move. You know that was supposed to be our trip.

Tess held her middle finger up at the phone and didn't respond. It continued to astound her how she'd become the bitch in Gabe's narrative, especially in his endless discussions with his Babers. Tess was doing her best to take the high road in this situation, but a part of her – one that she wasn't particularly proud of – ached to show him just how much of a bitch she could be if she wanted to. Instead, Tess took a deep breath – one of many she'd had to take over the last several weeks – and dug out her Kindle to skim a book Elizabeth had recommended. It was essentially a playbook for dealing with cheaters. Ah, Gabe had moved into the angry phase, Tess read. Sinking into the book, she was actually delighted when her phone buzzed again. This time, consulting her playbook, she smiled in glee – he was right on schedule.

I'm sorry, that was mean. It's just that trip was supposed to be about our future. And I can barely afford to get gas, let alone travel and stay in a swanky hotel.

Hmmm, halfway contrite, Tess thought, and found the chapter on that. But what she was reading basically summed up her assessment of Gabe's current mood – temper tantrum 101. Gabe wasn't the center of her universe anymore, would have to fend for himself, and didn't know what to do about that except lash out in anger. Though she desperately itched to respond to his texts with a tirade of messages defending herself and her choices, the book suggested that silence was a more powerful tool at this point. There were a million things she wanted to scream at Gabe. "Boring, unimaginative, narcissistic asshole," Tess spat, and then shook her head, tugging her hands through her tumble of hair. "Take the high road, Tess. Take the high road." She turned her phone off, tucked it in her purse, and headed out.

Tess walked the streets of Boulder aimlessly and thought about what would come next. It was like her mooring lines had been cut, and she drifted, seemingly at the whims of fate. She worried about whether Gabe would fight her for more money. Tess swallowed down the dread of losing part of her business, and instead berated herself for not working on her current book. She had brought her laptop. Without the distractions that surrounded her at home with everything she had to do, this would be a perfect time for her to edit her manuscript and send it off to her editor, easily making the deadline that loomed at the end of the month. She should go back to the hotel. Instead, Tess continued to listlessly walk the streets, pausing to people-watch.

A busy boulevard, Boulder's main street was blocked off for foot traffic only, and even though it was the middle of the week, the cobblestone street teemed with groups of moms pushing their baby carriages and drinking much-needed coffee, hungover college students executing the dreaded walk of shame, and a happy couple tugging each other to watch a street performer sing a song while strumming a faded ukulele.

You wasted my sweet time... do you think that's all right?

Had she given Gabe the best years of her life? Tess

stopped in front of a jewelry store, her eyes drawn by all the fancy wedding rings in the window, promises of love and forever-after sparkling in the sunshine that beamed through the clouds. Tess glanced down to her bare hand, missing the weight of her rings but knowing now that a ring was an empty symbol if the person giving it knew nothing of promises. Despite herself, Tess was drawn inside, quietly walking past the glass cases, peering into each to see the delights they held. The shop was funky, much like Boulder itself, and offered much more than the standard jewelry. There seemed to be mix of vintage and new, with fresh designs that had a playfulness and whimsy that Tess found endearing.

"Looking for something for someone special?" A young woman, fresh-faced and looking like she had the world ahead of her, smiled easily at Tess from across the counter.

"Oh, no, I was just..." Tess trailed off and thought about it for a moment. She was someone special, wasn't she? Glancing down at her bare hand again, she met the woman's sparkling eyes. "Actually, yes, I am. I'm someone special."

"Perfect, what are you thinking you'd like to treat yourself to?"

"Well –" Tess looked at the woman's name tag – "Stephanie, I just kicked my cheating husband out and I want to buy myself a ring that I can wear, knowing full well that I'll keep the promises I make to myself."

"Ohhh, perfect. I've got just the designer," Stephanie gushed, not batting an eye at the "cheating husband" part. She led Tess to a case filled with rings that were both eclectic and delicate, and made Tess smile.

"This designer is quite new, but I love her use of negative space and the touch of fun she adds to her designs," Stephanie said, sliding a tray out. "These are all gold and have varying levels of diamonds in each of them, depending on how blingy you're looking to go."

"Just something simple. The bling isn't what I'm looking for, so much as a symbol to myself," Tess murmured, trailing her fingers over the rings.

"What do you want to promise yourself?"

"To trust my instincts, listen to my voice, and to never let someone treat me like less than a queen." Tess laughed at the last part, knowing full well she didn't need to be treated like a queen – she just wanted some damn mutual respect.

"This one." Stephanie pounced, and handed Tess a delicate ring. "See how it has hints of a crown in the design?"

The ring, a slim gold band leading to a triangle of circles inlaid with two small diamonds, hit all the right notes. Tess smiled as she held it up to the light.

"This is lovely."

"Which finger will you wear it on?"

"The middle finger," Tess said automatically, smiling. "So when I flip Gabe off it will have a touch of sparkle to it."

"Classy," Stephanie laughed. Tess tried to slide the ring on her finger, but found it just a bit too tight. "Our jeweler is here today. He can resize it for you if you'd like to go get some lunch? I can even deliver it to you once it's done."

"Really? Can you leave here?" Tess asked, not seeing another salesperson in the store.

"Sure, I'll come over on my lunch break. Where will you be?" Stephanie helped Tess choose a restaurant, rang up her total, and before Tess knew it, she was sitting at an outside table, sipping on a cocktail, and watching the world go by. She felt suspended in time. No forward movement, no backward movement. Waiting. Waiting for what came next, not sure where to go, uncertain how to navigate these waters. Is this why people stayed in bad marriages, Tess wondered as she took another sip of her cocktail, better the devil you knew and all that?

She couldn't remember the last time she'd just sat at a table and done nothing. It had probably been years since she'd eaten alone without her phone, except for writing in coffee shops on her laptop. Instead, Tess sat, watching the passersby, and tried to give herself a pep talk.

It's not a big deal to eat alone, Tess told herself. This doesn't mean you'll eat alone forever. No, you haven't given Gabe the best years of your life; you're still young and lucky to have your health. Yes, you can move forward and work from anywhere, you're lucky to have a job where you can support yourself. Tess looped these thoughts around in her head, willing herself away from a pity party, reminding herself over and over how lucky she was to be able to make the decisions she could.

But in reality, she was hurt and sad.

Before the tears could well up, Tess saw Stephanie prancing down the street, a small silver and purple bag in her hand, and waved to her.

"Hi, Stephanie," Tess said, blinking back the sheen of tears in her eyes.

"Here you go, all sized and ready for you to wear," Stephanie said brightly, and reached out to squeeze Tess's shoulder. "Good luck with everything. I'll always smile thinking about you giving the haters a 'fuck you' with our pretty ring on your finger. Don't let 'em get ya down, Tess."

And off Stephanie went, as carefree as only people in their early twenties can be, before the world had scarred them too much, her walk bouncy as she waved at a friend across the street.

"I want to be like that again," Tess said, and slid the bag

open to find her ring box, prettily wrapped in silver. She smiled. "Correction: I will be like that again."

Sliding the ring on her middle finger, Tess beamed down at it, delighted with her purchase. She held her middle finger up just as the waitress came with her food.

"Whoops, sorry – that wasn't for you."

"No worries, honey. There's more than one person I'd flip off if I had the choice."

Tess laughed, this time feeling a knot of pain loosen a bit in her stomach, and settled back to enjoy her lunch. Holding her middle finger up again, she made a mental 'fuck off' gesture to her old life. If she had to start over, there were far worse places than lovely Colorado to do so.

CHAPTER ELEVEN

"Are you running away, or are you starting over?" Tess's therapist, one who had known Tess for years and had helped her through the grief of losing her parents, settled back into her chair and studied Tess from behind yellow-framed glasses.

"Both? It depends. Are you talking about my trips or the move to Colorado?" Tess asked, pulling a pillow on her lap to hug it, an old pattern of comfort for her.

"Well, let's talk about your trips. You've always loved to travel, but that changed a bit when Gabe came along. What happened there?"

"I mean, I think we both know a lot of the traveling I did when I was younger was a combination of wanting to see as much of the world as I could before I died, as well as just running away from dealing with the death of my parents."

"You were shown, very closely, that time is our greatest gift, and you chose to use yours to explore the world." Her therapist studied Tess with a small smile.

"And I loved it. I still do. The first time I tried scuba

diving? I was hooked! It was as though I'd entered into this beautiful underwater oasis. I loved not having a routine, being outside the mundane, and exploring new places. I miss scuba diving."

"But you let that go. Because of Gabe."

"I did. It seemed weird to go pursue a hobby on my own without him."

"Why couldn't you take a vacation where he could stay on the beach while you go for a dive?"

"I...I don't know. I guess we just never made vacation decisions like that. He only got a certain amount of vacation time a year and was more interested in going places like cities and whatnot."

"How did that make you feel?"

"Fine, I guess? I like traveling, so I'm always happy to go anywhere and get out of routine. But I do miss going to the water."

"Do you feel like you're running away by traveling a lot at key times during a fairly tumultuous time in your life?"

"I mean...the Colorado trip was already planned," Tess pointed out. "But, so what if I am? Who says I have to sit at home and cry during this whole divorce process? Why can't I do things that make me happy?"

"You can and you should. Does it feel like I'm judging you when I ask you that question?"

"Yes," Tess admitted, hugging the pillow a bit. "It does. I guess I hear Vicki's voice. I should be staying at home, fixing my marriage, working on my books."

"Do you believe that?"

"I trust myself to get my work done and manage the career I've built for myself. And, I love traveling, I have an amazing dog sitter who loves Red and Ringo like her own, and I don't want to sit in the house waiting for it to sell."

"I can understand." Her therapist smiled. "You are also someone who struggles with feeling trapped – by convention, routine, or expectations. It makes perfect sense why you love traveling so much. It's your freedom."

"I did feel trapped growing up. We argued so much, and I had no way out. Except to dip my head into books. I suppose that's why I've been drawn to be a writer. It's my escape, but also a world that I can control."

"How is your writing?"

"Well, I'll admit it's been a bit of a struggle finishing off my romance novel in the middle of all this," Tess said.

Every morning she showed up at her computer, and prayed to the muse to let her focus on her work today. By each afternoon, she'd been pulled away by another distraction – like prepping the house to get ready for sale. Her deadline had been pushed back more and more. Usually, she found writing cathartic, but at the moment, she was so distracted that it was becoming increasingly difficult to get words on the page.

"Is it because you don't believe in love anymore?"

Tess looked up at her therapist in surprise. "No, I absolutely believe in love. I think there's many iterations of love. I couldn't write my books if I didn't believe in love. But, I'm really angry right now. And all of that is pouring out on the page instead of words of love."

"Maybe you need to let that come out." Her therapist crossed legs clad in checked trousers. "What makes you the angriest?"

"That he abandoned me like my parents did," Tess said automatically.

"Ah, interesting. You view this as abandonment?"

"Isn't it?"

"I think cheating can be viewed many ways. But how it

resonates with you is going to be the area we need to work on and build your trust again. I'm happy to hear you say you believe in love, but we'll need to work on you believing that not everyone in your life will abandon you. And, if you want to get all spiritual about it – which I know you sometimes enjoy – the truth is the only person who can abandon you *is* you. So, how are you going to show up for yourself?"

"By giving myself permission to be angry, but also to live my life? To make the choices that I need to make, irrespective of what anyone thinks?"

"And how do you see that manifesting?"

"Ideally? With more travel in my future. Preferably to a warm locale with beautiful reefs to dive on."

"That's a start. Time's up for today, Tess. I just want you to know that I'm really proud of how you're handling this. Everything you're feeling is totally normal. Stay your path, dear, and you'll find your way out of this."

"You gotta go through it to get out of it," Tess agreed.

CHAPTER TWELVE

I t was only for five days.

Tess reminded herself of that as she and Elizabeth arrived at their hotel in Cozumel. She'd handled all the details of her life, hadn't she? One of her books was now with her editor, and she'd even started outlining a mystery novel. She didn't quite need the added pain of trying to write romance at the moment, so murder mystery seemed much more fitting with all the emotions swirling inside of her.

"Look! They have flamingos here," Elizabeth laughed at where a few flamingos milled around a pond in the open-air lobby of the hotel.

"And a peacock," Tess pointed to where a magnificent bird strolled nonchalantly down a paved path and into the trees, seeming like he was in command of the place. Tess admired the confidence in which he carried himself, as though he was certain anyone would bend to his bidding.

"Are you excited to dive?" Elizabeth asked as they made their way to their bungalow. Instead of a big block of rooms in one building, the hotel was laid out in little bungalows that sprawled all the way down to the sandy beach. Their bungalow turned out to be fairly close to the beach, and the dive shop, which would make things easy for them in the morning to meet the boats.

"I am. It's been a while, so I'll be happy to do a refresher course. But, I think it is just what I need. Listen, do you hear that?" Tess paused and listened to the waves hitting the shore. "That's a sound I could live with every day."

She'd been right, Tess realized the next day, as she leaped from the boat and into the crystalline blue waters of the Caribbean. The ocean *was* exactly what she needed. For the first time in weeks, she had complete peace. Nobody demanded anything of her, and all she had to do was remember the main rule – don't hold your breath. Just breathe, Tess reminded herself, as she floated above the reef, the current kicking her along so all she had to do was cross her arms and enjoy the ocean's beautiful show. And what a show it was – turtles, reef sharks, seahorses, parrot fish…Tess lost count of all the sea life that swam by. It felt like being in her own little aquarium and for the first time in weeks, her heart and soul were at ease.

Tess found herself envying the dive instructors at the dive shop. They all seemed good-looking, happy, and at ease with life. Hailing from all over the world, Tess enjoyed tuning into the accents that danced around her ears each morning at the dive briefing. She was even certain she'd heard a Scottish accent one morning, but never saw to whom it belonged. Which was too bad, considering her love for the Celts, Tess thought. With one of her book series focusing on Celtic romance, her readers would have loved a photo of her meeting a cute Scottish Scuba Instructor.

Tess even found herself making friends on the boat. She'd forgotten what a tight-knit community divers were. Why hadn't she just gone to her local dive shop and joined a group? It wasn't like she couldn't have hobbies outside of her marriage, Tess thought, and yet she'd never pursued it. She hadn't realized how much she'd put to the side once she'd married Gabe. Looking back, she realized how easy it would have been to meet platonic dive buddies if she'd just put herself out there. One woman, Kathy, had turned out to be one such enthusiastic dive buddy.

"My husband just had back surgery, so he's staying mainly on the beach," Kathy supplied one day before their dive. They typically went down in groups of eight with one instructor, though they still stayed in their buddy pairs or threesomes within the group.

"Doesn't that bother him?" Tess asked.

"How so? I mean, of course he misses being on the dives," Kathy shrugged.

"But does he mind you going without him?"

"Are you kidding me? I think he prefers it. I travel alone constantly. I'm always leading photography trips and he's used to not seeing me for up to a month at a time," Kathy had told Tess that she was a National Geographic photographer, and traveled quite often.

"A month at a time! Wow," Tess shook her head, the idea shocking her. She'd never even taken a weekend away from Gabe, let alone a month. If she had...would they have divorced sooner? Knowing what she knew now, Tess doubted Gabe could last that long on his own. The man had never been without a girlfriend since he was thirteen. Ever. He didn't know how to be alone or who he was as a person. And she'd fallen right into the role of constantly being the one to take care of his wants – at the expense of her own needs.

"It's good for us. I've always been really independent, and so has he. It's a good balance. We also travel together, but enjoy our time apart too. We've found a healthy balance that works for us," Kathy said, checking her dive computer, "Hey, we're coming back here in October. You should come!"

"Um, hmm, I don't know. I think the divorce is scheduled for some time around then. It depends when the courts get back to us with dates." Tess had filled Kathy in on her current dilemma.

"Well, if you can, let me know. My daughter's coming as well, and it will be her first dive trip. It would be fun! Plus, what a great way to celebrate a divorce other than to go diving? You won't be alone, we'll be here!"

"Thank you for the invite," Tess grinned at her as they geared up, "I'll definitely keep it in mind."

Later that night, she brought it up to Elizabeth as they sat, toes in the sand, with a bucket of beers between them. They were sitting on the beach in front of the dive shop waiting for the fire show to start. Each night the hotel would provide some sort of entertainment. While it should have been cheesy, Tess found herself admiring the skill of the dancers and acrobats. These people worked hard for the guests, and to remember a different show every night and all the complicated dance moves involved? It was pretty amazing.

"You should definitely come back. Why not? This is your life now. So long as you have your dogs looked after with someone you trust? You can work from anywhere. You *do* work from anywhere. So? Why not? It's not that costly to come down here to visit."

"No, you're right. It still just feels weird to be making these decisions on my own," Tess admitted, taking a swig of her Corona and digging a hole with her big toe in the sand. A mosquito buzzed near her head, as they always managed to find her, and Tess swatted it away as she thought about it. "I guess I'll just have to see what happens. I'm going to try to be open to new opportunities."

Tess glanced back as she heard laughter at the dive shop and caught a glimpse of her dive instructor, Stevie, walking toward a truck with another man who had blonde curls. Her heart fluttered and she looked for a moment longer, but they never turned around. Tess wondered where they lived... where did they go after work each night? It must be a fun life, she mused, being able to dive all day and then meet your friends for dinner and drinks later. A part of her craved that care-free lifestyle.

"Speaking of new opportunities..." Elizabeth pulled her phone out and looked at Tess, "I think it's time for you to do what I did after my divorce."

"What's that?"

"You're going to write down a list of what you want in a man. I truly believe it matters. I swear that's how I met Joe. He meets everything on my list, though I haven't told him that yet." Elizabeth had been dating an amazing man for a year now, and Tess could see they had a real future together.

"I don't know. I doubt that works." Tess drained her beer.

"Humor me. Just tell me and I'll write it down and email it to you. Someday you'll look back on it and see that when you put your intentions out into the universe, the universe delivers."

Usually, Tess was pretty open to all the universe and spirit-guides type of talk – she wrote paranormal romance, for god's sake – but she was having trouble getting in the mood for this.

"Fine. Number one – doesn't cheat," Tess said, and Elizabeth dutifully wrote it down.

"How about – worthy of your trust?"

"Okay, that works. What else?"

"What are things you didn't like about Gabe or things you'd like to do with someone? You love the ocean and scuba diving... what about that?"

"I do. It was one hobby I truly missed. I basically gave up diving because he never wanted to go on trips near the ocean," Tess admitted.

"Okay, loves the ocean. Loves to scuba dive or open to learning to dive," Elizabeth wrote down.

"Compliments me," Tess said, warming to the subject. "Gabe only criticized. I would spend all this time getting ready and he would ask me how *he* looked."

"Narcissist," Elizabeth commented, continuing her list.

"Makes me feel confident – comfortable in my own body." Gabe had always commented on her weight.

"Supports your business," Elizabeth added.

"Yes, isn't threatened by my success or being a career woman."

"Is a true partner."

"Adventurous."

"What about likes to travel? You've always wanted to travel more than you have. Well, until recently," Elizabeth laughed.

"Yes, loves to travel."

They continued working their way through the list as the dancers trailed onto the now dark beach, flaming torches in their hands.

"Oh... and taller than me." Tess laughed when Elizabeth looked at her. "I hated that Gabe is the same height as me. I know that shouldn't matter, but it's my list and I want a man taller than me."

"Done and done. I've got it down," Elizabeth said. "This is a great list, Tess. I've got a good feeling about this."

"That remains to be seen," Tess murmured. But as the

dancers lit the beach up with fire, and pounded their feet in an intricate circle of fire and tribal dance movements, it almost felt like they were sending her wishes up to the sky. In one final benediction, the main dancer, a lithe woman clothed in gold, shouted to the stars while fire circled her. A phoenix rising from the ashes, Tess thought, and wished she could take some of that courage home with her.

CHAPTER THIRTEEN

"Yes, Gabe hated purple. Make it purple."

"Yes, ma'am." Macy, her hairstylist who was known for doing a range of colors, brushed Tess's long hair back. "First, I have to lighten you, then we can add in the color. It's going to be a long appointment."

"That's fine," Tess said, not wanting to go back to packing her house.

A few weeks had passed since she'd returned from Mexico, and the days had returned to the same blur as before – an endless loop. But now added to the text messages from Gabe, discussions with her lawyer, and inability to get her writing done were conversations with her realtor and the weight of an unending list of things to do to prepare the house for sale. She'd taken to sitting on the floor of the back room late at night, obsessively reading Gabe's messages with "Babers," drinking vodka sodas, and watching countless reality shows. She told everyone she was doing fine. From the outside, she was. Tess was handling. Her. Shit.

But on the inside? Not so great.

Tess hated nothing more than a holding pattern and she was smack dab in the middle of one. She couldn't move forward until the divorce was final – the house couldn't be sold; she couldn't move out of state. Gabe hadn't been pleased that she was leaving, but at the same time, his refusal to look for full-time work was helping him to push her toward selling the house. She'd agreed he could get a third of the proceeds, as she'd contributed a significant down payment from the sale of her condo, and he was still getting more than he deserved. Still, at any moment, Gabe could hire a lawyer and everything could blow up. This time period of running in place was making Tess's nerves raw. All she wanted was to slam the door shut, ignore all the feelings bubbling up inside, and go.

Her therapist told her this was normal. But Tess didn't feel normal. In fact, she didn't know who she was at all anymore.

"Bright purple or just like light purple highlights?" Macy inquired, arching an eyebrow at her over the dye mixing bowl.

"Purple. All over. Like a brilliant lavender."

"Your wish is my command."

It was time for her to stop reading Gabe's messages, Tess thought, for the thousandth time. No good was coming of it, but much like picking a scab, Tess returned to the computer each night to torture herself with the latest saga of Gabe and his young lover. She supposed she'd been like this girl once, blind to Gabe's lies and shady half-truths, head over heels for him so much that it was easy to justify the way he was. Tess found herself fascinated by the way they spoke to each other, how quickly they flipped from adoration to disdain and back to this weird obsession about their love for each other. It was almost like they had to desperately convince themselves they were in love, that nothing could keep them apart, in order to justify their horrible behavior. From the outside, it was glaringly apparent that Gabe quite simply couldn't handle being alone. He needed his ego – and something else – stroked and Babers was giving it to him.

Meanwhile, Tess was restricting his access to herself as much as humanly possible. She'd yet to actually see him since the day she'd kicked him out almost two months ago. But that didn't mean he wasn't constantly in her life.

You're on fucking Tinder! It had taken less than three days for Gabe to find out.

How would you know? Don't you have a girlfriend?

Shut up, ass. My friend screenshotted it and sent it to me.

So?

So?! Certainly didn't take you long to start dating. Guess I didn't mean much to you after all.

At least I waited until after I filed for divorce, Gabe. Something you didn't have the courtesy to do.

Whatever. You don't even want to fight for this marriage. You're just going to go whore your way around town now. Everyone will laugh at you… the desperate divorcee.

And you? The aging cheater who predictably hooked up with his intern coworker? You think you're the one people are going to look up to?

She'd forced herself to stop responding after those texts. Ultimately, who she did or didn't hook up with, date, screw, or flirt with was entirely her concern.

She'd started a Tinder account to take her first shaky steps, flirting with a few of the guys who messaged her. It didn't mean she'd actually gone on any dates. She was just dipping her toe in the proverbial dating pool to see what was what. Frankly, she needed the confidence boost. It wasn't like being cheated on with a girl ten years younger than her was doing anything for Tess's ego.

"How's the writing going?" Macy asked, as if reading her mind.

"Um, I'm struggling a bit with writing happily-ever-afters right now," Tess admitted, watching as Macy unfolded the tin foil and checked Tess's hair.

"I can imagine. Maybe switch over to your murder mystery series?"

"That's the plan, after I get this book off to my editor. My readers are not very happy with me right now."

"That's life. Look how long people wait for the *Game of Thrones* guy. You write your books when you can and that's that."

Tess wished it was that easy. It was hard enough not feeling like a failure with her marriage in pieces around her, let alone missing her deadline with her editor. She knew she had to get back on track soon.

"I know, I know. I'll have to address it at some point. I'm still telling people that I'm getting a divorce, so, you know, not quite ready to make a more public statement about it, I guess." Tess shrugged. Vicki had been berating her for weeks now to tell the more extended family about her divorce, and then had just taken it upon herself to do so. It didn't matter that Tess wanted to tell them in her own time or that she needed to wrap her head around her feelings about it – what Vicki wanted to do, Vicki did. And holding back a juicy story like a divorce? It wasn't happening. Frankly, Tess was surprised Vicki had waited as long as she had before telling their cousins.

"Why do you have to tell anyone at all?" Macy asked, motioning Tess toward the shampoo bowl. "This is entirely your business."

"Because of social media – people pay attention, questions get asked about where Gabe is. I know I don't have to tell people, but at the same time, if I don't say anything at all, it's going to just look weird. Eventually, the truth is the truth and that's life. I'm getting a divorce. I won't be the first person or the last to deal with something like this."

"Doesn't mean it hurts any less." Macy patted her shoulder gently and then doused her hair in warm water while Tess let her mind wander.

"I just want to be on the other side of all this," Tess admitted while Macy massaged her scalp. What was it about hairstylists that made people want to confess their deepest truths?

"I get that."

"I want to skip all the icky bits. All the embarrassment, the hashing out of the story with people, the friends choosing sides, dividing the house... I just want to be past it all, lick my wounds, and heal on my own."

Macy hummed a non-committal note, nudging Tess back toward her chair and swiveling her away from the mirror as she blow-dried and straightened. Talking was useless at this point anyway, until she finally pronounced Tess finished. Turning the chair, Tess's mouth dropped open at the vision in the mirror.

"Now, does this look like someone who needs to go lick her wounds in private?" Macy asked.

Tess just shook her head, speechless at the transformation. For years she'd worn her hair dark, in long tumbling curls. But now? This brilliant lavender color that hovered around her face seemed to light her up, and Tess automatically straightened her shoulders.

"No, it doesn't. Oh, damn, Macy, this is so good."

"Of course it is. I do excellent work." Macy blew on her nails and then leveled one tattooed finger at Tess's face. "And you know what I see here?"

"What?"

"You may be wounded, but you're not out of the fight yet. You're one bad bitch, my friend."

Tess laughed, despite herself, and let the strength of those words flood her. Interesting how Gabe used the same word to try and take power from her.

"Bad bitch, indeed," Tess agreed.

For the first time in a long time, a punch of confidence bounced through Tess as she made her way to the car, even giving a cheeky wave to a guy who smiled at her in the parking lot. Feeling lighter, and happy with the new hairstyle, she decided to drop by Vicki's and show her nephew her new look. She knew David would get a kick out of it.

"What did you do to your beautiful hair?" Vicki shrieked, pouncing on Tess the moment she opened the door.

"It's purple! Gabe hated purple," Tess laughed, dancing inside and making a face at her awestruck nephew. "And I love it."

"It's so cool," David breathed, coming over to stroke it. Tess whooshed him up in a big hug.

"It *is* cool, isn't it?" Tess smacked a kiss on his cheek and ignored the eyerolls as he pretended to be disgusted by her affection.

"Yup. I want to do green, but Mom won't let me," David pouted.

"That's because drug addicts and thugs dye their hair and get tattoos. Is that what you want to be?" Vicki shooed David inside, glaring at Tess.

"Maybe, if I get to have a cool color in my hair," he replied.

Tess snickered as David scampered into the basement, chuckling the laugh of a boy who knows he's annoyed his mother.

"Great, just great, Tess. Now the only thing I'm going to hear about for ages is dying his hair," Vicki grumbled, moving into the kitchen and automatically pouring a cup of coffee for Tess. Tess settled on the stool and studied her perfectly coiffed and exceptionally uptight sister across the white marble countertop.

"Is that such a bad thing? Childhood is a great time to experiment – there aren't too many rules, you know?"

Vicki's eyes narrowed. "If I let him dye his hair green, then all the other mothers will be mad at me."

"Or maybe they'll be happy because then all the kids could experiment without fear of judgment from the mommy cliques?"

"You know nothing about parenting, so I suggest you shut up," Vicki snapped.

Tess rolled her eyes, but closed her mouth. In all fairness, she wasn't a parent and it probably wasn't smart to poke the bear any more than was necessary where Vicki was concerned.

"I'm sure it will be just a passing phase and next week he'll be on to something else," Tess said lightly, sipping her coffee from a mug that read *Live, Laugh, Love*. Was it bad of her that she wanted to throw it across the room? There was something about that phrase being painted on every piece of wall art at Home Goods that made Tess incredibly cranky.

"So, is this like some sort of breakdown then?" Vicki asked, gesturing to Tess's hair. "Like, I am woman – hear me roar?"

"No, I just wanted a change is all. It's fine," Tess said, the wind knocked out of her sails a bit.

"What's going on with the divorce? Has Gabe signed the agreement?"

"No, my lawyer is still drawing it up. We need to discuss

who gets what, how to divide up our assets and all that. I've been stalling a bit, I suppose, because it means I'll need to see him. I'm not ready," Tess admitted.

"Well, if you're going to insist on going through with this divorce, which I still think is a mistake, you might as well do it right. In my opinion, you're being entirely too nice. I can't believe you're even willing to divide up property with him. This man cheated and lied to you for months – even years, from what you told me you found – and now you're going to just nicely handle this divorce and let him get half of every-thing? What about the student loans you paid off? The truck you bought him? He has a 401k, doesn't he? You should get half of his savings too, you know. Plus, the proceeds from the house when you decide to sell. Don't tell me you didn't put more money in than him, I *know* you did." Vicki paced the kitchen as she punctuated each point with a stab of her finger.

"Vicki, I've told you this before, I'm trying to be nice. I want this over quickly. I don't need this to draw out into some long legal battle over 401ks and who gets the couch. It just doesn't matter." Tess's stomach began to knot up. She shifted on the cool white stools that Vicki had found for her counter. Tess had pointed out at the time that everyone hated backless stools, but Vicki had insisted. Now all her guests shifted uncomfortably every time they sat at the kitchen counter.

"It does matter. This is your life, Tess. You've worked for this and now you're going to just hand it off to Gabe like a fucking prize for cheating on you? What a joke."

Tess recoiled at her words. "I'm not handing it off like a prize, I'm taking the high road so I can protect my assets. Do I need to remind you he could hire a lawyer and turn this into a drawn-out blood bath," Tess said, all but pleading with Vicki to understand where she was coming from. "I'd squish him like a bug on the concrete if he did, but why take it that far, Vicki? Being nice and agreeable will get this done faster and we both can walk away and start over."

"It's complete bullshit, is what I think. You should slaughter him and take him for everything he's got. He's only benefited from this marriage with you," Vicki pointed out.

Tess's head began to throb. Why had she thought coming here was a good idea?

"Vicki, this is my divorce, and this is how I am handling it. Period. Might I remind you that you always tell me I'm too combative? Now, you want me to be more? Just stop. You have not gone through something like this. Much like you tell me to shut up because I'm not a parent, I'm going to have to ask you to do the same when it comes to how I handle my divorce." Tess was firm, but tried her best to keep the sting from her voice.

Vicki slapped her coffee cup on the counter and started rummaging through drawers, pulling out food for dinner.

So much for *Live, Laugh, Love,* Tess thought.

When the silence drew out, Tess rolled her eyes. Typical of Vicki – if Tess didn't fall in line with what she wanted, she got the silent treatment. Manipulation at its basest, Tess mused, annoyed that her sister still tried to control her so.

"In other news, I made a Tinder account," Tess said brightly, and Vicki slammed a drawer, turning around with a whisk in hand.

"You shouldn't be dating already. What do you think you're doing? First the hair, and now you're going to slut your way around town?"

"What's a slut?" David asked from the doorway to the basement.

Tess cocked her head at Vicki, raising an eyebrow in

amusement even though anger simmered hotly below the surface of her skin.

"It's a woman who dates too many men at once," Vicki said, her eyes on Tess.

"Why is that a bad thing?" David asked.

"It's not, David. Your mom just needs to learn a little bit more about being a feminist, is all," Tess said, smiling gently at him to diffuse the tension.

"What's a feminist?"

"A feminist is someone who wants women to have the same rights as men. So, for example, in this scenario if a man was out dating a lot of women he'd often be referred to as a ladies' man, and applauded for being charming. Whereas if a woman is popular with a lot of men, she's often shamed for doing so and considered to have loose morals."

David nibbled his lip, pondering her words while Vicki whisked a saucepan violently.

"Hmm, that doesn't seem that fair," David finally decided.

"Life isn't fair, kiddo. But if we raise more feminists, we may even the scale a bit." Tess smiled at him.

"Does being a feminist mean I can dye my hair if I want to?" David asked, sliding his eyes to his mother at the stove.

"Being a feminist means you wouldn't judge anyone for dying their hair – especially a woman," Tess said, trying to tiptoe her way through this particular landmine.

"I think you're cool for dying your hair," David pronounced, "which makes me a feminist."

"Awesome, my little man. Go on and conquer the world," Tess said, and a delighted David grabbed a juice box and raced back to his game in the basement.

"Tess –" Vicki began, and Tess knew that tone.

"Vicki, just stop. Stop trying to control my life, stop telling me what to do. For once, could you just support me? Without

judgment? This is an incredibly difficult time in my life and
I've asked you for nothing, nothing! You know why? Because
I don't need to sit here and listen to your judgments. If you
want to be in my life, then – just for once – can you try to be
my sister and not some judgmental asshole who thinks she
knows what is best for me? Because you actually don't. We're
completely worlds apart in who we are as people. If you want
to love me and support me through this, could you please do
just that? I get to handle this my way. Full stop. My divorce.
My life. My new beginning. You're either with me, or you're
not."

Vicki turned and crossed her arms over her chest, and
Tess's heart fell as she saw the stubborn look cross her sister's
face. "If this is your attitude, then as far as I'm concerned, I'm
out."

Tess stared at her. "You've got to be kidding me, Vicki,"
she said slowly. "You're saying if I don't handle my divorce
and my life the way you want me to, you're not going to be
there for me?"

"I don't even know you anymore. You're booking all these
vacations, dying your hair different colors, now you've
signed up for some one-night-stand dating app."

Tess stood, slapping her own coffee cup down so hard she
was surprised it didn't break.

"None of this is good for you, you know," Vicki continued, all but ranting now. "It's all going to blow up in your
face and you'll end up lonely and sad, one of those middle-
aged divorcee women that collect too many cats and do
things like meet for Scrabble parties and knit too much. And
forget about having time to have kids."

"I don't want to have kids. You know that," Tess said, her
own words soft as she absorbed the blows of Vicki's.

"You might with a different man. You don't even know

yourself, Tess. You're too impulsive, too headstrong, and that's why you always end up in these messes. The next one will be the same. Another deadbeat guy, another relationship to bail you out of, and who's to say where you'll be at that point? Yeah, I don't think I'm interested in being around to clean up any more of your messes."

"I have never asked you to clean up my messes." Tess moved around the counter and snatched up her purse. "I have always gotten out of them on my own."

"Really? What about that summer job in the Caymans? I told you not to take the job and I told you it would end up a disaster, and it did."

"How could I have known the boss would be an asshole? Sure, I called you crying for a plane ticket home. You're my sister, you're supposed to be there for me!"

"And I was." Vicki rounded the counter, shouting now, her hands on her hips. "I paid for that extremely expensive ticket to get you home!"

"And that was fifteen fucking years ago! I was barely twenty, and I was still learning. You bring it up at every single family dinner. Why? Why do you need to keep laughing at me for that failure? Why can't you just say you were sorry it didn't work and hope I learned something? But no, over and over, you bring this up to friends. You sit and laugh and make those boo-hoo motions with your hands about how I cried to you on the phone from the island. Frankly, Vicki, I think you just love when I fail. It gives you a reason to feel powerful over me, a reason for me to come running back to you, and a reason for you to keep trying to control me," Tess shouted, her hands trembling as she dug her nails into her palms. She strode through the house to the front door.

"If you would just do what I'd say, your life would be a

hell of a lot more successful, wouldn't it? I told you not to marry Gabe," Vicki shot back, following her.

"A divorce doesn't mean I don't have a successful life, Vicki." Tess yanked the front door open. "I've built a wonderful career for myself, I have amazing friends, awesome dogs, good credit – what the actual fuck?"

"A divorce is a failure. Even you'll have to admit that," Vicki said, prim as prim could be.

"And? Okay, so I failed at this marriage. And I'll fail again. And I'll learn and I'll grow, but I'll tell you this much, Victoria, I'm going to do it on my terms," Tess said, slamming the door in Vicki's face.

But she still heard her sister's parting words through the paned glass of the front door window.

"Then have a nice life."

CHAPTER FOURTEEN

M aybe she cried a bit, but with only Red and Ringo to see, Tess would swear to anyone that she hadn't. Like she'd give her sister the benefit of her tears, Tess thought, as she viciously swiped on eyeliner. Her friend, Cate, had been on the way to meet Tess at her house tonight. She'd generously volunteered to help Tess start packing all her stuff so she didn't have to sort through everything alone. The realtor had been pushing Tess to get the house in order so pictures could be taken for the listing, but Tess had been dragging her feet, hating to think about the immense amount of work ahead of her.

It wasn't that she didn't want to move – jeez, all she wanted to do was move forward – it was just so much damn work. She smiled into the mirror, still pleased with her hair color though her previous elation had been profoundly dampened after the vicious interaction with her sister. It had been just over two months since she'd kicked Gabe out. Ironic that her birthday in a few weeks was basically the halfway marker between kicking Gabe out and officially being divorced. Tess pulled on leather leggings and a shimmery navy camisole, and threw on some dangly earrings that highlighted her new hair color. After her fight with Vicki, Cate had issued a change of plans and they were meeting at a bar downtown that one of their friends owned.

Her phone pinged, signaling the arrival of her Uber, and Tess kissed her puppies.

"Best doggos in the world. Love you boys," Tess said, before tucking them into their beds and heading out the door.

She'd scored a chatty driver that night, and while normally it would annoy her, tonight Tess was more than interested in being distracted from her thoughts.

"Love the hair," her Uber driver – Max, the app told her – proclaimed.

"Thanks, I just did it today." Tess smiled.

"Uh-oh. Bad breakup?" He peered back over at her. Tess sized him up – probably early sixties, comfortable in his plaid button-down tucked into creased khakis, and an honest-to-goodness driving cap on his gray hair.

"Why do you say that?"

"Women, I tell ya. You're all so predictable. As soon as they break up, they change their hair and they start working out. I've seen it time and time again." Max grinned as he took the side streets to avoid rush-hour traffic.

"Well, Max, as much as I hate to say it, your theory must be correct because I just kicked my cheating ex-husband out."

"I knew it." He held up his hand to show her his wedding ring. "Took me three marriages to find my special lady, but this one's going to stick, I can promise you that."

"I hope for your sake it does, Max," Tess laughed as he pulled up to the bar, a funky speak-easy called the Tin Horse.

"Good luck with your new life. It stings for a bit, but keep your eyes open – there's always love waiting around the corner if you're open to it," Max said.

Tess said goodbye as she left the car and strode into the bar. Her friend, Meredith, a co-owner, waved to her from where she wiped a long wood bar that spanned the length of the narrow room. Candles flickered on shelves strewn haphazardly along the walls, dotted with books and doodads, and low-slung comfortable velvet couches were tucked in back. The bar had a friendly vibe – warm on cold winter nights, welcoming on spring days. It was an easy stop-in for many of their friends on their way home from work and Tess tried to make it by a couple of times a month to see people.

"Love the hair. 44 North and soda?" Meredith asked, after smacking a kiss on Tess's cheek. They'd been friends for years, had nursed each other through all manner of break-ups and woes, and had an easy friendship that stood the test of time. "Oh, wait. Break-up drink. Let's go with a whiskey."

"Manhattan works for me," Tess agreed, and Meredith bent to mix it as Cate strode in the door, a concerned look on her face. She scanned the bar until she spotted Tess and laughed.

"Here I thought I'd find you crestfallen, but instead, you've got purple hair and are sipping whiskey," Cate said, smiling as Meredith slid her drink across the bar. "I'm sorry it's taken me so long to see you."

"Girl, we've both been mad busy. It's okay. I don't expect everyone to stop their real life just because I'm going through a divorce."

"Still, I should have been here sooner," Cate berated herself.

Tess held up her hand. "Stop. You're an amazing friend, you always have been, always will be. Leave it at that. Now, can we talk about how awful Vicki was being?"

"I wasn't going to say it... but holy shit, Tess, from the little bit you told me, I have to say... what a bitch," Cate said, smiling at Meredith as she brought her a Guinness.

"Talking about the mistress?" Meredith asked, leaning over the bar, settling in for a chat.

"No; Vicki," Tess said, rolling her eyes.

"What happened?"

Tess recounted their argument, with both her friends wholeheartedly siding with her. She finished her second drink, feeling the warm cocoon of alcohol soften her mood a bit.

"It's a tricky word, isn't it – 'bitch'?" Tess mused, fishing out a cherry from the bottom of her drink. "Like, I totally know Vicki is being a bitch. But I was also proud of myself for feeling like a bad bitch today. Still, as much as I try to make it positive, Gabe has hurt me by calling me a bitch repeatedly since I kicked him out. It's a powerful word. It kind of takes and gives..."

"It's certainly one of the more versatile words in our language," Cate agreed.

"So how come I can confidently use it to give myself power and then hours later use it to malign my sister?" Tess wondered, introspection running as deep as the whiskey coursing through her.

"I suppose it's a word you've got to own, one way or the other," Cate said.

"What word is that?" A voice over her shoulder had Tess turning, and she immediately jumped out of her seat. "Owen! I haven't seen you in ages."

"I almost didn't recognize you." Owen tugged on her hair. "Love this."

"Thanks. You playing tonight?" Tess motioned toward the little platform at the front of the room where a small band could tuck themselves into the corner to play. Owen, a hipster finance guy, liked to throw off his suit coat after work, roll his shirtsleeves up his tattooed arms, and sing a few nights around town. She'd known him for years, and they had a relaxed friendship in a similar circle of friends.

"I am. Just me and my guitar tonight, keeping it easy. Is Gabe here?"

"Ah... about that. We're getting a divorce." Tess kept her tone light.

"Shut up! Oh, no, I'm sorry to hear that," Owen said, hugging her once more. "What happened?"

"He had an affair. I kicked him out. Is what it is," Tess said, feeling rather blasé about the whole thing. Or the whiskey was making her blasé. Either way, she didn't feel like rehashing it with Owen.

"His loss. But perhaps another's gain?" Owen winked at her and moved toward the stage to get ready to sing.

"He was flirting with you," Cate informed her.

"Oh, he was not. We've known Owen for years."

"Which is how I know he was flirting."

"Please. He's friends with Gabe too."

"Is he? Didn't you know him first?" Cate waved to Meredith for more drinks.

"What is this?" Tess laughed, but found her eyes going back to where Owen strummed his guitar on stage, "Finders keepers? I saw him first, he's mine?"

"Kind of. Isn't that how divorce bingo goes?"

"Who the hell knows?" Tess blew out a breath and was grateful when Owen's voice filled the room, drowning out whatever Cate was going to say next. For a moment, Tess's heart pounded. Could she hook up with Owen? Was that even allowed? Was it crossing weird friendship lines? Did it even matter? What would it be like to touch a different man?

"Whoa, what's got that look on your face?" Cate whispered in Tess's ear.

"Just... considering," Tess admitted.

"Yes! Do him. Do all the men. Go for it," Cate insisted. Tess laughed, but found her eyes going back to Owen, his black-framed glasses and tattoos looking cuter by the minute. Or, she supposed, by the drink, as Meredith slid her another drink across the bar.

"I don't think 'all the men' is necessary. But we'll see." Cate clapped as they enjoyed the rest of Owen's set before he wrapped up his show for the night and wandered back over. Cate immediately moved one stool over so he could sit between them.

"Great show, Owen," Cate said.

"Thanks. I always have fun here. It's low key, but lets me work out some of the stress from my day. Though I do prefer the more rowdy nights when my band can join me," Owen admitted, smiling his thanks as Meredith got him a beer.

"Oh! Speaking of rowdy! I can't believe I forgot," Cate crowed, slapping her hand on the bar. "I know what we're doing for your birthday. Well, if you're comfortable with it. But I say you're comfortable with it and it's going to be awesome and we'll take over the city."

"Um, slow down." Tess chuckled at her friend, who was clearly enjoying her buzz. "What city are we taking over and why?"

"Because it's your birthday, and you always say you want to travel more, and we need to do something fun, and I know we both harbor an unhealthy obsession with the sweet guitar stylings of one badass eighties rocker."

"Um?"

"Slash!" Cate all but bounced out of her chair. "Guns N'

Roses are touring again and guess where they're going to play?"

"Here?" Tess guessed.

"Nope! New Orleans! And you and I are going."

"What? No!" Tess gasped, both elated and horrified at the same time. Her last trip to New Orleans had been anything but pleasant.

"Yes. And we should go. I know it's where you got married. And I know it's a town with a lot of memories. But you love New Orleans. You loved it before Gabe. Don't let him take the town from you," Cate insisted, leaning over Owen to squeeze Tess's arm. "Please? It will be amazing."

"Um, I don't even know what to think," Tess said, "I just went to Mexico a few weeks ago."

"So? It's only a weekend. What? You're going to sit in that house alone all summer while Gabe lives it up with his mistress?"

"Ouch," Tess said, picking up her whiskey.

"Tough love time," Cate shrugged.

"I'm in," Owen declared, and Tess's mouth dropped open.

"You are?"

"Oh, I'm so in," Owen said, leveling her a heavy look that had Tess's insides turning liquid.

"Ohhhhh," Tess breathed, blinking at him.

"Yes, yes, yes! Let's all go. That's it, it's decided. I declare it so," Cate insisted and despite her misgivings, Tess found herself agreeing to a trip to New Orleans.

As she snuggled into bed that night, the dogs curled at her side and the buzz of whiskey pulling her into sleep, Tess blinked when her phone lit up with a message from Owen.

I see you're on Tinder.

Oh yeah? Did you swipe on me? Tess chuckled at her boldness.

Guess you'll have to swipe back to see.

When no more texts arrived, Tess bit her lip as she considered what to do.

"Screw it." Tess swiped through the app until she found Owen's grinning profile picture. Swiping on him before she could think, she giggled as the message popped up.

It's a match!

CHAPTER FIFTEEN

"I can't believe Owen's coming with us. This is going to be a blast," Cate crowed, all but dancing through the security line in her eagerness to get the trip started.

"It's going to be fun," Tess agreed, even though her stomach had been turning with nerves all morning.

She and Owen had been lightly flirting via text messages for the last few weeks, and while Tess enjoyed the attention, a part of her knew exactly what this would be: a mild fling to scratch an itch. Or, if she was to be honest with herself, someone who would get her through one of those first after-divorce hurdles – another man touching her body. Owen was... well, he was Owen. She knew he had a strong commitment to never *ever* settling down. Coming from a broken home, he'd eschewed long-term relationships for the easier lifestyle of love 'em and leave 'em. Which she reiterated to Cate once again.

"Which is perfect," Cate insisted as they walked toward their gate. "You aren't ready for a relationship anyway;

you've said so yourself. Owen's a nice guy, you know he won't gossip about you or hurt your feelings, and you can have some fun. Is that possible? Can you just have fun with him without catching feelings?"

"I think so. I mean, I'll admit, I'm attracted to him. Or the idea of him at least. Or maybe, I might just be starving for some attention and he's giving it to me right now. But, yeah. It doesn't matter in the long run, since I'm moving to Colorado."

"Which I hate you for, but I'll be out to visit you all the time."

They were going to go over the marriage settlement agreement when she got home. It all sounded so legal and final, and the man who had once been her husband now seemed a stranger. "I need out. Vicki still won't speak to me, and if it wasn't for Chad letting me text message with David, I wouldn't have any contact with my nephew at all. The house will be gone, family dropping out of my life, friends picking sides – it's just not the place for me anymore," Tess admitted. They found a spot at the breakfast bar where they could see Owen approach, and promptly ordered sandwiches and mimosas.

"It'll be a fantastic fresh start for you. It's crazy though, isn't it – how things change when you go through tough stuff?" Cate asked, clinking her glass against Tess's.

"I guess I had just thought I'd lose my husband and the house. I wasn't expecting to lose family and a few friends along with it," Tess said, annoyed at the friends who had fallen to Gabe's side, even though he'd been the one to lie and cheat. "But I've been through this before. People don't handle trauma well. I remember when I lost my parents in college... it was like an entire group of friends that I thought were my girls suddenly disappeared. I was too... sad for them to be around. And I get it. We were young, everyone wanted to have fun, nobody wanted to deal with real life stuff. And real life Tess was messed up in the head over their deaths."

"What was Vicki like then?"

"Even more controlling, if you can believe it. She swooped in and tried to take over all my finances, the choice of guys I dated – even my career choices. She's mortified that I'm writing romance novels."

"But you love it so much. You've worked really hard for your career. I think she'd be proud of you," Cate said, tucking a curl behind her ear.

"I don't know if she's proud of me. I think she feels like she needs to force me into the life that she thinks my parents would have approved of. Then she's done her job somehow? Paid a debt to them? Either way, she barely acknowledges my career even when I've told her repeatedly how happy I am and that I'm so lucky to have found something that I love doing. For me… just for me."

"I think people fear what they don't understand," Cate said. "And Vicki, well, she's not a creative. She understands the corporate world, not the creative. Making a living as an artist is likely her own worst nightmare."

"I suppose I can see that. But who's to judge what is successful? If I'm happy, I can pay my bills, and I manage my career all on my own – isn't that a good measure of success? Why does it have to be done her way? I bet if I'd gone to law school, like she wanted me to, she'd be raving about me."

"I suspect that would have made her happy."

"And my parents would have been proud of me." Tess shrugged.

"I'm proud of you. I think you're incredibly badass for teaching yourself to write books, to go out on a limb and start your own business – it takes courage. And to put yourself in the court of public opinion is not easy, my friend."

"No. No, it is not," Tess admitted. "But I feel like I've grown a tougher skin. Kind of. It depends. I have days, that's for sure."

"We all do." Cate scanned Tess's face with worry in her eyes. "Will you be okay on this trip? Like, I know I kind of sprung it as a surprise, but you wouldn't go if it hurt too much, right?"

"Like I said, thick skin." Tess smiled and squeezed Cate's arm. "I even booked us at my favorite hotel, because it's a great place to stay and easy to get around the city. It'll be fine. We're going to have a kickass weekend, I'll erase Gabe from the city I love, and it'll be a few more steps forward."

"Speaking of steps forward, how about some leaps and bounds for down there," Cate said, motioning to Tess's pants before waving to where Owen was sauntering toward them.

"Right, yes, about that," Tess said, suddenly nervous.

"Oh, shush. It's not like you've never been with a man before, jeez." Cate laughed at her.

"True," Tess said, smiling at Owen.

"And when in doubt, a few cocktails should loosen you up."

"On it," Tess breathed, shaking her glass at Cate and laughing.

THE TELL-TALE SOUNDS of New Orleans greeted them as their taxi rolled into the French Quarter. On one corner a ragtime band danced and played the washboard, on another, a woman offered up delicious grenade drinks.

"Don't drink the grenades," Tess cautioned, seeing Owen's attention caught.

"Bad?"

"Horrible alcohol and loads of sugar. Not worth the hangover."

"Duly noted," Owen said, brushing his thigh against hers and smiling. All day, he'd been touching her, grazing her hand on the plane, leaning over her to look out of the window. Though her nerves had escalated, she'd been playing it cool. As the city she loved enveloped them in her warmth, Tess tried to push memories of what had been into the past.

"Is this the hotel? It looks awesome," Owen said as the taxi rolled to a stop in front of a lovely gray hotel with arched doors, beautiful wooden balconies, and green shutters framing the paned windows. Gas lanterns framed the doors, and a bellman approached their taxi.

"It is awesome," Tess said. "It's a great location because it's not on Bourbon Street, but central enough that we can walk everywhere we want to go. We can even walk to the concert tomorrow night."

"Perfect," Owen said, and they got out and greeted the bellman, waving away his assistance as they all just had carry-on bags. Walking into the grand lobby, Tess chuckled at a woman draped across a man's lap, already clearly a few drinks too deep in her day. They stepped to the front desk, and Tess gave her name. She'd booked through their website, finally agreeing with Cate to book two separate rooms instead of a suite where they all could stay. While she and Owen hadn't exactly had a conversation about the room situation, it was implied they would be staying together.

"Mrs. Campbell, so lovely to have you both join us again. We took the liberty of upgrading you as you've stayed with us several times before. Your room is on the fifth floor, and Ms. Linden's is on the seventh. Please let us know if there's anything else we can do for you during your stay." The pretty woman behind the counter beamed at her and Tess smiled numbly back, realizing they'd assumed Owen was her husband. Nerves kicked low in her stomach as she berated herself for booking here. There were so many other hotels they could have stayed at.

"It's a great hotel," Cate said, having been there for Tess and Gabe's wedding weekend. "Don't worry about it. That rooftop pool is killer. We can float there and laugh about everything when we're hungover tomorrow."

"Okay, you're right. It's fine," Tess said, taking a shuddering breath in and then smiling brightly at Owen. "All good?"

"Let's get this party rolling," Owen said, smiling at her, seeming to communicate with his eyes that everything really was going to be just fine.

"I'm going to go to my room and unpack, change, and all that. I'll meet you guys in your room in an hour? We'll go explore?" Cate asked, and then mouthed at Tess behind Owen's back, 'Is that enough time?'

Tess rolled her eyes.

"Yes, perfect. Let's hit the streets and explore." No way was she having a quickie with Owen. She needed more time. And liquid courage. Thank goodness, New Orleans was a drinking town.

The elevator deposited them on their floor and with a cheeky wink from Cate, they walked down the corridor. A corridor that looked decidedly familiar. Tess gulped back a lump in her throat as Owen counted down the rooms, heading unerringly toward where Tess had a sinking suspicion they'd been upgraded to.

"Hey, look, it's the Tennessee Williams suite," Owen said. Of course, the hotel had to ferret out her name among the thousands of people that booked regularly with them from their online booking engine and deposit them in the same room. She was sure they'd thought they were doing something sweet at the time, and while she could applaud their customer service, her stomach wanted to unload itself all over a beaming Owen. He took one look at her face and paused.

"Uh-oh. Is this bad? Tell me," Owen demanded.

Another couple was strolling toward them, and the last thing Tess needed to do was fall apart in the hallway, so she silently motioned for Owen to open the door. He did so, ushering her into the room.

A corner suite with two bathrooms, a grand living room, and a huge wrap-around balcony, the Tennessee Williams suite was what New Orleans dreams were made of. With windows that ran from ceiling to floor in the living area, and a balcony that showcased the best of street buskers below, it invited the essence of the city directly into the room. Now, as she stood here with Owen, she wondered how stupid she had been to decide to come here.

"Hey, it's okay. I'm your friend, first and foremost. Talk to me," Owen said, guiding her inside the room and sitting her down on a green velvet sofa. From there, she could see directly into the bedroom where a king-sized bed was piled high with pillows and a bottle of champagne chilled on the sideboard.

"We came here for our five-year anniversary. About six months ago," Tess said, twisting her hands in her lap. "As in, here. This room. Gabe upgraded us without me knowing it."

"Ohhhhhh." Owen drew the word out in one long syllable and then looked the room over with a keen eye. "And the hotel automatically upgraded you to it again."

"Yup," Tess said, looking down at the floor and wondering what kind of batshit crazy this man would think she was.

"Well, then," Owen cleared his throat, "looks like we'll have to have all sorts of fun in this room. Replace some bad memories with good."

"Wha…" Tess gasped as Owen pulled her off the couch and all but tossed her on the bed, pouncing on her so that he straddled her. On the king-sized bed. The one she'd lain in with her husband. Never in a million years would she have predicted she'd be here again, this soon, with another man.

She doubted anyone could have.

Too nervous to think, Tess sank into Owen's kiss, letting his touch soothe her nerves, reveling in the feel of another man's body on her own. It was weird, after being with someone else for so long, to taste another man's lips, to feel the weight of his body, inhale the scent of his aftershave. Despite her misgivings, Tess began to feel the tension leave her as a more pressing need arose.

Pulling back, Owen grinned at her.

"This room is beyond fantastic, and we're going to have a blast this weekend. I know it's ridiculously weird for you right now, but we'll do our best to help you. And I'm going to do my best to make this your most delicious stay in the hotel yet."

At that, Tess laughed so hard that tears ran down her face. She silently thanked whatever angels were looking down on her that she had some pretty amazing people in her life.

"You're awesome, Owen. Thanks for not freaking out on me, I know this is pretty weird."

"I love weird. Let's make it weirder. I'm going to do all sorts of naughty things to you this weekend, Miss Tess. But we don't have enough time before Cate comes down for happy hour. So let's get the party started and as they say here... *Laissez les bons temps rouler.*"

Tess raised an eyebrow at him.

"You've been practicing that."

"For weeks."

CHAPTER SIXTEEN

The weekend blurred into one of those perfect extended moments of fun, and Tess never wanted it to end. They laughed their way through the French Quarter, dancing on the street, poking their heads into various odd stores and bars, and even taking a late-night dip into one of the many dance clubs that dotted Bourbon Street. As they stumbled their way home the first night, laughing the whole way, Tess barely realized they were walking in front of where she'd gotten married to Gabe until she saw Cate casting a few weird looks at her.

"Oh." Tess stopped and gazed into the courtyard where she and Gabe had promised to love each other forever.

Seeming to understand, Owen wrapped his arm around her waist, and Cate hugged her from the other side. They stood in silence for a moment while Tess just looked, breathing it in, and said a silent goodbye to her past. It was going to be okay, she realized. Maybe there was some good to coming back here, to visiting the ghost of herself from five years before. Even then, she'd been nervous about the marriage. Looking into the courtyard now, she forgave herself for not trusting her gut sooner. So she'd picked the wrong man for her. Hell, at least she'd tried.

"I don't care what Vicki says," Tess said suddenly, startling her friends. "This wasn't a failure. I'm exactly where I'm meant to be, and I've learned a hell of a lot. More to go, for sure, but I'm going to look at this as a lesson I needed to learn. Maybe the hard way, maybe not the way Vicki wanted me to learn it, but it's my life to live and my lesson to learn."

"That's my girl," Cate said, and they danced their way down the street, leaving her wedding venue exactly where it needed to be.

Behind her.

Back in the hotel, when Owen tumbled into bed with her, Tess didn't even blink. She had enough whiskey coursing through her to feel bold and, channeling the inner badass bitch that her new purple hair called out in her, she'd pounced on him, delighting in exploring a new man and the beginnings of a new life. True to his word, Owen made sure she had all sorts of fun in the bed, on the couch, and in the shower. Certain she'd have bruises in the morning, she'd collapsed into the best sleep she'd had in months, only awakening when she heard the insistent buzzing of her phone the next morning.

"What time is it?" Owen grumbled from the bed next to her.

"Dunno." Tess squinted one eye at the phone. "Almost one."

"Shit. We need food and the pool. It's too hot to walk around hungover," Owen said, heading toward the bathroom while Tess blinked the sleep from her eyes and tried to ignore the headache that pulsed between her eyes. Stretching, she felt the tenderness between her legs, and smiled to herself, pleased that she'd finally moved past the first big first after Gabe. It gave her power, she realized, to make these choices again.

You're in New Orleans with fucking Owen?

Are you fucking kidding me? OWEN.

You stupid bitch.

I can't believe you'd fuck Owen in our town.

I knew you'd slut it up, but I can't believe you'd be such a dumb bitch to do it with Owen.

That guy is such a dick. A total pansy.

You'd fuck him? After me?

Tess blinked at the tirade of anger that washed through her phone, message after message detailing, repeatedly, what a dumb bitch she was.

"What?" Owen was standing naked in front of her.

"How does Gabe know we're here?" Tess asked, glancing up from where she was still scrolling through all his messages.

"I posted the photo of the three of us at the bar last night." Owen shrugged. "Is it a big deal?"

The photo had just been the three of them leaning in together, raising their glasses to the camera.

"Not to me, it's not." Tess looked down at where her phone buzzed again. "But someone has his panties in a twist."

"Fuck him," Owen said, and tossed her phone across the bed, diving onto her and tickling her, causing Tess to start laughing.

"You're absolutely right, Owen. Fuck him."

Tess wished she could be so black and white, like men seemed to be, she mused later that day as they floated in the pool, soaking off the last of their hangovers before they had to get ready for the concert later that night.

"It must be nice to shrug things off," Tess said, and Owen looked at her from behind his shaded glasses.

"How so?"

"Like, as a dude. You can compartmentalize things much more than women can."

"Guys are like that," Cate said from her lounge chair next to the pool. "It's like if they are playing video games, that's all they think about. Having sex – they are only focused on that. Cooking dinner, it's cooking time. While I'm cooking dinner while thinking about sex and also wondering how to level up in the next video game."

"It's true. We do have a remarkable ability to compart-mentalize," Owen agreed. "Keeps our lives easy. Until women come in and complicate them."

"You've kept yourself pretty free of complications," Tess teased.

"And for good reason. I'm not meant for long-term rela-tionships. I don't believe in them and I've rarely seen them work out. Almost everyone I've ever known has broken up or divorced. Honestly, the odds aren't in your favor." He'd obvi-ously come to terms with his views on relationships a long time ago.

"Don't you think that's a bit sad, though? To think you'll never have a life partner?" Tess asked.

"How's that life partner thing working out for you?" Owen asked, but stroked a hand down her arm to let her know he was teasing.

"Touché."

"It keeps my life easier. Granted, I get women who think they'll change my views, and then things get complicated because inevitably I hurt their feelings even when I've been expressly clear from the beginning about what I want and who I am. It never fails though – women always think they'll change me."

"You're safe with me." Tess smiled, reaching out to pinch Owen's cheek. "While I find you delightful, you're not my future. You're much too cynical."

"Careful, Tess, I might actually fall for you with those sweet words." Owen chuckled, but Tess felt a knot inside her ease. This really could be the perfect hookup weekend for her. They would walk away friends, go back to their lives, and move forward – no harm, no foul. As rebound flings went, Tess mentally gave herself a round of applause.

"Guys, I hate to break up this sweet moment where you both agree you're only each other's booty calls," Cate said, "but we have a concert to get to. Let's roll."

THE CONCERT WAS EXACTLY what it needed to be. Guns N' Roses made no apologies for embracing what they were – a loud eighties rock band with one of the best guitar players around.

"Slash," Tess sighed, as they laughed their way down the street, arguing over which song had been their favorite. The band had pulled out all the stops, from crazy video graphics to fireworks, and... Slash.

"His leather pants," Cate sighed, fanning herself.

"You girls are ridiculous," Owen grumbled.

"Shut up, my teenage hormones have come alive once again," Tess declared, laughing. "Just imagine how well he'd play a woman's body."

"Yum," Cate said.

They found a hole-in-the-wall bar, deciding to hang out there and avoid the worst of the crowds that pulsed from the stadium, gleefully singing along to Guns N' Roses songs with others who had just seen the show of their lifetime. Trays of shots were passed, new best friends were made, and everyone agreed that Slash had been the star of the show. By the time they made their way back to the hotel, it was dangerously close to dawn.

"Let's finish that bottle of wine in the room," Owen said. "Come on, Cate. We can sit on the balcony for a while and watch the sun come up."

"Don't you have a flight to catch?" Cate asked. Owen was leaving a day earlier than they were, due to work.

"I can sleep when I'm dead. But what I've never done is sit on a balcony and watch the sun rise over New Orleans."

And so they found themselves content on the balcony, lounging in silence as they watched the city of New Orleans sleep in the hour before dawn.

"I don't think I've heard this city be this quiet yet," Owen commented as they sipped their wine, each lost in their own thoughts.

"Sunday night – well, technically Monday morning. I suppose it's the quietest it will get," Tess said, tilting forward to lean her arms against the balcony rail. Six months ago, she'd sat in this same spot. She glanced back through the window to the bedroom. For a moment, she could see Gabe lying there, silhouetted in the glow of his phone, leaving her alone on the balcony, a robe wrapped over her sexy lingerie, to look out at the city and wonder why her husband didn't see her anymore.

"Hey, pretty lady!" Tess shook herself from her memories to see a man below carrying a white bucket, a jaunty bounce to his step. "Good morning to you, darling!"

"And to you, good sir," Tess waved down to him, and Cate and Owen leaned over to wave as well.

"Ah, a crowd. My favorite," the man declared, hugging his arms to his chest before turning the pail over on the middle of the sidewalk and settling onto it. He cleared his throat for a moment, and then held his hands up to Tess. "I've got just the song for you."

The city seemed to settle into itself, taking a giant inhale, and Tess froze as the man began to sing.

"I know your pain...darling..."

A surprisingly beautiful tenor voice boomed from the depths of his soul, floating across the silence of the street up to their balcony. The words hung, crystalized in the air. Tess's eyes filled as the song punched her, his voice prophetic. Her dreams of an idyllic future with Gabe shattered at her feet, the promise of a new destiny as sure as the sun rising on the man who sang his heart out below.

"Let your worries drift...running with the river...change is coming...oh yes, my darling...change is coming."

CHAPTER SEVENTEEN

The weekend away had only begun to whet her taste for traveling. Coming home to a house that was staged for showings, a shell of what it was, made Tess even more anxious to get out, get away, and get after life. She craved the carefree attitude of the weekend she'd had in New Orleans, where she could laugh with friends and forget about all that troubled her for a while.

"At least I am still writing," Tess said to Red, who had settled himself at her feet, her little shadow. She'd spent the last couple of weeks feverishly writing, getting absorbed into the murder mystery she was working on. Red cocked his head at her while Ringo ran to get a toy, always assuming she'd be up for some playtime.

Writing a book was hard enough, Tess mused, absent-mindedly tossing the ball for Ringo as he scampered across the room after it. Writing a romance novel while going through a divorce? It had been like sticking a knife in her gut. Repeatedly. She'd finally broken down and politely announced to her readers that she'd found herself going through an unexpected divorce and to anticipate delays in the romance series they loved. While most had been sympathetic, many had dug deeper for the specifics of what had happened. Tess couldn't blame them – she wrote drama for a living, after all, and everyone loved juicy stories. But, knowing he was checking her public page, she'd refused to comment and had stayed strictly professional.

Once again, she found herself adrift, struggling to write her book and feeling listless and sad that she couldn't really take charge of her future.

"Do what makes you happy," Cate had advised on the way home from their trip.

"I wonder…" Tess murmured, remembering that Kathy, her new friend she'd met in Cozumel, had invited her to come diving with them again in the fall. Before she could think more about it, she messaged her friend to see if they were going with a group and if there'd be any spots open on the dive boat. "Who knows, Red? Maybe I can get back in the water again. Wouldn't that be nice? A whole week under-water with nobody talking to me?"

Red licked her ankle in response.

Her phone beeped with an email – like it did constantly these days. Tess had been handling everything for this divorce – as in *everything*. Gabe hadn't bothered with getting a lawyer or helping with the packing and staging of the house, or anything really. She'd repainted the living room, something she'd asked him to do repeatedly when they were together, and had spent hours decluttering. It had taken every ounce of her willpower not to toss Gabe's old records in the garbage when she tripped hauling them up from the base-ment and skinned her knees. Even more infuriating? When this was all said and done, he'd prance away into the sunset with a good chunk of money in his pocket, half the household goods, no student loan debts, and a young mistress on his arm. Resentment burned in her stomach at the thought – it seemed like he was getting rewarded for being the unscrupulous one – but she shoved it down.

Play the long game, Tess reminded herself. Be nice. Be nice. Be nice. Get out with as little struggle as possible, and just move on. Your prize is that you'll be free from ever having to deal with someone who treats you like shit again, Tess thought, and picked up her phone to scan her new messages.

There were a lot of unread emails that had piled up while she was focused on finishing her novel. Another house showing this afternoon. Tess sighed, annoyed with how often she had to gather the dogs and leave the house. Another message from her attorney.

Nothing from Vicki, Tess noted as she skimmed through, and tried not to let that particular resentment curdle up inside of her. A lot of emotions bubbling around inside today. She'd tried a few times with Vicki since their big argument, but her phone calls went unreturned, and her text messages ignored. Frankly, at this point, if Vicki didn't want Tess in her life, that was on her. Much like with Gabe, Tess kept trying to take the high road and somehow was left feeling like she was on the losing end of the stick.

A new e-mail popped onto her screen, and she clicked on it immediately.

Hey Tess! Great to hear from you – yes, we'd love to have you come dive with us! That would be so much fun. You should totally come down, get away from all the life crap that you're dealing with. Nothing better than blowing some bubbles to take the stress away. Here's our dates. Let me know! – Kathy

Tess fist-bumped the air. "Yes!" Until she took a second look at the date and her heart fell. They were traveling the week of her divorce date. She had to be in court to go before the judge to dissolve her marriage. Crestfallen, she thanked Kathy and explained the situation.

Let us know if anything changes. You can always book last minute. It's low season there and flights are a steal.

Tess would have stomped her feet on the floor and had a bit of tantrum if Red wasn't currently sitting on them. She really wanted to go on this trip – no, she *needed* to go. Why? Tess had no idea, but for some reason, once the thought took hold, it consumed her. It was as if her last trips had awakened her passion for travel, and now she craved the freedom and new experiences it brought.

Tess sighed, working her way through her messages, starting with the most recent. Her attorney had asked her to call. She might as well check in now.

"Hey, Sandra," Tess said, "How are you?"

"I'm good, and you? Hanging in there?"

"Yup. Taking the high road like we discussed." Tess glanced at the clock, knowing they were on very expensive billable hours. "What did you want to talk about?"

"Have you had a chance to go over the settlement agreement with Gabe?"

Tess thought back to his tirade of messages when she'd been in New Orleans.

"No, he hasn't been in the best frame of mind."

"I understand. But I know you want to get this over with, and it would make the proceedings go much more quickly. The sooner I get the papers signed, the sooner I can submit them to the court and get this wrapped up."

Tess froze.

"Sooner? As in…can you get the divorce date moved up?"

"Yes, if we have a signed settlement agreement, we can probably get the date moved up." Tess almost dropped the phone. "I can't promise by how much, but courts like to see agreements and will typically try to move them earlier in the schedule when they can."

"I didn't know that."

"Have you been checking your emails?"

"I'm a bit backlogged at the moment," Tess admitted.

"Check them. You've got an updated agreement that has been delivered to both you and Gabe. All we have to do is get signatures and you're rounding the corner toward home plate."

"Wow. Okay, thanks, Sandra. I really appreciate it."

"No problem. Good luck, and let me know how it goes with Gabe."

"I will."

Hanging up, Tess glanced back to her computer where the message from Kathy was still open. If the divorce date got moved up, she might be able to go on the scuba diving trip. Sun, sand, and a week of nothing but the peace of floating underwater and smiling at turtles and pretty fish. Tess craved it so much, she actually gasped out loud. It could be a way to establish the beginning of a new way of life where she put herself first. Perhaps she could take more dive trips and that would become her thing, Tess thought, picturing herself diving around the world. It was a hobby that she could do as a single person; all she had to do was join a dive boat to make friends and she'd have built-in dive buddies.

"That's it. I'm going on this trip," Tess said and Red leaned over to lick her ankle once more. "Don't worry, buddy, your favorite dog sitter will come stay with you guys, I promise."

Picking up the phone, she pressed Gabe's name.

"Gabe, it's me."

"Hey," Gabe's voice sounded uncertain over the phone.

"There's another house showing today." Tess plucked at a crease in her shorts. "And we've got two tomorrow."

"That's cool."

Tess rolled her eyes. No mention of asking if she needed help cleaning the house or to watch the dogs, she noted. "We need to go over the settlement agreement," Tess said, keeping her tone even.

"I know, I know."

"So? When can we do it? I know you don't have an attorney, and I want to make sure that you're comfortable with what you're going to be signing. It's only fair that you understand everything."

"Yeah, I get that."

"So? When can we do it?" she pressed.

"Why does this need to be done again? Can't we go over it in court?"

"If we sign it now, the divorce date can be moved up." Tess wondered if he would even care.

"Really? I didn't know that. Sure, let's go over it after my trip," Gabe said, an edge of gloating creeping into his voice.

"What trip is that?"

"I'm road-tripping to Portland. On my own. I've never done something like this and I just really feel like it will be good for me."

Tess bit back the gazillion questions that immediately popped into her head. How was he going to pay for that if all he did was complain about money to her? Shouldn't he be looking for a job instead of trekking across the country? Wait – did he say alone? She almost laughed. Gabe could barely spend the afternoon by himself, let alone travel cross-country on his own. Tess had a good idea who this road trip was going to be with.

"When do you leave?"

"In two days."

Tess tamped down the frustration that boiled up inside of her. So he'd go galivanting off across the country with his mistress while she handled all the house showings and negotiations? Typical of Gabe to do exactly what he wanted, when he wanted.

"I'd like to sign this before you go," Tess insisted.

"I don't know that I'll have time." She could hear the stubborn note in his voice.

"Gabe, please just do this. I'm not asking you to stay in town and handle the showings or help at all with the selling of this house, which you're getting a healthy amount of proceeds from. My lawyer did suggest that if you're going to be absent from helping to sell, perhaps we need to take the agreement back and readjust the percentage of proceeds," Tess said, her tone sweet as sugar.

"No, no, no. I think it's fair where it's at. I'll be by tomorrow night," Gabe said. Tess thanked him before hanging up.

Kathy… I may just be lucky enough to swing this trip after all.

CHAPTER EIGHTEEN

G abe, we're going to have so much fun on our trip. I can't believe I'm moving out there – it'll be better than this town. I'll find us a great spot.

I know, I can't believe you are either. I dig it though. I've always wanted to live out that way.

I know, babers. We'll leave all this behind.

Yup.

What time are you meeting Ryan tonight? Do you think you'll be out late? I'll wait up for you.

Don't wait up, Babers. We're having a boys' night. I'll just Uber home so I'm not annoying you when you have to get up for work early.

You sure, babers? You know I like it when you wake me up.

I like waking you up, with my tongue...

Tess rolled her eyes and clicked out of the messages, promising herself that she would, indeed, one day soon – very soon, she swore to herself – stop reading these messages. They had become like a daily soap opera – as her grandmother had called it, her stories – and Tess tuned in each day to read about how awful she was, how poor Gabe had no direction, and what Gabe and Babers were arguing about in the moment. And, boy, did they argue, Tess mused, wondering for the hundredth time if they could sense the disdain and distrust in the way they spoke to each other. She knew he lied, even to his new love.

Glancing in the mirror in the front hallway, Tess studied herself. Had she spent a little extra time getting ready? Damn straight, she had. Leaning forward, she wiped a smudge of mascara away from under her green eyes and sighed. At thirty-six, she certainly couldn't compete with the skin of a twenty-two-year-old, Tess admitted to herself, studying the few lines around her eyes and one in her forehead. Gabe's cheating had caused a serious blow to her ego, and she was working every day to remind herself that she wasn't in competition with the college kids of the world. Someday, maybe – if she found the right man – she wouldn't feel the need to compete at all.

And, still.

Tess straightened her shoulders, adjusting her pretty summer dress, and felt nerves skitter through her stomach at the knock on the door. The dogs went wild, as their favorite thing was guests at the door, and then leaped all over Gabe when he entered the house without Tess opening the door for him. It annoyed her that he hadn't waited, but she swallowed it down and just looked at him.

Four months since she'd seen him in person. He looked ever the same, his hair in perpetual need of a haircut, and he smiled the same quirky smile at her, trying to hide his crooked bottom teeth.

"Hey," Gabe said, his eyes lighting up at her.

"Hey," Tess said, struggling to process the emotions that flooded her. A part of her wanted to hug him, and another part of her wanted to kick his ass through the window behind him.

"Hey guys, good to see you." Gabe bent to the floor, making a show out of petting the dogs. "Wow, they really missed me."

"They do that with everyone who walks through the door," Tess said, breaking the moment and moving into the kitchen. She needed whiskey.

"No need to be bitchy. I miss my boys," Gabe said, coming to stand by her in the kitchen. "I miss you, too."

Tess shrugged, his nearness unnerving her. Their sex life had never been an issue, and even now, she wasn't immune to the man she once professed to love forever. She'd been with the man for years, it had to be a natural response. Though she now saw him through a new lens, one where the shine had long worn off revealing the insecure boy who needed constant attention from anyone who would give it to him.

"Thank you," Tess said lightly, mixing herself a Jameson and ginger ale.

"Can I have one?" Gabe nodded to the glass, before looking around the house. "The place looks nice."

"It has to. We're trying to sell it, remember?"

"I'm well aware, Tess."

"The agreement is on the counter." She motioned with her glass to where the paperwork was spread out, two pens neatly placed on top. The expectation was clear – sign it and get out.

"Fine, fine, all business," Gabe grumbled, and pulled out a stool – not backless, and something that she'd agreed to give to him in the agreement, Tess noted. It had taken ages of back-and-forth with emails to sort out who got what, and she certainly couldn't recommend this process to anyone, but finally, hopefully, the end was now near.

Tess paused for a moment, unsure what to do, before rounding the counter and sitting on the stool next to him. Taking a healthy gulp of her drink, she nodded to the paperwork.

"Okay, let's get through this."

Three drinks later, and with a minimal amount of fuss, they finished going through the agreement. She watched, silently, as his pen scratched his signature across the page. Tess leaned her arms on the counter, turning her head to really look at Gabe.

"So that's it."

"Yeah, it is," Gabe said, his eyes meeting hers. Eyes she'd known for ages now, eyes she'd once looked into and promised forever with.

"It's a little surreal, sitting here and doing this," Tess admitted.

"I know. After all this work we put into refinishing this kitchen," Gabe said. "Tess... I..."

"Gabe, don't. Just don't, there's nothing you can say," Tess said, dangerously close to... something she wasn't sure of.

Instead, he leaned over and kissed her, his lips sliding over hers. The comfort of what once was surrounded her. It surprised her, that she could still want the touch of a man who had hurt her so.

"Tess...I miss you," Gabe breathed against her lips, and Tess's stomach flipped in turmoil, "I miss being with you. It's so lonely going to bed by myself every night." Gabe stood and tried to tug her toward the stairs, toward their bedroom. However, his words stopped Tess from moving from her seat.

"But that's impossible," Tess stood, crossing her arms over her chest and meeting his eyes.

"What's impossible? I love you, Tess. Of course, I miss being with you. I miss our life, I miss this house, I miss our dogs. I want to be with you – I want to make this work."

Tess closed her eyes. She'd wanted this from him – she'd wanted Gabe to fight for her. But even now, she knew he only had his mind on one thing and that was not on repairing their marriage.

"It's impossible that you could be lonely every night when you're sleeping with your mistress," Tess said, her tone sharp as she stared him down.

"I've told you a million times – that's over!" Gabe said, running a hand through his hair, exasperation lacing his voice.

"And I know you are lying to me. Still, you lie! For once, I wish you could just be honest with me. Hell, if you can't be honest with me – then be honest with yourself. This isn't real, Gabe. None of what you are saying is real. You need to leave," Tess pointed toward the door, fury ripping through her.

"Seriously? You're making me go?" Gabe asked, incredulous.

"Yes, Gabe. We aren't going to be together again. We're getting divorced, the house is on the market." Tess swept her hand out to the room. "All of this is going away. And so are you. You need to leave. You don't get to stay and cuddle and pretend that all is forgiven. Because it's not. This is goodbye."

"That's a hell of a way to say goodbye, Tess."

"Don't act so offended. What did you think would happen? That I'd take you upstairs and you'd tell your girl-friend that you guys were done? All would be forgotten and we'd start over?"

Gabe stared at her, his face mulish. "I don't have a girlfriend."

Tess's hands clenched, barely swallowing down a scream. "Yes, you do. I know you're going on your road trip with her." Tess searched his face, wondering if he would finally, just finally, be honest with her.

"I swear I'm not," Gabe said, lifting his chin, his eyes darting away. "I'm doing this trip alone – for *myself*. For me, Tess. Don't you see how this has torn me apart? I've been lost without you! Lost! I don't know what I'm supposed to do with my life. I have no job, no direction, I don't even want to be in this damn city anymore. I can't even go out because all our friends judge me."

Pity party for one, Tess thought, narrowing her eyes at him as she struggled to calm the rage that threatened to spew out of her.

"Those are all choices *you* made, Gabe. You decided to cheat. You decided to quit your job. You decided to go on this trip with your girlfriend," Tess said, crouching to pet a whimpering Red. He was her most sensitive dog, and hated when Gabe yelled at her.

"I don't have a girlfriend. It's over," Gabe lied again.

"Bullshit. But you know what? Who you screw is no longer my concern. This is your life now, Gabe. Figure it out."

"Oh, like you've been some angel?" He paced the kitchen. "You went to fucking New Orleans – *our* city – with Owen. Made me look like a laughingstock to our friends. The fact you'd hook up with that guy, over me? How do you think that makes me look?"

Tess stared at him, completely astounded at how self-absorbed he was.

"I don't think my choices have any reflection on you anymore, Gabe," Tess said, her voice quiet. She was tired – bone-deep tired – and she just wanted him to go.

"I'm going on this trip alone. I'm going to find myself and

I'll show you, Tess. You just watch – you'll realize what you're missing out on." Gabe turned to leave.

"Absolutely nothing, Gabe. That much I know for sure. *Trust me*, you're the only one that's going to be missing out." Tess said, hugging Red to her. Gabe stood in the doorway for a moment, silhouetted in the light from the hallway, looking at her. A myriad of emotions crossed his face and she watched as he danced from sadness to rage. At least they were finally on the same page about something.

CHAPTER NINETEEN

The hallway was eight tiles across. Tess paced, counting each tile, refusing to look at the woman who wept gently in the corner, waiting for the doors of the divorce court to open. Their divorce was first on the docket, and Tess had shown up early, her nerves strung thin from a sleepless night.

It would be the last thing they would do together as a couple, and Tess pushed down the memory of their wedding that rose unbidden to her mind. A part of her felt like a race-horse at the gate, itching for the door to swing open so she could run away, leaving the past in the dust, blinders on to everything but a new future.

"Tess."

Tess turned to see Gabe, fidgeting with a button at the cuff of the blue button-down shirt he wore.

"Hi," Tess said, not sure what the exact protocol was for greeting the person you were ending a future with. Luckily her lawyer, Sandra, strode up at that moment. Clad in a red jacket and kick-ass heels, she held her hand out briskly to Gabe.

"Sandra Moriarty. You must be Gabe?"

"Yes, nice to meet you," Gabe said automatically.

"Yes, well, under the circumstances, I'd say likely not so nice. However, I would like to ask once more if you're comfortable with the agreement that's been signed, and if you understand all the paperwork?"

Gabe nodded once, brushing a too-long lock of hair from his face. "I do."

"Great. This should go fairly smoothly then. The judge will call each of you forward, and he'll ask you to state your name and if you understand and agree to the terms of the agreement. If at any point, you don't understand the question or you need clarification, please don't hesitate to ask." Sandra checked a slim gold watch at her wrist. "It's time for us to go in; they'll be calling us shortly."

And so Tess sat before a judge, in a courtroom with a grating fluorescent light that turned her skin an odd shade of green, and looked Gabe in the eye when the judge asked her if the marriage was beyond repair.

It was. Tess knew that in her heart. Yet it hurt – it hurt to know the marriage had failed, that she hadn't trusted her instincts with this man, and that she'd let herself be so consumed by someone, she'd lost who she was as a person. A part of Tess wanted to promise herself that she would never again put herself in the position where a tired judge had to be the final say on whether she could move on with her life or not, but that might have just been the smell of failure in divorce court clouding her brain.

They walked to the carpark after, wordless, as Tess thought about how strange it was to feel comfortable walking in silence with someone who was no longer going to be a part of her future. Stopping at her car, she turned.

"There's a house showing with a highly interested couple right now. I'll let you know how it goes. Otherwise, no showings next week as I'll be gone."

"Is it really the best time for you to go on a trip?" Gabe asked, annoyance flashing over his face. Tess wondered how tight money was getting with him, as he still hadn't tried to find a job.

"After a divorce? Yes, Gabe, I'd say it's exactly the perfect time to go on a trip," Tess said, lifting her chin at him as she leaned back against her Jeep and crossed her arms over her chest. The light was dim on the lower floor of the parking garage, and the lot was silent but for the tapping of someone's heels toward the elevator.

"It's just that... I need, I mean we need the house to sell," Gabe said, shrugging a shoulder.

"I understand, but much like you just took a road trip with your girlfriend, I deserve to take a trip as well." Tess tried to bite back a smile as Gabe's face settled in his normal mulish lines.

"I wasn't with her."

"Save it. I don't care, Gabe." Tess shrugged. "You're not my problem anymore."

"As you've already told me many times. You don't have to be like this." Gabe moved to stand closer to her. "What are you doing now? I thought we might go get breakfast, and you know... hang out."

"Are you serious?" Tess asked, her mouth dropping open as Gabe flashed her a smile – a smile that had once worked its charm on her – and leaned in to put an arm on either side of her.

"Yeah, wouldn't that be just like us? Saying goodbye the right way – for old times' sake?"

Tess closed her eyes, taking a deep breath. "No, Gabe. I don't think so. I will say this – I wish you'd learn from this," Tess said, her eyes meeting his, eyes she knew as well as her own. "I truly mean that. I hope you learn and grow from this. We all have experiences in life that are meant to change us. This is one of them. For your girlfriend's sake, I hope you don't ever hurt someone the way you hurt me again, but your track record isn't looking so good at the moment."

"I can change – anyone can change, Tess."

Tess just shook her head at him, deciding not to point out the fact that he'd just propositioned her while fully involved with another woman. The irony would be lost on him. "I know, Gabe," she whispered and let him hug her, breathing in his scent once more and saying goodbye to the man she once knew – the good and the bad. She stepped back. If Gabe was a lesson for *her* to learn, she needed to acknowledge that as well.

"You'll let me know about the house?"

"Of course." Tess got in her car, nodding to where he stood, hands in his pockets, an incredible sadness on his handsome face. She pulled away. Tamping the emotions down, Tess sang her lungs out all the way to Mae's house, where she had promised to be waiting.

It wasn't until Mae opened the door, a mimosa in hand, that Tess allowed herself to cry, gratefully accepting the offered alcohol.

"I wasn't sure what drink was best for saying congrats on your divorce," Mae fussed, and Tess laughed, wiping the tears from her eyes with the back of her hand and snuggling into the couch to cuddle Mae's baby while her friend listened in rapt attention to her morning.

When her phone binged with a text, she was comfortably ensconced in a light buzz of champagne and baby snuggles.

The couple offered on your house – one hitch, they want a three-and-a-half-week close as they have an accepted offer on their house. Can you make it happen?

CHAPTER TWENTY

Three things have been difficult to tame: the oceans, fools, and women. We may soon be able to tame the oceans; fools and women will take a little longer.
  – Spiro T. Agnew

"Whiskey soda," Tess ordered, turning back to stare out the window at the clouds that flitted past her first-class window seat. She'd upgraded her seats for this trip and hadn't thought a thing about it. This trip was going to be all about what *she* wanted. Her drink was delivered quickly with a smile and a cup of warm almonds, and Tess settled back, enjoying the pampering. A part of her wanted to nap – in fact, she felt like she could sleep for a week, as the last five days had been hell – but no way was she missing out on luxuriating in the full first-class experience.

They'd accepted the offer on the house. It threw a huge wrench into Tess's plans, but Gabe had been eager for the money and Tess was fed up with feeling like her life was on hold. Knowing that Tess was leaving for the trip, and that a dog sitter would be staying at the house, they'd rushed the inspection process through to ensure there were no major kinks that would derail the agreement. Once it was determined the house was in good shape, Tess had hopped on a last-minute flight to Colorado, toured several properties, and picked a house to rent that could accommodate her tight time schedule. She'd stayed one night, had dinner with Elizabeth, signed a ten-month lease, and headed home to pack for her dive trip the following day. Tess had no idea if the house she had rented was a smart choice, but the lease was only for ten months. It would be a starting point for her to move on with her life, and Elizabeth assured her it was located in a good neighborhood. All she really cared about was a fenced yard for the dogs and a garage spot for the car. With both of those items checked off her list, she'd signed, and now had a place to move to in – Tess gulped – *three* weeks.

Luckily, she'd found a moving company that would take her half of the furniture; Cate had volunteered to drive out with her and the dogs; and the last hurdle would be signing the papers and giving Gabe a chance to move the rest of his big items out of the house. When all was said and done, Tess had worked like a maniac, checking things off her list with ruthless efficiency, and now she finally felt like she could breathe for the first time in months. From this trip forward, Tess was determined to explore what living life for herself meant. Finally, it seemed, Tess would get to really test her wings. Perhaps it was coming later in life than for most, but without the weight of Vicki's controlling voice and having to placate Gabe, Tess felt like she could finally learn who she was as a person.

And wasn't that a scary thought, Tess mused as she sipped her whiskey.

So much of her life had been defined by other people's

wants and needs that it had become second nature to question her decisions, to ask for advice constantly, to step carefully along every road she took. Writing novels had been the first thing Tess had done – in the face of much criticism from her family and Gabe – that had finally felt like her. It had only been when she'd started making a name for herself that those in her life had flipped their scripts and started speaking warmly of her accomplishments.

Vicki had refused to acknowledge her books when Tess had first started writing. It had been a deliberate power play. For the first year or two of Tess's writing career, whenever they'd been together as a family or at a party and the topic of Tess's books had arisen, Vicki had swiftly changed the subject – glaringly so – and brought the focus back to her own accomplishments. It had stung at the time, as it had meant to, and now Tess wondered sadly why Vicki had felt the need to compete with her.

They'd been at a happy hour the year before, just a small gathering of friends and a few of their cousins, and Tess had just had her first big success – one of her books had made it onto the *USA Today* bestseller list. Their cousin William had been congratulating Tess on making the list when Vicki had wandered over.

"Thanks, I'm really excited about it." Tess smiled at her cousin, feeling proud that her creative work was being recognized. As an artist, it was difficult to put her books into the court of public opinion. She did her best to not let negative reviews sting her, but Tess was still working on building a thicker skin. The *USA Today* bestseller recognition was a huge step toward building Tess's confidence.

"How much money have you made from it?" Vicki, her eyes glittering with the tell-tale sheen of too many vodka sodas, had nudged her way into the circle. It was the first time she had directly acknowledged that Tess had even written any books, let alone asked her a single question about her work.

"Excuse me?" Tess raised an eyebrow at Vicki as their circle of friends shifted uncomfortably around them.

"How much money have you made? I mean, you're this big bestseller, right?" Vicki laughed, turning to try and include the group, who all found other things to look at. "You must be rolling in it now."

"It's nice to enjoy some success from this book," Tess demurred, her cheeks heating in embarrassment at Vicki's continued questioning.

"Blah, blah, blah," Vicki said. "Give us the goods. How much?"

"Vicki... I don't really know. I'd have to look at vendor costs and all my expenses," Tess stammered.

"Yeah, right. You know," Vicki said, shrugging and turning to the group, effectively dismissing her. "Did I tell you guys that I got a huge promotion at work? Plus, I get three weeks more vacation. I think maybe we'll finally put in that pool we've been talking about."

Tess had faded away from the circle, dipping into the bathroom to pat water on her cheeks, and to force herself not to cry. It didn't matter, not really, what Vicki thought of the books or if she was in some sort of silent competition with Tess on who made the most money. All she'd ever wanted from Vicki was a sister – in the truest sense: a relationship where they could celebrate each other's wins and support each other during their lows. Instead, every time she and Vicki had a conversation she felt like she was trying to cross the street with a blindfold on.

They had the pool now, Tess realized, and smiled at the stewardess who brought her lasagna with a warm roll served on actual dishes instead of throwaway plastic cartons. Vicki had the pool, the promotion, and the perfect family – though Tess suspected her marriage still struggled – and from what Tess could see, Vicki was none the happier for it. If anything, the strain of trying to be perfect, of constantly working toward the next big thing to buy or show off to the neighbors, was winding her into a tight ball of anxiety.

Tess bit into her flaky roll and looked back out the window where blue water could be seen far below. Perhaps that was why Vicki was so angry with her, because she didn't give a shit about keeping up with the proverbial Joneses. As far as Tess was concerned, the Joneses could have their perfect house, indiscernible from every other house on the block, and they could spend their time gossiping over the neighbors, basing their self-worth on a sliding scale of comparisons, all while silently drowning in their own unhappiness.

If this was a competition, Tess happily conceded.

CHAPTER TWENTY-ONE

The island welcomed her like a lover returning to bed, enveloping her in sunshine and scents, the colorful rhythms of scooters weaving in and out of traffic, tourist stores hawking their wares, and music – music everywhere – making Tess's pulse pick up in excitement. Here was a vibrancy of life, a casual comfortableness of being, that Tess craved. To wake up next to the ocean each day, wave to people you know on the street, and to live somewhere that people used their precious vacation time to visit was something that fascinated Tess. Did the people who lived here take it for granted? It wasn't without its issues, Tess noted, as she observed more than one run-down shack, drunken tourist, and wandering stray dog from the cab window on the way to the hotel. But wasn't that every city? No place was perfect, and no matter how hard the suburbia of America tried, striving for perfection had a way of intoxicating people so they ignored the cracks in the foundation. Or, as one of her friends used to say, a polished turd was still a turd.

"It's best to examine the ugly side, for it's the broken bits that make it interesting," Tess whispered, pressing her fingers to the glass as they passed a smiling woman sitting on a crumbling stone wall, bouncing her baby on her knee.

"Pardon?"

"*Lo siento.*" Tess smiled at the cab driver. "*Yo hablo conmigo.*" She hoped she'd just told the driver in her halting Spanish that she was speaking with herself. He just gave a friendly nod and pulled to a stop at her hotel. In moments, she was deposited on the curb. Sweating in the heat that clung to her, she rolled her suitcase to the check-in desk where a cheerful young woman greeted her. Tess half-listened as they tried to entice her into viewing a presentation in the morning on joining some sort of special members' club, which she knew meant watching a slideshow on timeshares. She gave her thanks when they finally handed over the key to her room and directed her down a wooden pathway that wove over a small pond where the same flamingos she'd met earlier this year honked at her. Happy to be on her own, miles away from real life, Tess all but bounced her way to the little bungalow that housed her room, grateful to be truly disconnected for the first time in months.

The irony wasn't lost on her as she immediately connected to wi-fi and checked her messages, but how else was she supposed to check in on her friends' arrival? Seeing a message from Kathy asking if she could get them reserved on the first dive boat of the morning, Tess checked the time and realized the dive shop was closing shortly. She'd just have time to get there and put their names on the list if she hustled.

Couldn't they have built this hotel less sprawling? Tess grumbled as she hoofed it over to the beach where a little hut of a dive shop was nestled, its large gear room and changing areas tucked behind it, a brightly colored red-and-white dive flag blowing in the wind. Tess arrived, dripping in sweat, with ten minutes to spare and looked around for someone to help her. A cheerful laugh caused her to turn, and for a moment, Tess was blinded by a ray of sunlight piercing across the ocean, the late afternoon sun casting a warm glow on the man who now smiled broadly at her over the counter of the dive hut. Tess froze, her gaze drinking in the bluest eyes and brightest smile she'd seen in ages. When he beckoned to her with one finger, she went – immediately sucked into this man's gravitational force.

"Welcome! What can I help you with today?" the man asked, his blue eyes dancing, the faint wisp of the Scottish Highlands tingeing his accent. For the first time in her life, Tess understood what it meant when a woman felt like swooning.

"My…" Tess desperately wanted to say it was her sex life he could help her with, but cleared her throat, and handed him her dive certification card instead. "My paperwork for diving this week. I need to reserve spots on the boat for tomorrow for myself and two friends."

"Sure thing, here you go." The man – Aiden, his name tag read – handed her a form and took her dive card, turning to answer a question from another diver who had stopped by the counter. Tess did her best to sneak glances at him, surreptitiously wiping the sweat from her face as much as she could, annoyed when her arm stuck to the paper she was filling out. Of course, the island had to have about a thousand percent humidity going on at the moment, Tess thought, then smiled brightly when Aiden returned to her.

"All set?" Aiden asked, his blonde curls haloing his head, and Tess almost caught herself sighing.

"Yes, I'm good." Tess peeled the paper from her arm and handed it to him with a sheepish grin. Clearly used to sweaty tourists, he didn't blink an eye as he reviewed her questions and then picked up her dive card again to fill in the necessary information.

"Hey, that's a really beautiful photo," Aiden said, holding the card up to look at the photo and back to her. Tess blushed at the compliment, doing her best to not fidget under his assessing gaze.

"Thanks, it's my author photo." Her hair had been professionally styled and makeup carefully applied, a far cry from the frizzy-haired drippy mess that she was certain she presented to him now.

"Is that so? What do you write?" Aiden leaned in for a chat and Tess blinked up at him, for a moment having lost the power to speak.

"Um... romance. And murder mystery. Mainly romance though," Tess stammered, then reminded herself that she was a writer, for god's sake, and she could at least make an attempt to be more articulate.

"I'm a character in a book," Aiden said, gracing her with his smile once more. "But my mate killed me off. Not very sporting of him, but at least I died in glory."

"Doesn't sound like he's a good mate if he killed you off," Tess pointed out.

"Nah, it's the Scottish way. A bit of banter between friends is all." Aiden shrugged, confirming the accent for Tess.

"Gruesome banter," Tess mused. "Seems about on par for a Scotsman."

"'Tis the best kind, lassie." This time Tess almost *did* swoon. Never in her life had she thought she'd actually hear someone say 'lassie' in real life and mean it. "I've got you all set for tomorrow, though I'm sad to say I won't be diving with you."

"You won't?" This made Tess suddenly incredibly sad as well. "That's too bad."

"I'm set to leave for a dive show in the UK in two days, so I am on dry land until then. We dive so much here that I'm just giving myself a little extra time out of the water before a long flight like that."

Tess felt herself oddly deflated at the notion he was leaving. "That makes sense, I know the no-fly regulations after diving are quite cautious." She just stood there for a moment, but realizing she had nothing left to say, she took her dive card back. "I'll see you in the morning then. Thanks for your help."

"No problem, always glad to help." Aiden held her gaze for a moment longer than necessary. She wondered what else he'd help with if she was brave enough to ask. Biting her tongue, Tess hightailed it away from the dive hut before she sweated all over the handsome Scotsman and fainted at his feet.

"Lassie," Tess repeated and laughed, clutching the image of him to her heart, and wondered why it felt like this man was going to have a place in her life. This happened to her sometimes – a knowing about a thing or a place, where she could almost see the impact of something or someone on her future. It had happened, just there, with Aiden. For once, Tess decided not to examine it too deeply – they lived in different countries and the man was leaving for the UK in two days – so she shoved the feeling aside and navigated her way back to the bungalow across the palatial hotel.

Tomorrow would bring what it would bring.

CHAPTER TWENTY-TWO

"So, what's your favorite book?" Aiden asked. He had found Tess straightaway the next morning among the group of divers that crowded the dive shop in various stages of undress as they geared up to go out on the boats for the day. Tess's insides warmed at his nearness, as yesterday they'd had the buffer of a counter between them. Now he stood before her, barefoot and smiling, and she realized she still had to look up at him. It was nice, she realized, to have a man taller than her to look up to.

Not your man, Tess reminded herself, though her dreams the night before had told a wildly different story. Maybe it had been the tequila at dinner, or the tropical locale, but when Tess had finally found herself back in her room for the night, she'd immediately drifted into a sleep that involved some decidedly naughty dreams about the Scotsman. Now, standing next to him once more, Tess's gaze landed on his mouth and she blushed at the thought of where that mouth had been in her dreams.

"Um, that's hard to say, really," Tess stammered, her brain

refusing to pick an answer. "I read a lot and having just one favorite is almost impossible to choose. From childhood? Recent years?"

"Sure, any of them," Aiden said, and Tess noticed he was careful to keep his eyes on her face, though she stood before him in a bikini top and wetsuit half-pulled on. Buying herself a bikini for the trip had been a big deal for her, as she'd always worn tasteful one-pieces. Gabe had tended to grab her stomach and tell her she needed to work on her problem areas. Tess would never be a skinny girl – she just wasn't built that way – but she was trying to overcome her confidence issues.

"I really liked *The Power of One* growing up," Tess blurted out, forcing herself back to the conversation and away from past insecurities.

"The little boxer kid in South Africa?" Aiden squinted in thought and Tess found herself admiring the laugh lines that crinkled at the corners of his eyes.

"Yes, that's the one."

"I don't think I've read it, but there was a movie, no?"

"Yes, there was. I haven't seen it, though." Wanting to know more about him, she leaned forward. "Do you get a chance to read much?"

"I try to, but honestly, I'm so knackered after a day here that I'm lucky if I stay awake for dinner. It takes me a while to read books because I fall asleep quickly when I'm reading."

"Is this a tough job?"

"It's an amazing job, but you have to love diving. Sometimes we're doing four to five dives a day and it really does take a toll on your body. It's not surprising that many of us use our days off to sleep." Aiden smiled at her, and the call went up for the boats to leave.

"I guess I have to go," Tess said, suddenly far more interested in staying on land.

"You're with a great instructor today and diving on some stunning reefs," Aiden said, fading back into the group as he waved to her, already turning to answer questions as divers clamored around him. "Have fun!"

"I will," Tess murmured, but he was already gone, swallowed up by the seemingly endless rush of people around him. Tess could now see why he was exhausted at the end of the day. She couldn't imagine having to answer that many questions, let alone dive every day on top of it.

She wondered if he had a girlfriend.

Shaking her head, Tess followed the dock to where Kathy and her husband, Brian, waited for her by one of the five dive boats boarding to leave for the day.

"Who's the guy?" Kathy asked, her shrewd eyes missing nothing.

"Just an instructor here." Tess shrugged.

"He's cute," Kathy said, "though I'd cut his hair."

"I like the hair. It's kind of got the surfer vibe going," Tess said automatically, and caught Kathy giving her a sly grin.

"Oh, stop." Tess laughed. "He's leaving to go back to the UK. He won't even be here this week." She handed her gear over to a crew member on the boat.

"Doesn't mean you can't get to know him," Kathy pointed out.

"Maybe," Tess demurred and then shut her mouth as the boat left the dock, motoring across water so blue it made her eyes sting. She listened dutifully as the instructor gave the dive briefing. Despite herself, she kept gazing back toward the dock, wondering if she could just catch one more glimpse of blonde curls.

"Girl, you got it bad," Kathy whispered, bumping her shoulder against Tess's.

"Oh, hush, I do not." Tess shoved Aiden from her mind, letting the excitement of her first dive in ages clamor in.

And what a dive it was, with crystalline waters and the current whisking them over reefs teeming with life. Feeling instantly at home in the water, Tess delighted in floating past a turtle, who poked his head up to eye her balefully as she took a picture from a respectful distance. When a nurse shark cruised by, she smiled around her regulator. She'd hoped to see sharks on this trip; they were her absolute favorite. The water soothed her battered soul, seeming to fill the cracks, reminding her there were many ways to mend a broken heart.

When they surfaced, waiting as a group for the boat to pick them up, Tess took her regulator from her mouth and laughed. It didn't matter the stress that waited for her back home, or the raw newness of having to start her life over again – if she could steal moments like this for herself, her future wasn't looking so bad.

The boats dropped them back at the resort for a lunch break, the divers chattering down the dock in excitement over all the beautiful things they'd seen that morning. Tess had already made several new friends, and loved how a hobby like diving could bring people together so quickly. She supposed it was the element of danger that helped to form fast friendships, for when you were underwater with some- one, you needed to practice good buddy skills. It was nice knowing that people had her back, Tess thought, because not everyone in her life had been that reliable.

"We're sitting over by the pool if you want to join us," Kathy said, motioning with a tray in her hands to where a group of divers clustered under a thatched palm umbrella.

"I..." Tess spied blonde curls across the dining area and

saw Aiden sitting by himself. "I'll see you on the afternoon dive boat."

Kathy followed her gaze and, though she smirked, didn't comment on the direction Tess was already heading.

"See ya in an hour," Kathy said, a smile hovering on her lips as she went to meet the group.

Tess wandered over to where Aiden sat and stood awkwardly by his table until he looked up from the paperwork in front of him.

"Mind if I join you?" Tess asked, uncertain of her welcome.

"Of course, please, sit." Aiden pushed his paperwork away and leaned back to smile easily at her.

"You sure? I know you must do customer service all day long." Tess felt a little awkward about intruding on his alone time.

"It's never a hardship to spend time with a pretty lass." Tess felt her insides go liquid as his eyes crinkled at the corners again with his smile. She liked how free he was with his compliments, and even though she was sure he probably said it to everyone, it still made her feel nice inside. Gabe had rarely given her compliments, instead choosing to criticize, and her wounded ego lapped up Aiden's kind words like a kitten with a bowl of cream.

"That's sweet of you." Tess sat down. She speared a piece of sliced fruit with her fork and smiled at him. "I really enjoyed my dives this morning. I was here earlier this year and have missed the ocean like crazy since."

"I don't blame you. The reefs here are some of the best in the Caribbean. When were you here?"

"In May," Tess tilted her head and realized he had been the Scottish accent she'd heard and wondered about.

"I was here then. That's strange that I didn't meet you," Aiden said, tilting his head to look at her more closely.

"I guess the timing wasn't right," Tess said, feeling her heart clench as she met his eyes and then looking away, her cheeks flushing.

"Yeah, that's random. I don't have a lot of days off here, and I'm pretty good with faces. Have you been certified long?" Aiden asked.

"Yes, I got certified in college when I took a summer job working in the Caymans teaching marine biology. It wasn't my major, but my friend was leading the course and needed an assistant who was able to identify the fish and was super comfortable in the water. Luckily, I fit the bill. It was a great experience, even though the boss was horrible. Besides the fact that he practiced zero safety procedures, and almost got several of the students killed, he sexually harassed me incessantly."

"What happened? Did you say anything?" Concern creased Aiden's handsome features.

"I up and quit after he shoved me one day. He'd been embarrassing me in front of the other teachers all summer, making lewd comments about me going up to my room to masturbate and awful comments like that, but the end came when I told someone about a cave he'd found with skulls in it. He wanted to keep it a secret to profit from it, and I thought that was part of the Caymanian history. When he found out, he was so angry he shoved me against a wall. I quit on the spot and hitchhiked to the airport."

"That's horrible. Of course you should have said something. It's so typical of people trying to profit off another's culture. If that cave had true history in it, then, yes, it should have been given to the Caymanian government." Aiden ran a hand down her arm. "I'm so sorry."

"It's okay. The worst was my sister giving me such a hard time for years after because I called her crying for help." Tess shrugged away the question she saw in Aiden's face. "Anywho, after that, I tried to get to warm water when I could, but I couldn't afford to travel a ton at the time. Unfortunately, I live in a pretty cold area of the States and didn't dive as much as I would have liked after that." Tess shrugged.

"I don't blame you. I'm a fair-weather diver myself," Aiden laughed. "I have zero interest in putting a dry suit on."

"How did you end up teaching here?"

"I've bounced around a fair bit, teaching in Vietnam and so on, but when I learned about Cozumel, I decided to come over and see what my options were for teaching here. This is actually the longest I've stayed somewhere," Aiden said, absentmindedly tugging a hand through his blonde curls and Tess found herself wanting to do the same.

"Oh yeah? You're a wanderer?"

"You could say that. I've over fifty passport stamps." Aiden laughed. "I like exploring the world and seeing what's out there. I've volunteered all over. I volunteered at a bear sanctuary in Bolivia where I'd walk the bears every day through the rainforest. I volunteered at a children's orphanage in Honduras. Ran a party company in Vietnam and owned a hostel in Australia called: The Last Resort." At that, Aiden laughed and ran a hand through his hair, "And it really was the last resort for weary travelers. It was fun though. See, I worked in California for ten years, teaching at a surf camp in the summers and saving my money to travel in the off-season. I really liked the flexibility of the lifestyle and was able to venture to loads of countries."

"That's amazing," Tess said, thinking how lovely it must have been to be so free. "Do you have family back home?

Anyone expecting you to settle down and take over the family business?"

"I do have family in Scotland, but no – they know I'm happy living the life I've chosen. I did try the corporate route for a year or two after my masters degree, but it just wasn't a fit for me."

"What made you stop?"

"I used to be in sales for a large computer corporation, and I'd have to travel to all these companies and sell the software programs. At least once a week, I'd pass this fairground and I'd nip in, in my full business suit, and ride a roller-coaster. Just one coaster, and then I'd be on my way to my next meeting. Eventually, I realized I wanted the exhilaration of that coaster ride more than I wanted to close a sale on a software program."

Tess paused, struck by the image of Aiden in a staid business suit, his eyes alight with joy as he rode the coaster, probably to the amusement of the mothers with children in the car next to him, and thought about what a metaphor it was for her life. Chasing freedom, caged in by expectations, craving the rush of the next ride. He'd just figured it out sooner than she had.

"I love it," Tess said, smiling at him. "I'm so impressed you were able to trust your gut and go after the life you wanted."

"It hasn't always been easy, but when I'm eighty I'll be able to look back and say I have no regrets," Aiden said.

"No regrets is a nice way to live." Tess shook her head a bit, realizing she sounded sad. "But you plan to stay here, you think? Since this is the longest you've been in one spot?"

"I'm not sure," Aiden admitted, and Tess marveled at the simple way he mused over decisions that many of her friends would take years to decide. "I do own property in Glasgow that's a nice little nest egg for me. Sometimes I think about returning to live there, but I don't think I ever will. However, I know that I am getting burnt out diving as much as we do with little days off and suspect I'll need a break soon. Maybe I'll move on elsewhere – maybe to Indonesia. I'd like to explore there."

"Sure, Indonesia, right." Tess laughed. "You say it so casually, like you can just pop up and move to other countries."

"You can. It just depends what you want out of life," Aiden said. "What about you, Tess? What do you want out of life?"

"I don't know," Tess admitted, pushing food around on her plate as she thought about it. "I love writing and am happy that I found my way into this career. But, well, I'm kind of at a new transition and I guess once the dust settles, we'll see."

"Divorce?" Aiden asked, crossing his arms behind his head and treating Tess to a view of an intricate tattoo on his bicep.

"How'd you guess?"

"Most people wouldn't use the word transition unless they got fired or divorced, and it doesn't sound like you can fire yourself from your writing gig."

"Excellent point." Tess met his eyes. "Yes, divorced not even a week, actually."

"Congratulations," Aiden said, and Tess found herself smiling at him. "Then you've gone and treated yourself to a dive trip. The first step in discovering what you want out of life."

"True. More diving, that's for sure."

"Water is the best medicine, they say. Nothing like blowing some bubbles to clear the mind for a bit." Aiden reached out to touch her arm. "Are you okay, though?"

"I... I actually am," Tess stammered, struck by the kindness she saw in Aiden's eyes. "It hasn't been a fun time, and I know I still have a mess of yucky feelings to deal with, but yeah, I'm going to be just fine. When I get back from the trip, I'm moving to Colorado and starting my life over."

"See? It's not as hard to get up and go as you may think," Aiden said, then nodded out to where divers had started heading toward the boats. "Speaking of get up and go... I think it's time for us to head back to the shop."

Had an hour passed so quickly? Tess had barely noticed the time, she'd been so caught up in basking in the nearness of this man.

"Right. I need to stop back at my room first." Tess barely resisted telling him which bungalow was hers – right, like he'd actually sneak into it at night like in her dreams – and stood. "Thanks for letting me crash your lunch. I enjoyed talking with you."

"You too. Have fun today, Tess. You deserve it."

She did deserve to have some fun, Tess thought as she walked away, though she was certain she and Aiden were thinking of two different kinds of fun.

CHAPTER TWENTY-THREE

The next morning, after another night of dreams that left her aching in need, Tess searched the hustle and bustle of the dive shop for Aiden, but to no avail. Had he left for his trip already? It would be just her luck to have met someone who truly captured her interest and to never see him again. Not that she was likely to see him again anyway, Tess reminded herself, irrespective of whether he was gone on his trip or not. It wasn't like Tess would be visiting Cozumel again any time soon, and she doubted he'd be trekking his way through Colorado if his sights were set on Indonesia.

Resigning herself to the inevitability of the nature of life, Tess geared up and met Kathy at the boat.

"How'd you sleep?"

"Great, thanks," Tess said, handing her gear over to the guide who was loading the boat. The wind was still today, and the water looked like glass. It was going to be a great day for diving.

"Where's your man?"

"He's not my man," Tess grumbled, having already

taken some ribbing from Kathy and their friends last night. All the people they were traveling with were coupled off, and more than one of them had taken an interest in her crush.

"Aww, did he leave already?"

"I don't know, I haven't seen him," Tess admitted, annoyed with herself for not asking him to go out for a beer or something the day before when she'd had the chance. She'd never been good at flirting, and now her chance had passed her by.

"Well, I'm sure he'd say goodbye, no?"

"Why? I'm just another customer in the sea of endless customers he deals with. I doubt it even crossed his mind." Tess boarded the boat, annoyed at herself for even feeling grumpy at this situation. Here she was in paradise, about to go on another day of amazing dives – she'd even signed up for a night dive – and a man she didn't even know was distracting her thoughts.

"Maybe, maybe not." Kathy shrugged. "But I think I see blonde curls by the pool."

"Really?" Tess shot up and shaded her eyes. Sure enough, she could just make out Aiden by the pool, speaking to two people in the water and holding up a regulator.

"Girl, you got it bad." Kathy laughed.

"Shut it," Tess sat down, unable to wipe the grin from her face. He wasn't gone yet! Maybe, just maybe, she'd work up the courage to ask him out for a drink after her dives tonight.

"Oh no, I'm doing the night dive," she exclaimed.

"So? Cancel and go out with him."

"You make it sound so easy."

"Don't overcomplicate things. Your life is tough enough as it is right now," Kathy said and then they both shut up to listen to the briefing. But all Tess could think about was the fact that Aiden was still at the resort. Now she just needed to put her big girl pants on and make a move. Any move.

The dive was amazing, again. And Tess was looking forward to talking with Aiden about it at lunch. But she saw nothing of him all day. By the time the sun was nearing the horizon, she resigned herself to the fact that she'd missed out on an opportunity. Perhaps she'd been reading too many romance novels – and erotic ones at that – where having a fling with the sexy scuba instructor was just what happened. If she'd written the story, he would have asked her to dinner yesterday at lunch and they would have spent all night exploring each other's... depths. Tess smirked, giving herself a mental high-five at her scuba pun, and then made her way to the shop where a smaller cluster of divers was waiting to go out on the boat for a night dive.

"Tess! Hi – I was wondering if I'd see you," Aiden's voice came from behind her and Tess gulped, closing her eyes and mouthing a silent thank you to the universe.

"Hey, Aiden! I thought you might have left," Tess said, turning to smile at him. He looked just as cute today, a long-sleeved shirt hugging his arms, highlighting the blue of his eyes.

"I'm heading out tomorrow, but I have night duty tonight," Aiden said, gesturing toward the shop.

"I thought you couldn't dive?"

"Someone stays at the shop while the boat is out in case they need to radio in for anything. It means a late close for me, but I'm all packed for my trip anyway."

"That's good," Tess said, nodding lamely as she tried to work up the courage she'd promised herself she would have if she saw him again, "Um, so how late will you be? Maybe we could get a beer." There. She'd said it.

"Ah, I'm afraid I won't be going out on the town tonight."

Tess felt herself deflate. "That's too bad. Just thought I'd ask."

"But if you can grab a beer from your mini-fridge, I can have one here with you while I close up shop," Aiden said, smiling at her.

"Ah, yeah, I totally can do that. They restock beers every day." Tess knew she sounded dumb, but was too delighted she'd get to spend a little more time with him to care.

"So I hear. Have fun on your dive – find an octopus for me. They're so cool to see at night." Aiden brushed a hand down her arm before stepping behind the desk to answer the phone.

Okay, so maybe it wouldn't be like her erotic romance novels, Tess thought as she all but skipped down the dock, but at the very least she'd get to spend a little more time with Aiden. And so what if it would only be fodder for a few naughty dreams down the road? It was nice to spend time with a sexy man who complimented her – and for now, that was enough for her.

Baby steps.

CHAPTER TWENTY-FOUR

"Tell me more about these romance stories of yours... are they naughty ones? Do they have women on the covers being hugged by the Fabio types?" Aiden asked, and Tess laughed, sipping her beer. The night dive had been gorgeous, and she'd not only seen a sleeping turtle but also two octopus on the hunt. She couldn't decide what she was more thrilled about – the dive or having a beer with Aiden – but as far as she was concerned, this was a perfect night.

They sat at the end of the dock, their feet dangling just above the water, the fire lanterns illuminating the walkways of the beach flickering warmly under the palm trees. A breeze brushed her hair, keeping the mosquitos at bay, and Tess leaned back on her arms, looking to see the first of the stars blinking out above them.

"No, I don't have any bodice-rippers, but yes, my stories definitely have some naughty bits to them." Tess laughed. "But they're not full on erotica either."

"Have you ever written erotica?" Aiden asked, his eyes

lighting in interest and Tess laughed again, a faint blush tingeing her cheeks.

"Maybe, a time or two. Under a pen name. Which I shall never reveal," Tess said, already cutting off the question she saw dancing on his face.

"Oh, a secret pen name of sordid stories. A woman of mystery."

"Not quite," she said, though she liked his portrayal of her. "But it's always interesting to write in different genres and see what you like."

"I think that has to be really gratifying – to be able to write something creative and sell it. I admire that. It takes some cojones to put creative work out there." Tess felt a wash of pride rush through her.

"It is satisfying, actually. Sometimes terrifying, and I always get really nervous before I publish, but it feels good to work my creative muscles." She sipped her beer quickly as her mind flashed to other muscles she'd like to work. Her skin flushed with heat.

"That's awesome. I really admire creatives. You should be proud of yourself." Tess was struck once more by how genuinely kind this man was. It wasn't just a customer service spiel, she could tell; he really meant it when he gave compliments.

"Thank you, I am working on it," Tess said. Then before he could ask her a question, she continued, "So will you go home to see your family after the dive show?"

"Yeah, I'll pop in for a few days to see my parents and my niece, eat some haggis, have a wee whisky or two with friends… the usual." Aiden laughed at Tess's expression, his smile lighting up his face.

"Haggis?"

"Yes, it's delicious."

"Erm, we may have to disagree there." Tess shook her head.

"Have you tried it?"

"I don't have to try it to know I don't like it," Tess insisted.

"Can't knock it 'til you try it."

"I'll leave that to you." Tess stretched her legs out in front of her and sighed, knowing their beers were almost finished and he would have to go soon.

"Are you excited about Colorado?" Aiden asked.

"I'm excited to move my life forward," Tess admitted. "I feel like I've been in this holding pattern for the last five months and finally, I get to do what I want. I'm nervous, I'll admit, but I have friends in Colorado. I'll be okay."

"Do you miss him? Your ex?"

"I don't, not really." Tess was surprised to find it was true. "I think he hurt me so horribly that I just kind of shut the door on my feelings for him. But I do miss being in a couple. I'm used to someone being there at night, to go to dinner with, or watch a show on the couch together with. Just that kind of thing… the nearness of someone."

"He cheated," Aiden said, and it wasn't a question.

"Yeah, he did. And once that foundation of trust is broken – well, for me at least – there was no getting it back. Love him or not love him, it doesn't matter anymore. A relationship without trust has no future." Tess looked up at the stars once more as the waves lapped lightly below them.

"I completely agree. There's nothing I despise more than a liar or a cheat," Aiden said, his handsome face twisted in a grimace.

"Been there?" Tess asked, studying him.

"I dated a girl recently who stole from me. It really messed with my head."

"I'm sorry." Tess reached out to touch his arm. "That's really tough. You should feel safe with the person you're with."

"Live and learn, right?"

"Some lessons are harder than others." Tess shook her head, her hair still drying from the dive and tumbling in wild curls down her back. "But hopefully they're ones that will stay learned."

"I hope so for your sake too, Tess." Aiden turned, bumping his shoulder to hers. "I have to go, there's loads for me to do still before my flight in the morning."

"Thanks for having a beer with me." Tess stood and they wandered back down the dock. "This was nice."

"It was nice," Aiden said, stopping by the door to the shop. She looked up at him, the light hanging over the door silhouetting his blonde curls in a halo. "Think you'll be back to dive?"

"Someday, hopefully." Tess wondered if he'd still be living there. Working up the courage, she smiled at him. "Care to stay in touch?"

"Yeah, I'd like that." Aiden reached into the office. She heard a little stamping sound and then he handed her a piece of paper with his full name and dive instructor number on it, circled by a bear claw. "Sorry for the stamp; it's just an easy way for me to sign dive logs."

"I like it," Tess said and smiled at him. "I'll find you on Facebook. It was nice meeting you."

"You too." Aiden leaned against the doorway, his arms crossed over his chest. Tess smiled and, not knowing if she should hug him or not, gave an awkward half-wave. Turning over her shoulder, she looked at him once more, smiling in the glow of the light, watching her as she walked away into the darkness.

"Goodbye!"

"I prefer saying 'until our paths cross again' instead of goodbye," Aiden called.

"Until our paths cross again, then," Tess said, his words warming her. Maybe, someday, that would be true.

CHAPTER TWENTY-FIVE

For the first time in a week, Tess barely slept as she tossed and turned, thinking about what the morning would bring, as well as everything she had to accomplish on her to-do list. Lists, that is. Lists upon lists. Groaning, Tess rubbed the sleep out of her eyes and rolled to cuddle Red, who had wiggled his way across the bed on his belly to snuffle in her face. Ringo popped his head up from the nest of blankets he'd made at the bottom of the bed, interested to see if it was time for breakfast. The consistency of life – the routine of feeding the dogs, taking them outside, and making a cup of coffee – propelled Tess from bed and reminded her that this was just another morning, in a slew of many, that she would handle. It wouldn't be her worst day, nor would it be her best, but the gift of hardships in life was knowing she could get through tough days.

After Aiden had left, the rest of her vacation had passed much too quickly, as vacations are wont to do. She knew she should be excited, for in a matter of weeks her new life would start, but she still had a mountain of work to do, several sad goodbyes to make, and, well, today to deal with.

Gabe was coming to the house with his father to load the rest of his items and officially move out. Tess needed to be here, as there were a few items they still hadn't agreed upon, and he had asked to say goodbye to the dogs. All Tess wanted to do was get in the car, drive to the airport, and fly back to Cozumel.

As she hauled herself out of bed and started her day, she kept picturing Aiden's smiling face behind the dive shop counter. She'd only known him a short time, and yet she'd found herself crushing hard on this man. Whether it was his easygoing manner, the kindness in his eyes, or his carefree ability to wander the world with confidence, Tess was drawn to him.

The night he'd left she'd immediately gone to her room and done what any normal person would do – stalked his Facebook page. True to his word, it was filled with pictures of his travels around the world – from him smiling while feeding peanuts to an orphaned bear at an animal rescue sanctuary in Bolivia where he volunteered, to holding the attention of a class of smiling children while teaching in the jungle of Honduras.

He really had lived an amazing life. Tess had friend-requested him and a warm glow had filled her when he'd accepted. Though she hadn't worked up the nerve to message him right away, she'd foolishly downloaded a delightful Scottish romance novel. When she'd happened on a passage about haggis, Tess had giggled and, deciding to initiate communication, photographed it and sent it to Aiden.

See? Apparently, haggis is quite popular in romance novels, Tess typed.

Ah yes, the Scots way of wooing women, Aiden had replied.

They'd chatted a bit more, but he'd been on his way to Scotland after the dive show and he'd signed off fairly quickly.

The trip had been good for her, Tess realized. The diving had kept her mind focused on the beauty of nature, taking joy in the world to be found beneath the waves, and the simple pleasures that came with watching the sun set over the water. Flirting with Aiden had been a welcome distraction, and even though her heart wanted to tell her there could be more there – *pay attention*, it seemed to say – it had made her feel more confident about starting over again. Sure, Owen had helped her get over the first hurdle after Gabe, but meeting someone new in person and flirting? That was another big step for her. For so long now, she'd automatically shut down any attempts at flirtations – she'd been married, after all. But Aiden had opened her eyes to the world of actually dating again.

Sooner than she would have preferred, the knock she'd been dreading sounded at the door. As the dogs went crazy, skidding across the floor barking, Tess shook her hair back and answered the door with a composed smile.

"Gabe, Matthew, hello," Tess said, nodding to Gabe's dad, a shorter, older version of Gabe. Instantly, she felt bad for Matthew, as he shrugged sheepishly at Tess, unsure of how to proceed in this situation. Taking pity on the man – he hadn't cheated or lied to her – she gave him a quick hug and invited them both in.

"Well, I'm sorry to hear about all this," Matthew said, glancing around at the boxes lining the hallways and clearing his throat as he shuffled his feet on the bare floor.

"Me too, Matthew. Give my best to Shelly, please," Tess said, patting him once on the shoulder and then turning to where Gabe wrestled with the dogs on the floor. "Most of your stuff is in the basement or in the garage, but there were a few pieces you wanted to go over with me?"

"Yes, I was wondering if I could have..." Gabe launched into a list and Tess followed him around the house, tamping down annoyance at some of the things he wanted specifically. The nautical mirror they'd bought together in New Orleans? She bit her tongue, wanting to point out that the man barely knew how to swim. He was the furthest thing from a sailor there could be, and yet he wanted a ship's porthole mirror for his wall? It didn't matter, she told herself. Things were just that – things. Her freedom was much more precious than a stupid mirror.

"Have the mirror, Gabe, I really don't care," Tess said, crossing her arms over her chest as she leaned back against the wall.

"Yeah, I know you don't care, Tess. You don't really give a shit about me at all, do you? You didn't even try and fight for us," Gabe said, his face stormy. "You didn't even give me a chance."

"I did give you a chance, Gabe. Marrying you *was* your chance. I took a chance on a life with you and you bailed. You didn't fight for me, you never even told me you were truly sorry for what you did." Tess spoke calmly, and held Gabe's eyes. "Instead, you told me how much shame you felt for your actions and how sick to your stomach it made you. It was always about you. If you had wanted to fight for me, you would have had your butt in therapy and done everything possible to try and win this marriage back. Instead, you were spending every night with your mistress and moaning about your lack of a job. I wouldn't exactly call that fighting for this marriage, Gabe. You're out of chances – well, with me at least. We'll see how many your babers gives you."

"Don't be such a bitch," Gabe said, stomping over to the

wall and pulling the nautical mirror down, tucking it under his arm. "I would've fought for us."

"Too little, too late," Tess murmured, wondering why Gabe hadn't realized that she'd used his pet name for his mistress. Gabe glowered at her, opening his mouth to speak, but she cut him off. "I'll be upstairs with the dogs. Let me know if there's anything else to discuss. Otherwise, I think we're done here."

Tess let Gabe stride out of the room and whistled for the dogs, hightailing it upstairs to the master bedroom and closing the door behind her. Sitting on the bed, she realized she was shaking. How could this man – who had professed to love her – come at her for not trying to save this marriage? And why was she suddenly feeling guilty, as if it were her fault for choosing to no longer allow shitty behavior in her life. Why should the burden be on her to forgive and fight for the marriage when he'd barely tried to apologize, let alone learn from his mistakes? He'd done nothing – *nothing* – to show Tess he was willing to learn and grow from the destruction he'd done to their relationship.

Tess's thoughts flitted to Vicki, and for the first time, she saw some strong parallels in the foundational relationships in her life. The cycle remained the same, Tess realized: The people she loved would say or do what they wanted, and when there was an explosion, it was on Tess to make amends. Startled at the revelation, Tess leaned back against the pillows of her bed, automatically opening her arms as Red and Ringo jumped up for cuddles. Was this a toxic cycle she'd found herself in with both Gabe and Vicki? Look what happened when Tess removed herself from the pattern of constantly making amends, constantly saying she was sorry, constantly bending to their will – they left her. What kind of relationship did that make if it was always on Tess to fix things? And what did that mean for her future with Vicki, Tess wondered, as she dropped a kiss on Red's forehead, caressing one of his floppy ears. For the first time, Tess hadn't come crawling back to Vicki after Vicki had exploded on her, saying horrible and hurtful things. Since then, Vicki had completely cut her out. It was a manipulation tactic, and one that had worked for years on Tess, one she now realized Gabe employed. When Tess neatly stepped outside the cycle – removed herself from the pattern – they looked at her as if they didn't even know her anymore. As if *she* was the bitch.

Fascinating, really, Tess thought, and glanced toward the window.

Below, Gabe and his dad loaded a large tool chest – a gift from Vicki – onto a trailer attached to Gabe's truck. A truck she had paid for. It was a little surreal. Many times before she'd watched from this window, wondering when Gabe would come home from the bar or the gym or wherever, and now she was watching him leave her life for good. Even though he'd hurt her, incredibly so, Tess still felt sadness fill her as they separately packed their lives up. This was the door closing and even though Tess knew it was right and good for her, there was a finality to the moment that made her feel so incredibly lonely. Gabe had someone to hold him that night; no matter how he professed to mourn the loss of their marriage, he still had someone waiting in the wings, ready to soothe him.

Tess was alone. She let that thought sit for a moment.

Actually, it might not be as scary as it seemed, she realized.

Her phone beeped on the bedside table, signaling a message. Tess leaned back on her pillows, holding the phone above her head and then grinned when she saw it was a message from Aiden. Had he read her thoughts?

I'm in my Airbnb in Glasgow. Look what I found for my reading pleasure – are these the type of books you write?

He'd sent a picture, and Tess laughed at his cheeky grin as he held up a tattered copy of *Fifty Shades of Grey*. Tears pricked her eyes, and Tess dashed them away with the back of her palm, before Red stood on his little legs to lick them from her cheeks. Tess glanced outside once more to where Gabe and his father hefted a couch into the trailer and back at the photo of a grinning Aiden.

"Okay, okay, okay," Tess said, focusing on the warmth that flooded through her at getting a message from Aiden. "Eyes forward, Tess."

When Gabe finally left, with a last goodbye for the dogs, Tess walked downstairs to Gabe's office, empty except for the computer that sat on the floor. Though it might have been petty of her, she hadn't budged on giving it to Gabe. It was her company's property, after all. Signing on, she clicked on where his Facebook page was still open and studied it for a moment. It was time for her to move on, Tess realized, and give up that certain level of control she felt she wielded over Gabe by reading all his private messages. Her friends were right – this was not a healthy mindspace for her to be in. If she really wanted to start her life over, it was time to conclude the soap opera that was the Gabe and Babers show.

Tess signed off.

CHAPTER TWENTY-SIX

T ess thought a lot about paths as she packed up, said many tearful goodbyes, and piled the dogs into her Jeep. Was her path to the mountains a dream from her younger self? Moving to Colorado had always represented freedom in Tess's mind, but fresh from another trip to the ocean, she wondered if near water was where her home was really meant to be.

The paths people chose had such a lasting impact on their lives, each decision affecting the next, and sometimes the road diverged. She'd chosen, once, to take a chance on love with someone who had proven to be untrustworthy. Her gut had tried to tell her, but she hadn't known herself well enough at the time to decide differently. Instead, she followed the path that had been laid out before her and had worked to build a future from there. It wasn't like her path hadn't had many glaring signposts warning about the upcoming fork; had she just been too busy daydreaming to read the signs? Hope could be a blindfold, but she'd chosen to wear it.

"I don't want to lose the hopeful side of myself," Tess said to Elizabeth as they unpacked her boxes at her new place. Cate had been awesome in driving down with her, but had to leave almost immediately. Luckily, Elizabeth had shown up as soon as they arrived, and stayed to help, leaving Tess no chance to be lonely. "I'm scared I'll become bitter and afraid to take chances again."

"Understandably so," Elizabeth said, efficiently organizing Tess's new kitchen space. "I was the same. But wouldn't it be sad to miss out on life because you were afraid of getting hurt again?"

"I guess. But there has to be a line between believing in a fairy tale and protecting your heart." Tess leaned to look out the window at where the dogs chased squirrels in the yard. This house had been a good rental, Tess realized, quite simply because it had a large yard where the dogs could race in a full circle around the house.

"I say believe in the fairy tale," Elizabeth said, meeting Tess's eyes. "What's the point if you don't? Life can be as amazing and wonderful as you want it to be; you just have to keep believing."

"Nothing comes easy for us, that's for sure," Tess said, slicing a knife through the packing tape on a box. Elizabeth's divorce had been even more traumatizing than Tess's had. It had amazed her how Elizabeth had stayed focused on building her life again, open to love, and had not let her past shroud her from finding happiness once more. Now, her current boyfriend was a brilliant match for her, and Tess wouldn't be surprised if there were wedding bells in the future. She'd never seen a couple so at ease and happy with each other. It gave her hope for her own future.

"Would it mean as much if it came easy?" Elizabeth asked, breaking down boxes and moving them to the back hallway.

"I don't know, I'll let you know when something is easy for me." Tess laughed.

"Tell me about this scuba guy." Elizabeth had only gotten a brief run-down via text message as Tess had been so busy packing and selling her house to do much more than shoot off a message here and there.

"Oh, Aiden? Well, hmmm. He's super sexy, funny, and a really nice guy. I had a lot of fun meeting and flirting with him," Tess admitted, folding towels on the kitchen table. "But you know, it's just that – a flirtation. He's something fun to fantasize about, I guess."

"Can it be something more?"

"How? He lives in Mexico."

"Yeah, I guess that would be tough. Though at least he hits some of the notes on your list, right? Loves the ocean, loves diving, taller than you… I know you can't tell if he's worthy of your trust and the other things you were looking for, but it sounds like you're headed in the right direction."

"Girl, I have no direction. I'm rudderless. I've been so focused on just getting here – to this place, to my freedom – that I can't see what comes next."

"Maybe you don't have to right now. Just take it a day at a time," Elizabeth said. "How about some energy healing?"

"Yes, I'm all in. Talk to my therapist, get some reiki, talk to a psychic." Tess laughed. "I will do all the things to clear my energy."

"I think for now, you need to rest. Remember self-care is about also not doing all the things and saying no once in a while too."

"I swear that's what I had planned for the next few days. I just want to read on this big front porch and sleep for days. With no agenda."

"Then do it. Absolutely do it. For now, let's get you as

unpacked as possible. I know it sucks, but hey – once it's done it will feel so amazing to have everything sorted out."

"I agree. Thanks for helping me, I really appreciate it," Tess said.

"Any word from Vicki?" Elizabeth asked, waving away Tess's thanks as friends of years and years do.

"Ah, no, unfortunately. I was allowed to go say goodbye to my nephew, but that was only after going through Chad."

"Honestly, she sucks." Elizabeth snapped a towel fiercely as she folded it. "She has never been supportive of you. It's either fall in line with what she wants or she's competing with you. I'm telling you, she's toxic for you."

"I did have a revelation recently," Tess admitted, smiling as Red raced into the house, knowing his dinner time was near. He danced at her feet, and she wondered once again how it was that her dogs knew what time of the day it was.

"What's that?"

"Just that I'm in this pattern of doing what they want and even when something goes wrong, it's on me to make things right. It was the same way with Gabe as it is with Vicki. This cycle of 'do it my way' and when I don't, somehow I still have to be the one to apologize. It's really frustrating."

"It's toxic," Elizabeth insisted. "People don't withhold love or give you the silent treatment if you don't divorce the way they want you to, or follow the career they think is best for you, or any of the other million little things they've pushed you into. Their way is not the right way, at least not for you, and obviously Gabe couldn't handle that so he went off and found someone who would only agree with him. And Vicki? Well, she's so mad at you for not acting the way she wants you to, that instead of listening or apologizing, she's stamping her foot like a two-year-old and refusing to speak to you. I hate to say it, Tess, but you're the adult in this situation.

Ugh, I can't stand emotional manipulation, it drives me crazy." Elizabeth shuddered. She'd dealt with her fair share with her ex-husband.

"It makes me question my instincts, you know? Like I'm legit questioning who I am and if I'm doing the right thing. But when I step back, it's like, duh, yes – I am doing the right thing. This man didn't love me enough to work on the marriage before he had multiple affairs and lied for months and months. Leaving that situation is allowed. Period. And how I handle it is my choice. Period. Not Vicki's or anyone else's choice. I honestly wonder when Vicki will stop treating me like a child. Except for the moments when she does treat me like a sister, and then she's in competition with me."

"She's jealous of you," Elizabeth said, and Tess looked at her in shock.

"Jealous? How so? She's got the perfect life."

"No, she doesn't. She's obviously unfulfilled. She keeps striving for perfection with family, job, perfect house, and so on – and for what? None of it is giving her the happiness she so desperately craves. She's following what she thinks is the dream because she's too scared to step outside the mold. While you are out here living your own life, building your own career, traveling, and not being afraid to leave your cheating husband. You're an anomaly to her – you've gone rogue. And when people like you go rogue, it makes the people who crave the norm wary of you."

"Huh, that's an interesting take. Gabe keeps calling me a bitch for it, and I think Vicki secretly agrees. But I don't think it's being a bitch to stand up for myself and protect my boundaries and choices."

"Absolutely not," Elizabeth agreed. "You scare them – and what they fear, they attack. Remember that."

"I just wish she'd try to understand me and realize that I

have no need or desire to compete with her. I want her to be my sister, my family, my friend."

"She may never realize that. And will you keep submitting yourself to her judgments and her expectations? Why does she get to set the rules of the relationship? Aren't you allowed to have your own boundaries too?"

"I absolutely am," Tess agreed and turned to see that her living room and kitchen were essentially unpacked but for a few bits and pieces to be hung on the wall. "Damn, girl, you're right. It does feel good to be unpacked."

"Welcome home," Elizabeth said as she hugged her. Tess smiled, feeling – for the first time in ages – a sense of peace with her new life. Even if it was only a ten-month lease, this was home for now and she planned to make the best of it.

No matter what lay ahead.

CHAPTER TWENTY-SEVEN

T rue to her word, Tess spent the next few days puttering around the yard and spending hours sitting out on the wide front porch that ran the length of the house. Set slightly up on a hill, she had a great view of the street and enjoyed people-watching as neighbors strolled past to visit the shops on the corner. It was nice living somewhere she could walk for a coffee, grab some groceries, or browse the local bookstore. It was a great little neighborhood, and Tess was enjoying the easygoing vibe of Denver and how smiley everyone was. Perhaps it was the sunshine, she thought, as back in Chicago snow had already begun to fall. But here? The weather was holding at a moderately comfortable temperature and the sun shone every damn day.

She'd noticed her neighbors to the right a few times – two handsome men with a small daughter – and she couldn't decide if it was the delicious scents that wafted from their kitchen or the booming laugh and distinct accent of one of the men that intrigued her more. When Tess was ready to come out of her self-imposed cocoon, she planned to stop by their house and introduce herself. For now, she curled up on a rocking bench on the front porch, her feet tucked into cozy slippers, and indulged in reading another Highlander romance, something of a recent addiction since she'd met Aiden.

When she saw her neighbor coming down the walk with his daughter in his arms, she waved, and was going to return to her book until she saw his face. The man looked positively traumatized.

"Hi," Tess said, coming to stand at their shared fence line. "Are you okay?"

"No, I'm really not," the man said, tears streaking down his face. "I'm just back from the emergency room with her."

"Oh no," Tess breathed, reaching up to pat his daughter's arm. She was tucked into his shoulder and looked sleepy, but otherwise okay. "What happened? Is she hurt?"

"She took a hard tumble and hit her head on the side of the concrete step outside. I just have to monitor her. Teddy met me at the hospital – he works there. Everything will be okay, but it was really scary," he said.

"Oh, I'm so sorry, I can imagine it was." Going with instinct, she gave him a big hug.

"I'm Daniel, by the way, and this is Delia." Tess smiled at Delia.

"I'm Tess, it's nice to meet you."

"Are you living here now? Or are you the new girl-friend?" Daniel bounced back and forth as he rocked Delia. She detected a slight British accent.

"No, I'm renting it. I wouldn't date my landlord. He kind of skeezed me out." Tess laughed.

Daniel shook his head emphatically. "Yes! Total creep. But the house is gorgeous. Listen, I need to get her inside, but come by for a martini tomorrow? We'd love to get to know you better."

"Oh, I don't want to intrude," Tess protested.

"It's not. I love entertaining. Please, come by tomorrow," Daniel insisted and Tess agreed to go. It couldn't hurt to have one drink and meet her new neighbors. She suspected they would be friends. Or at the very least, she'd score some of the deliciousness that was emanating from that kitchen into her living room every day. Smiling, she returned to her book and decided that tomorrow would be as good a day as any to start on a new routine – find a new gym, outline a new book, and make some new friends.

THE NEXT DAY she crossed the yard with a bottle of red wine in hand, excited to meet her new neighbors. It would be nice to have friends next door, Tess thought, and maybe they'd be able to offer some advice on areas to explore around town.

Daniel opened the door with a big smile on his face, Delia at his hip, and their big black lab at his feet.

"Hi! This is Elliot, who I'm sure you've seen around the yard."

"Hi, buddy." Tess bent to pat the dog who immediately leaned all of his substantial weight into her, begging for attention. "Aww, he's a lover, isn't he?"

"He's just the best," Daniel agreed and ushered her into their home. A stunning open layout spread before her with a large kitchen to the right, a massive dining table in the middle, and a funky living room just beyond with glass doors that showcased the backyard. Something that smelled heavenly bubbled on the stove. "This is my husband, Teddy."

"Hi Teddy, it's so nice to meet you. Thank you for having

me over." Tess smiled at the handsome man who greeted her, a wisp of the South in his accent.

"Hi, Tess, welcome. We've been wondering who had moved in next door. Where are you from?"

"Let me get you a drink. How about a Manhattan?" Daniel asked, popping into a small room that showcased a bar and more types of glasses than she would know what to do with.

"I'd love one, thank you," Tess said and smiled at Teddy, who gestured toward a chair at the table. "I'm from Chicago, and rented the house next door for the next year."

"That's great! We weren't particularly fond of the owner, I have to admit," Teddy said.

Tess grinned. "So I hear."

"He yelled at us for having outdoor lights in our back-yard. Can you believe that? Something about how it's impossible to sleep with the lights shining in his room. They don't even shine up at the room, just down into our yard."

"I haven't noticed them at all." Tess accepted the Manhattan that Daniel handed to her. "Plus, there are shades in the bedroom, so I don't see what the issue would be."

"Nasty man," Daniel said, bouncing Delia.

"How is she today?"

"All good, it seems. I might have been a bit overdramatic with the fall, but it sounded like she'd hit her head so hard and I was just so worried," Daniel admitted, a sheepish grin on his handsome face.

"Better safe than sorry," Tess said.

"That's what I said," Daniel said, shooting a look at Teddy, who just smiled and rolled his eyes. "Teddy works at the hospital, so he's probably less hysterical than I am."

"Just a tad," Teddy said, laughing into his drink.

"Are you a doctor?"

"No, I'm in operations. I oversee the staff and manage the financials, that kind of thing."

"And what do you do, Daniel?"

"I'm a realtor here, though I used to be a chef." Daniel checked the pot on the stove.

"That would explain all the delicious smells that waft into my house. I honestly thought I lived behind a restaurant!"

"That's our kitchen fan; it vents toward your yard."

"Well, keep on venting. It all smells divine."

"So what brings you to Denver?" Teddy asked.

"Ah, well, divorce does, I suppose, though my ex-husband and I had planned to move here at some point. Now it's just me and the dogs."

"Oh, I'm sorry. Was it rough?" Daniel asked.

Before she knew it, they were several Manhattans deep, full of delicious pasta, and shaking their heads in disgust over lying asshole men.

"You're better off without him, honey. Plus, there's so many yummy men here," Daniel exclaimed from where he lounged on the couch. They'd moved to the living room after they'd put Delia to bed, and Tess worried she was over-staying her welcome.

"I honestly wouldn't know. I haven't really dipped my toe in that pond yet," Tess admitted.

"What?" Teddy exclaimed, leaning forward excitedly. "You're not on Tinder yet?"

"Um, well, I did open a Tinder profile a while ago, but haven't really used it."

"Give us your phone," Daniel demanded and Tess laughed, shaking her head.

"No, really, I don't even know how to use the app."

"We do. We do this all the time for our friend Kristina. Tell us what you like," Daniel said, as Tess handed her phone over.

"It doesn't matter what she likes. She's just divorced, she needs to like all the men," Teddy insisted. They hovered over her phone, shaking their heads no or yes as they swiped delightedly through the profiles.

"No, he looks like he lives in his mom's basement," Teddy protested.

"He could just be the sensitive type," Daniel argued. "Look, he writes poetry. She's a writer, too."

They both looked at her in question and Tess shook her head no, giggling despite herself.

"That's a no. Too sensitive, got it," Teddy said, moving on, "Oh, he's cute. Hey, look – it's a match!"

"What? Who? How?" Tess asked, moving to look over their shoulders at a cute guy with a scruffy beard.

"Because Tinder is based on your location. So they've already seen your profile and said yes. Now it's on you to decide if you want to chat," Daniel explained.

"Oh jeez, I don't know if I'm ready for this." Tess felt nerves bubble up in her stomach. "I don't know if I can handle all that judgment online. Like what if I'm not skinny enough for some guys, or they see me and don't like me?"

"Honey, you're beautiful. You've got a full body shot in here so guys can see exactly what they're getting. Don't worry about it," Daniel insisted.

"Ugh, this feels so weird. I've never online dated before," Tess admitted. Her phone started pinging, making her curious. "Oh my gosh. Now what? Do I start messaging him?"

"Hell yes, you do! And come over to try on first date outfits. We love this stuff," Daniel said.

"My phone keeps pinging, what is all that pinging?" Tess said, nerves trickling through her.

"Matches. And messages. Girl, you're going to be busy." Teddy laughed, handing her phone back and Tess looked down in awe at the messages that poured in.

"Ew, this guy wants to put it in my butt," Tess said, gasping at the first message she opened.

"That's a bit forward for a hello, wouldn't you say?" Daniel laughed.

"Yeah, at least make him take you to dinner first," Teddy said.

Tess looked at the ceiling and took deep breaths. "Is this seriously how people date now? Like, let's meet up and have sex? That would freak me out! I could never just let some strange guy into my house for sex in the middle of the night," Tess exclaimed.

"Understandably so," Teddy agreed, leaning back into the cushions.

"Ew, this guy says he's divorced too, and just wants to pleasure women, no attachments." Tess held the phone out.

Daniel took it from her. "Is that what you want? No attachments?"

"I don't know what I want. I know I'm a bit shaky with all this stuff, that's for sure," Tess admitted, smiling when Daniel got up and crossed to make her another drink. "But I'm used to being in a relationship, so I'll have to learn to just date again, I suppose."

"You gotta start somewhere, girl," Teddy said.

"Not with the in-the-butt guy," Daniel ordered from across the room, and Tess snickered.

"Who's Aiden?" Teddy asked, looking at her phone curiously.

Tess lunged for it.

"Ohhhh, my my, does Miss Tess already have someone on the horizon?"

"He's not... he lives in Mexico." Tess wanted to open his message, but decided to save it for later. "I met him when I went scuba diving. He's Scottish and teaches diving there."

"A Scottish scuba instructor?" Daniel pretended to swoon as he carried their drinks back over. "Yum, yum, that sounds like just what the doctor ordered."

"I wish." Tess laughed, accepting the Manhattan from him and sipping it, glad she only had to walk next door after all these cocktails. "But it's not likely I'll see him again anytime soon."

"Why not? With your job you can fly down there anytime," Daniel pointed out, snuggling in next to Teddy on the couch.

"It's just... I guess I don't know. I've had so many big changes recently. I need to get my head on straight and start my new life here." Her phone beeped incessantly with messages and Tess flushed.

"Well, my dear, this looks like an excellent place to start. I can't wait to live vicariously through you."

"You guys! How many men did you swipe on?"

"Pretty much all of them." Teddy shrugged and Tess groaned, falling back into the cushions of the couch as her phone flooded with messages.

"Don't worry, you're about to have yourself a world of fun, honey. We've got your back," Daniel promised.

"I certainly hope so," Tess said and laughed, holding her drink up to them. "To new beginnings."

"To new beginnings!" they crowed.

"And to in the butt..." Daniel added and Tess almost choked on her drink.

At home later that night, more than comfortably buzzed and ensconced in her bed, Tess pulled out her phone and started responding to messages. It quickly became clear that this was a hook-up app, and she doubted she would find anyone actually interested in dating. Still, she had fun messaging with a few of the guys. It wasn't hard to weed out the jerks or unmatch with those that she didn't find desirable, and soon she'd narrowed it down to a few who seemed okay to have a bit of a chat with over a drink someday. Finally, she opened the message from Aiden.

Did you make it out to Colorado?

I did, and I am loving the new house and the location is great. I met my new neighbors tonight.

Are they nice?

Yeah, they are two great guys with a young daughter. One of them used to be a yacht chef and I predict many a delicious meal in my future.

That's awesome. I'm glad you're making friends.

They hijacked my Tinder account.

Tess paused and almost hit herself on the forehead. Now, why was she telling Aiden about her Tinder account? It wasn't exactly the flirtiest of topics to discuss with a guy she thought was cute. She should be asking about his day and trying to engage him, not talk about other men.

Uh-oh. Sounds like you're going to have some fun in Colorado.

I mean, I guess. I don't know. It seems like just a hook-up app.

Is that what you want to do? Just hook up?

Tess looked at the ceiling, suddenly interested in where this conversation was going.

This is such unfamiliar territory for me. I've never online dated before.

It could be fun for you. Help you get past the divorce. Have you dated at all since you kicked him out?

Just one guy. A friend. A little fling, nothing more.

So it's time for you to explore.

I guess. What about you? Are you on Tinder? Is there Tinder in Mexico?

There is, but I'm rarely on it. I meet a lot of people through work.

Oh, sure. Duh, I'm sure the ladies are lining up to meet the hot scuba instructor.

Tess hit herself on the forehead. "No, no, no, why are you saying that?"

Do you think I'm hot, Tess?

I mean, yes, I do think you're quite sexy.

I think you are beautiful. I especially think it's interesting that you're so creative – not to mention those erotic stories you told me about.

Oh great, she had to mention those, Tess thought, blushing at the thought of some of the hidden stories she'd written.

Right, those stories.

I'd like to read one.

Um, hmm. Really? I mean they're just... you know.

No, I don't know. But I'd like to.

Um, well, I guess I could send you one. I'll have to pick a favorite.

I would be very interested in which one is your favorite.

"Phew," Tess blew out a breath and fanned her face, squirming in bed, another need taking over her body.

I can do that.

Looking forward to it. I have to get to bed now, we're two hours ahead of you and I'm up early.

Oh shoot, I didn't realize the time. I'm sorry.

No worries, I like chatting with you, Tess. Speak to you soon.

Okay, sounds good. Sweet dreams.

Oh, and Tess – I can't wait to read your fantasies.

"Eeeeek," Tess screeched. She didn't respond, pulling a

pillow over her head. She didn't want to go on a Tinder date. She wanted to have Aiden next to her, telling her all the wicked things he'd do to her in his delicious accent. Taking a deep breath, she decided to attend to something else that she'd been ignoring as of late, and opened up a website where she could discreetly order a toy that would attend to some of her more basic needs. Scrolling through, she clicked on one that looked like it would be good, hit the order button, and put her phone on the bedside table.

Snuggling in, she found herself grinning into the pillow, decidedly delighted with the turn of events her life had taken. Maybe it was time to put herself out there, date a little, and just have some fun. The past months had felt like she was trudging through cement, and now nothing was holding her back.

CHAPTER TWENTY-EIGHT

"I have no idea, this guy seems kind of intense," Tess said the following week, as she sipped a coffee with Daniel in the backyard. "He wants to drive all the way from Boulder to meet for dinner, but has informed me that he is incredibly picky about the women he dates."

"Hmm, that's weird to say. But obviously he finds you to be up to his standards if he is going to drive forty-five minutes to meet you." They'd fallen into an easy friendship, and Tess had found herself speaking to either Daniel or Teddy almost daily. She was beyond excited to have neighbors who had turned into friends. It kind of felt like her college days, where she could call across the hallway to a friend to meet for a drink.

"He's from Brazil. I wonder if I would meet his standards. You know Brazilian women are knockouts." Tess felt her insecurities kick up. She'd never been on a blind date before, and she wondered how people did this on the regular.

"So are you, honey. Don't worry, it's fine. Though I'm

surprised he wants to have dinner. Most people just meet for drinks."

"I know; I've actually had a few requests for dinner. I'm kind of surprised at that. Shouldn't it just be one drink and then you decide if you vibe?" Tess asked, leaning back to feel the sun on her face. It had definitely grown colder now, but still nothing like Chicago, and sitting outside in a fleece and jeans was comfortable for her. The dogs loved prowling around the yard, and Tess was not missing the lake effect snow that Chicago so reliably delivered.

"That's how I would roll, but hey – why not? At the very least, you'll get to explore a new restaurant. I just love the place you're going to," Daniel gushed and then stood, pointing to her house. "Let's pick out an outfit for you."

"Oh! Fun," Tess said and they traipsed up to the bedroom, Daniel commenting on the layout of the house, already in realtor mode. Once there, Tess pulled out several options.

"I'm not sure leather pants on the first date is good, it may scream too much *bad girl*," Daniel decided, motioning for Tess to put the leather pants aside. "Keep it casual, but cool. Slim jeans, a sexy top, fitted jacket. Easy."

"Heels?"

"Mmm, no. What if you are taller than him?"

"Good point. Though if I was, I'm not interested. Does that make me shallow? I think it makes me shallow."

"You can be shallow. This is your time to do what you want, and if a tall man is what you want, then go for it."

"You say that because you're ridiculously tall," Tess said, smiling at him.

Daniel laughed. "Yes, I am. A lot of South Africans are." Daniel had told her he'd moved to the US from South Africa after a few years being a private chef on various yachts, and met Teddy in Florida. After that, they'd decided on Colorado and had happily renovated a few homes in the area, enjoying the community and the city.

"Maybe I should find me a South African then," Tess quipped, laying out a swingy tank in deep red.

"What about that Scotsman of yours?"

"He's not mine," Tess protested, blushing a little as she thought of Aiden.

"Anything more there?" Daniel pressed.

"We've chatted a bit, flirted here and there. Nothing much really. It's just kind of nice. Like every few days or so, one of us will send a message."

"Sounds like he's interested. A man does not just send messages every few days to someone he wants to be friends with."

"Well, I mean, really – what could possibly happen here?"

"Phone sex?" Daniel wondered, then laughed at Tess's shocked face.

"Who even does that?"

"Oh please, you write romance novels. I'm sure you know people engage in phone sex."

"Yeah, but like when they're in a long-distance relationship and know each other. You don't just have phone sex with someone for the first time of hooking up," Tess protested and then paused, considering. "Or do you?"

"Girl, you can do whatever you damn well want." Daniel grinned, standing and stretching. "It's your life."

"Right, well, I doubt I'll be phone-sexing with Aiden anytime soon."

"Keep me posted if you do. I want full details."

"Maybe I will. Maybe I won't. For now, let me get ready for this dinner date." Tess shooed him from her room.

"Also, keep me posted on that. Text when you leave and when you get there. We'll watch our phones. And if it's awful, come over for a drink after." Daniel waved to her as he left.

IT WAS AWFUL.

To start with, he'd been shorter than her, which Tess had told herself to overlook because he could end up being an amazing guy and then it wouldn't really matter. But instead, he'd looked her over head to toe, and then barely made conversation all through dinner. She knew it wasn't a language barrier, as he understood exactly what she was saying. After he only ordered an appetizer and refused a drink, Tess knew what was up. Why had he even bothered with dinner, she wondered? She had one drink, split his appetizer with him, and ordered an Uber home.

He'd tried to insist on giving her a ride, but after that less than scintillating date, she'd refused. Like she was about to get in the car with this potential serial killer? Heading home, she leaned her head against the back seat, grateful for an Uber driver who didn't feel like talking. She stared out the window at the city passing her by. She knew this was supposed to be fun, that dating again was meant to be a second chance to go wild with loads of different guys, but all it was doing was bringing her insecurities to a head. There was nothing worse than going out on a date with pleasant expectations only to have someone size you up and find you wanting. She only hoped it would get better from here.

Getting out of the Uber, she didn't even stop at her house, instead knocking on Daniel and Teddy's door.

"Girl, get in here." Daniel ushered her inside. "Bad?"

"So bad! He was so rude," Tess said, tossing her jacket on the front chair and gratefully accepting the glass of wine that Teddy had already poured for her. "He seriously looked me up and down, said like two words during his appetizer, and then tried to drive me home."

"Maybe he was so excited that he wanted to skip dinner and get right to the good stuff," Teddy suggested.

"Doubtful. Don't you think he'd at least try then? Flirt a little? Ask a few questions? Something?"

"Maybe you made him nervous," Daniel considered.

"He already told me he was exceptionally picky about women," Tess reminded him.

"He did? That's really… rude," Teddy said.

"It is, isn't it? Like, thanks for letting me know your high standards and then subjecting me to the fact that I don't meet them. Have you considered you might not meet my standards, you little pipsqueak?" It wasn't like she would have gone home with the guy anyway, but that long look he'd given her before he decided she didn't meet his standards had stung.

"Next," Daniel called, wiggling his hands for her phone.

"No, I'm not sure you get to use my account anymore," Tess grumbled.

"Oh please, it's one date. There will be many more," Daniel said. "Now hand it over. We want to look at all the horrible fashion choices straight guys make."

Tess handed her phone over. They were right: he was just one guy of many, and it certainly wouldn't be her first bad date – or her last.

"Oh, he's cute! And a firefighter," Daniel exclaimed and soon Tess found herself laughing, the stress and awkwardness of her first failed Tinder date fading behind her.

Onward.

THE WEEK PASSED in a blur of exploring Denver, tentatively

feeling out new Tinder matches, and finally diving back into her writing. Her readers had been fantastic through the divorce, kindly waiting for her book to be released, and now she was feeling like she was in a good mental space to start writing again. She'd slowly started outlining another book, watching as the days grew shorter and winter began to approach Denver. The mountains had snow, and Tess had even driven up to the front range to get a peek at the hills, marveling in their beauty, feeling like her problems were very small in the immensity of nature's awesomeness laid out before her.

Tess smiled as a ding from the Tinder app told her she had a new message. She'd been chatting with a guy who owned a used bookstore and hosted a radio show. So far, they'd had fairly interesting conversations, which was a step up from most of the guys on the app who just asked if they could come over at midnight. He seemed funny, smart, and into the arts – and Tess had decided she would definitely meet him for a drink if he asked. She smiled when she opened the message to see that it was, indeed, an invite to meet up for a salsa and margaritas. Deciding she would message him as soon as she got home, Tess sang along to the radio the whole drive home.

A box sat on her doorstep, and Tess idly wondered what she'd ordered now. It wasn't uncommon for her to click "Buy Now," and forget what she'd ordered by the time the box showed up. Which probably meant she shouldn't have ordered it to begin with, but Tess knew she wasn't the only one with a secret shopping addiction.

The dogs danced around her feet, always excited when she had a package in hand because there could be treats or toys at any moment.

"I don't know what this is, boys, but I'm sure you have

more than enough toys," Tess said, nodding to their wildly overflowing toy basket. Putting the package on the kitchen counter, she grabbed a pair of scissors and slit the tape open, popping the lid to see a large neon pink box. "Hmm." She took the box out, surprised at the weight of it. Opening it, she dropped it on the counter in surprise.

"Shut up!" Tess choked out, laughter seizing her as the sheer size of the vibrator she'd drunkenly ordered online weeks ago. "Nooooo, this thing is huge!" Tess pulled it out of the box and waved it around like a sword. The thing was massive, beyond anything she'd ever consider using or touching or buying unless it was as a joke for a bachelorette party.

"Dear lord, they need to post size comparison photos for these things," Tess groaned, laughing so hard that tears clouded her eyes. Laying it on the counter next to her hand, she took a photo of it to send to her friends.

"You have got to see this," Tess typed out, and paused as Ringo made a particularly high jump and tried to seize the toy. "Ringo! No, this is definitely not for you!" Picking up her phone just as it beeped, she sent the photo to Elizabeth, knowing she'd die when she saw the picture.

Her phone beeped again, several times in a row, and Tess, still laughing and eying the gigantic toy balefully, picked it up to talk to Elizabeth.

"Oh shit," Tess breathed.

Well, well, well… I suppose we could skip the margaritas and go straight to the fun stuff, then. I see you like to have fun in bed. Good thing I'm packing just what you need.

"Noooooooo," Tess screeched, realizing a Tinder message had come in at the same time she was texting Elizabeth and she'd sent the photo to the cute bookstore owner. "Oh for fuck's sake, I can't believe I did this."

The guy had seemed fairly normal, tall, attractive, gainfully employed and – up to this point – respectful. Now that she'd inadvertently sent him a sex-toy photo, it was like she'd greenlighted him to tell her all the naughty things he wanted to do to her. The messages poured in, increasingly lurid, and Tess bent over the counter, smacking her forehead lightly against the counter.

"Why, why, why do I do these stupid things?" She screenshotted the man's messages, for she knew Daniel and Teddy would get a kick out of this, and then very politely told him it had been a mistake and she was no longer interested. Unmatching with him quickly and deleting all messages, including the photo from her phone so she wouldn't make that stupid mistake again, Tess buried the toy in a drawer, planning to discreetly toss it in the bin on trash day.

"I shouldn't be allowed on these apps," Tess grumbled, plopping onto the couch. "I'm only a menace to myself."

Her phone beeped again, this time with an incoming Facebook message, and Tess saw it was from Aiden. She hadn't heard from him in over a week now, and she'd meant to send him a message but had been feeling shy. In a bold move, she'd sent him the erotic short story she'd written, and then hadn't heard anything since. She'd begun to think that she'd well and truly embarrassed herself, but after the last twenty minutes of her life, Tess realized she could dig that hole much deeper than she'd thought.

Hey, how's it going?

Good, how are you?

Good, it's been a crazy busy week. We're getting into high season now, so we're slammed.

See? He was just busy, not avoiding her, Tess told herself and relaxed into the couch cushions, pulling the blanket over her so Red could cuddle in her lap.

I forget how busy you guys must get in high season, I can imagine it's exhausting.

We have six boats going out five times a day – it's a lot of divers. I love it, I just wish I had more days off that I could plan around. It would be nice to do more than just the washing up on our day off. Plan a day trip or two…that kind of thing.

I can imagine that's tough to never know your days off. I'm jealous of your sunshine though. It's getting cold here. I think we might see snow soon.

Brrrr, better cuddle up and stay warm. Speaking of staying warm, how are those Tinder dates treating you?

Interesting, Tess thought, that he'd ask about her dating life. She wondered if he cared that she was dating, or if he was the jealous type.

Not so great, to be honest. I'm either making a fool of myself or being found wanting.

What do you mean being found wanting?

Like I went on this date with one guy who just scanned me up and down and decided I wasn't for him. He couldn't hightail it out of there fast enough.

Tess had no idea why she was telling him this stuff, other than he was a nice guy and easy to talk to.

He's an idiot. I can't imagine any man not being pleased to have you on his arm.

Awww, that's sweet of you. Thank you.

Don't let assholes get you down. You're beautiful and an awesome person. Any guy would be lucky to have you.

Tess beamed at the phone, simply taken with this man and his sweet words. Did they really make men who were this kind?

You're really a doll. I'm surprised some girl hasn't snatched you up.

Haha, you said snatch.

Tess laughed despite herself.

Yeah, yeah, yeah.

In all seriousness, I haven't wanted to be serious with anyone since my last girlfriend messed with my head. It's been better for me to be single for a while.

I get that.

Or maybe I'm just waiting until I meet someone who catches my interest more than most, you know?

I can understand that. Dating is tough, I'm not sure if I'm cut out for the online dating world.

Do you have any other dates lined up?

One this coming weekend, but I'm not even sure why I'm going except he's extra eager. He's kind of a young one though.

How old?

Young.

How old, Tess? Robbing the cradle?

Tess chuckled. Aiden was only a year younger than her, and she was more than certain he'd had many a young woman come on to him.

He's twenty-five.

Ohhhh, Tess. Naughty girl.

Stop it, I know it's ridiculous.

A girl's gotta do what a girl's gotta do. No judgment.

Sigh, we'll see. I already know it's going nowhere, but he's so excited to go out – another dinner date at that – that I feel bad canceling on him.

I'm sure you'll have fun. Hopefully not as much fun as in that story you sent me.

Tess's eyebrows shot up and she paused, holding her breath. How did she respond to that?

I wondered if you'd had time to read it.

I did... well, what I could get through without being too turned on. I like how your mind works, Tess.

Oh, well, thank you. Glad you liked it.

I didn't just like it… I loved it. Would definitely like to read more of what you've written. I can see why your readers like you.

Tess blushed and clapped a hand over her face.

Haha, I'm blushing.

I have to go, Tess, I think I'll read another chapter before bed… and think of you. Night night.

"Eeek!" Tess said, putting her phone down and fanning her inflamed face. Why was it she was having more fun texting with Aiden than any of the men who had messaged her through Tinder – the ones who lived within ten minutes of her that she could actually have a future with?

Maybe he had shown up in her life at the right time just to grow her confidence. He was exceedingly kind, and consistently complimented her, which in turn made her feel more comfortable with exploring the dating world again. No matter what came of her situation with Aiden, maybe she'd met someone who was meant to teach her the right things at the right time in her life. And if that was all it was meant to be, Tess could be grateful for the little things, like words of kindness and the thrills of new beginnings.

CHAPTER TWENTY-NINE

E *xcited for your big date?*

  Oh stop, not even. I don't even know why I'm going.

I don't blame the lad, I would be eager to go on a date with you too.

Tess smiled at her phone that she'd placed next to the bathroom sink as she ran a straightener through her hair. She'd kept the lavender color after her move to Colorado, having found a stylist right around the corner who was great at maintaining the right shade.

You're so sweet to me. I think you'd be fun to go on a date with as well.

I'm bummed we didn't get a chance to spend more time together when you were here.

So am I. Maybe next time…

Tess raised an eyebrow at her boldness as she leaned forward to the mirror, carefully applying her eye makeup. There was something about the fact that Aiden was so far away – unattainable really – that made her carefree in what she said to him.

Do you think you'll come down here again?

I don't know. I don't really have anyone to dive with.

Ahem *waves hands*

Yeah, but you're working. It's different.

Well, just think about it...

I will, but I have to go.

Oh, that's right, the teenager awaits.

Stop it! He's not a teenager, he's twenty-five, I think. Old enough to go to the bar.

Uh-huh. Just a wee lad, then. Just be careful, please.

Shush. I will, I promise.

It was such an interesting dynamic that had developed between her and Aiden, Tess thought as she swiped some tinted lip balm on and deposited her phone in her purse. They'd begun to message almost every day now, and the conversations ranged from friendly banter to bordering on naughty flirtations. He seemed to straddle the line between being her friend and hinting at something more... and it was the something more that was keeping Tess up at night.

Tess walked to the restaurant, pulling her coat tight around her, as the first snowflakes of the year began to fall. It was December already, and back home had already been hit with a few snowstorms. Her mind idly flipped to Christmas and she realized this would be the first year in a long time she wouldn't be with her family for the holiday. Not that it mattered much, she supposed, other than missing out on time with her nephew. Vicki was holding strong with her silent treatment.

Shoving those thoughts aside, Tess breezed into the Mexican restaurant, and searched for a guy sitting alone that resembled the photos she'd seen online. A man – well, more of a man-boy – waved to her from a back table and Tess bit down a sigh, thinking about Aiden's quips about robbing the cradle.

"Hi, Tess? I'm Micah. It's nice to meet you." Micah stumbled a bit as he stood and caught his windbreaker on the edge of the table. Why was he wearing a windbreaker in the middle of winter, Tess wondered, and then stumbled herself when he engulfed her in an effusive hug.

"Nice to meet you, Micah." Tess sat down across from him at the table.

"I, uh, ordered us some chips and guacamole, figured you'd like that. Oh, and some margaritas. I know it's good to order for the lady."

Tess sighed. He really was young, and so very eager. "Unfortunately, Micah, I'm allergic to avocado. But I'll be happy to indulge in a margarita." She noticed he'd already almost finished a margarita himself. She wondered how long he'd been waiting here for her.

"Oh man, I'm sorry. Let me cancel it, I can…" Micah raised his hand to flag down a waitress and almost knocked his drink over. Steadying it, he shook his head in disgust as the waitress appeared with the chips and guacamole.

"She can't have guacamole. Take it back," Micah ordered.

Tess raised an eyebrow at him. Turning to the waitress, she smiled. "It's fine, really. He didn't know I couldn't eat avocado. But if you bring a side of salsa, that will be lovely. And thanks for the drinks." The waitress beamed at her, setting the plate down before moving on to check her next table.

"So, Micah, tell me more about yourself." Tess sipped her margarita, noting that the restaurant had gotten the blend of sweet to sour just right.

"Well, I just graduated and I have a great job. I'm in finance at…."

Tess felt her eyes glaze over and her brain wandered as Micah pontificated on the finer points of personal finance. He continued talking, pausing only when they ordered their food – which Tess wished she hadn't even bothered with – and their second, his third, round of drinks. By the time her fajitas had come, Tess was blatantly looking around the restaurant, wondering if he'd even noticed that not once had he stopped talking, nor had he asked her a single question about herself.

"You know, Tess, it's best for you to have a 401k. If not, have you considered a Roth IRA or an investment portfolio? You can't be too smart about saving for your future," Micah said, slurping down his drink and signaling the waitress for another.

"Micah, let me be perfectly clear here. I'm thirty-six years old. I've owned homes, have no credit card debt, own my own company, have investment portfolios, and am fiscally responsible. While I thank you for your advice, I'm doing just fine in that department," Tess said, smiling at him to ease the sting of her words.

"Oh, well. Duh, I should've figured. You're much older than me."

Tess just measured a long look at him over the table.

"I mean... I, um..." Micah gulped his drink and looked gratefully at the waitress when she arrived with another. When she looked to Tess in question, Tess waved her away. It was clear where this night was going, and she wanted to have her wits about her as man-boy across the table got himself sloshed.

"So, Micah, what is it you like to do for fun?" At least she was enjoying her meal. She'd have to come back here with Daniel and Teddy.

"Party, go to concerts. My roomies and I like to go snowboarding and grill out."

"How many people do you live with?"

"There's six of us in the house, sometimes more depending on if we bring girls home." Micah flushed, realizing his mistake, and gulped more of his drink.

"Cool." Tess let the silence drag out, wondering if he would ask her any questions about herself.

"So, you're a writer, huh? I bet that has to be a tough gig. Hard to make money from," Micah said, moving directly into his next margarita. Tess raised an eyebrow at him, wondering why they were once more back to the money discussion, but Micah plowed on. "It's not like creatives can make a real living. I mean, most I know just dabble on the side of their real jobs."

"Writing is my real job," Tess interjected, but Micah continued. Tess quietly finished her delicious dinner.

"I mean, I like to write songs, but it's not going to get me anywhere, you know? It's more responsible for me to work for a stable corporation, with a retirement plan and benefits. Sure, I'd love to be a songwriter, but I can't make a living off of that."

It was the first interesting thing Micah had said all evening.

Tess leaned back, motioning to the waitress for the check. "Why can't you make a living as a songwriter?"

"It's too hard to break into. You get paid nothing until you work for the big names."

"But if it's your dream, isn't it worth giving it a go?" Tess inquired, smiling gratefully at the waitress who placed the check on the table.

"No, it's not worth it. I have bills to pay and student loans to pay off. Much more sensible to work for a stable company," Micah insisted, reaching for the check just as Tess did as well.

They had a silent tug-of-war over the table until Tess finally relinquished the leather holder.

"Can't you do both? If it's your passion, you make it work. You could write on your lunch hours, or take weekends to pour yourself into writing songs. That's what most people do until they can go full-time. It's what I did."

Micah looked at her like she was crazy. "Weekends are for partying and snowboarding."

Tess nodded, just wanting to be back at home cuddled with the pups. "Of course." She dipped into her wallet and pulled out some cash. "Here, I'd like to pay for my half of dinner."

"No, no. I insist, my treat," Micah said magnanimously. "It's on me."

"No, really, I'd like to pay half. I don't need you to pay for me." Tess felt awkward about the whole thing, considering the man was obsessed with money.

"No, but it's a date. I'm the man, you're a struggling writer, and I'm paying," Micah said.

Tess cocked her head, wondering how he managed to be both chivalrous and condescending at the same time. "Where did you get the impression that I was struggling as a writer?" Tess wondered out loud. He'd talked through the meal, barely asked her any questions, and had no idea if she was successful at her career or not.

"Well, I mean, most creatives are. That's just how it works. That whole starving artist thing." Micah shrugged, so sure of himself and the world at his young age.

Tess just nodded, deciding not to rock his boat. "Ah, of course. And all those famous musicians must be making peanuts." As they left the restaurant, Tess rolled her eyes at the waitress, who had overheard and was shooting her a sympathetic look.

"Well, I mean, they are one in a million. Most people can't make a living off being a creative," Micah scoffed.

Tess stopped outside the restaurant, standing in the chilly night, and met his eyes. "I do." When he opened his mouth, she held up a hand to shake his. "Thanks for a delicious dinner, Micah. Really, I'll have to come back here sometime, the food was excellent."

Before she could say anything else, Tess had a tongue halfway down her throat and an eager hand seeking its way into the waistband of her pants. Shocked, she pushed at him, then a little harder, until Micah stumbled back, grinning at her.

"Shall we walk to your place? I know you said it was in the neighborhood." Micah looked so happily sure of himself.

"No, Micah, I'll be going home alone tonight." Tess stepped back from him, unsure of how to clue in the clueless.

"You sure? Ah, I get it. You're one of those classy ladies. Not on the first date and all. I like that... playing hard to get. I'll call you later. I really can't wait to see you again, Tess." Micah rocked back on his heels, beaming at her.

Tess slowly walking backward away from him.

"Bye, Micah. Thanks for dinner," she called from the corner.

"You sure you don't want me to walk you home? To make sure you get in safe?"

"Nope, I'm all good, Micah. Goodbye," Tess said, hurrying to turn the corner, then dodging down an alley and out onto a different street just in case he followed her. She didn't think he would. Micah might have been an idiot, but he seemed fairly harmless aside from slobbering all over her outside the restaurant. She was more than happy to see the warm glow from the lamp on her front porch, and she all but bounced up the stairs, happy to be home and ready to cuddle up with the dogs and watch some girl shows. The dogs danced around her feet, and Tess unwound her scarf and tossed her jacket on the table, then poured herself a glass of wine. When her phone beeped, she rolled her eyes, assuming it was Micah.

How'd the date go?

Tess smiled at the message on the screen. She really wanted to talk to Aiden and see his face, not just text message with him.

Want to video chat? she asked, feeling bold.

Sure, I have some time before bed.

Tess grabbed her iPad, checking her appearance in the mirror, before she settled into the couch, smoothing her hair once more before she pressed the button to video message Aiden. When his smiling face filled the screen, blonde curls and blue eyes beaming at her, Tess felt herself go warm.

"Hi," Tess said, smiling back at him.

"Wow, you look gorgeous. I'm surprised you're back from your date so soon." Aiden leaned on his arms so that he was looking down at her. He must be stretched out in bed, Tess thought, immediately wanting to be stretched out beneath him.

"Are you though?" Tess teased.

"Nah, not really. I didn't suspect the lad had much to keep you interested."

Tess's phone buzzed with a message. And then buzzed several more times.

"Speaking of the devil...." Tess held up the phone for Aiden to see all the messages.

"Jeez, mate, you just left her. Play it cool, man." Aiden shook his head sadly. "Schoolboy error."

"He can't wait to see me, wants to make sure I don't want him to come over, or I could come party at his house tonight, or maybe tomorrow..." Tess listed off, reading through the messages. "I honestly don't understand it. He never even asked me anything about myself. Just talked through the whole damn meal. How could he know he wants to see me again?"

On screen, Aiden rolled his eyes. "Look at you, of course he wants to see you again."

"You're sweet to me," Tess said, smiling at Aiden.

"What are you going to tell the lad? It's not like he's going away anytime soon judging by how your phone's lighting up."

"Ugh, probably because he sucked down like five margaritas at dinner." Aiden shook his head once more. "I'll just be straightforward and tell him thanks for dinner, but that I'm not interested."

"That's nice. I prefer when women are direct with me, instead of playing games." Aiden nodded his approval. "It's best for everyone when expectations are clearly outlined or defined."

"Oh yeah? Play by the rules, do you?"

"Depends on the rules." Aiden laughed. "But I think I'm ethical to a fault at times. I just see so many people doing wrong in the world that I try my best to do right when I can."

"That's refreshing to hear. Not everyone thinks like that."

"I hate liars, I like strongly defined boundaries, and I don't like playing games," Aiden said. "Well, I like playing actual games, like card games and such, but I hate mind games."

"I suppose life would be easier if everyone was just straightforward." Tess paused to look at her phone again and grimaced at the messages.

"I don't know if it would be easier, but it would be at least clearer for people to navigate. Straightforward doesn't mean that feelings don't get hurt."

"True," Tess said, glaring at her phone once more.

"What did he say?"

Typical bitch move. Let the nice guy take you out for dinner, get your dinner paid, and go home without putting out. What do I get out of it? Nothing. What a waste of money.

"So, apparently buying someone dinner equates to sex then," Tess said, anger building up in her. "I tried to pay for my half of dinner – several times! I all but insisted, but he got pissy about it, so I let him. Where does that mean I agreed to take him home and have sex with him? I owe him nothing! Yet, I'm the bitch for not putting out?"

"Sounds like this guy is a total asshole," Aiden said, his eyes meeting hers through the screen. "A guy could take you away for a weekend vacation and you still owe him nothing. It's your choice when and who you share your body with. Period. Never, ever, let some wanker push you into sex because he thinks it is owed to him. That guy has a lot to learn about life."

Let me be very clear, Micah. Tess typed rapidly. *The only bitch here is you – for expecting that sex is given as a form of payment for dinner. If you want a prostitute, I suggest you go downtown and hang outside the clubs. Don't ever message me again.*

"Tell him off?" Aiden said, watching her.

"That I did." Tess turned her phone off, snuggling into the couch and smiling at Aiden. "Now, tell me about your week."

They chatted for almost another hour before Aiden yawned, and glanced at the clock.

"I'm sorry, Tess, I really have to go." She could see the sheer exhaustion in his face.

"I understand, it's high season for you."

"Have you thought about coming back to visit?"

"Um, not really. Like to come stay... and hang with you?" Tess asked, not sure at all what he was asking.

"Yeah, for a dive trip... you could get an Airbnb near my place instead of staying at the hotel and then come in and dive with me every day," Aiden said, his eyes ripe with exhaustion and something more.

"That would be fun." Tess's heart sped up at the thought of spending time with Aiden. But she could tell the man was falling asleep, and didn't want to hang her hopes on exhausted invitations. "We can talk more about it tomorrow."

"Night-night, pretty Tess."

"Sleep well, sweet Aiden."

CHAPTER THIRTY

Another day passed with no message from Aiden, and Tess shrugged it off. She had a book to focus on and a new life in Colorado that she was slowly building. She wasn't thinking too deeply about actually going back to Cozumel anytime soon, until she picked up her phone Sunday morning and found a very late-night message from Aiden.

I want to play with you.

Tess's eyebrows shot up. Well. *Then.* Somebody had been having some naughty thoughts about her late in the night. And, not at all to her surprise, Tess found she wanted to play with him too.

As do I… and how do you plan to accomplish that?

Come visit?

He was online! Aiden must have the day off, Tess thought, and smiled into the phone, then gasped when it rang.

"Hello?"

"Hi, Tess. And how are you this beautiful morning?"

"Lounging in bed. It is Sunday after all." Tess grinned at hearing his lilting accent.

"That it 'tis. Would you really come down and visit me?"

"I mean, in theory, yes. I'd have to look at flights and figure out a dog sitter, but so long as I have wifi for work stuff, I would love to come down." Tess smiled up at the ceiling.

"That would be amazing," Aiden said. "But I have to ask you a question first."

"Go ahead," Tess said, taking a deep breath.

"What are you looking for? From this?"

Tess remembered their conversation from the other night and how he preferred the straightforward over playing games. "Honestly? I can't say, Aiden. I mean, I'm recently divorced. I know I'm back out dating and stuff, but it's not like I'm seeking out anything serious," Tess admitted, knowing it was the truth. "I think I just need to have fun for now."

"Okay." Aiden sighed, which sounded like in relief. Tess narrowed her eyes. "Because I'm leaving Cozumel soon and I just didn't want to get too involved with someone before I go."

"Oh," Tess said, surprised to find herself feeling a little crestfallen. "Where are you going?"

"I'm leaving for the Philippines at the end of February. I'm burnt out on the job here and I had an opportunity to travel with someone who is heading the same way. It just made sense to go then."

"Right, totally, I get it," Tess said automatically, reminding herself that Aiden had told her he liked to wander the world, not stay in one place too long. "That's a long ways away."

"It is. I should be there about six months, then I plan to head over to Indonesia to pick up work there. I hear the diving is incredible."

"Yeah, so I've heard. Well, that will be awesome." Tess

took a deep breath. This was a good thing, she lectured herself. Aiden could be a fun fling for her with truly no expectations other than enjoying each other's company before he moved across the world. Because if she had thought Mexico was too far for a long-distance relationship, the Philippines wasn't going to be any better.

"That being said, could you visit before I leave?" Aiden asked, his voice hopeful.

"Let me look at dates, but it would likely need to be soon – so I don't hit the expensive airfares over Christmas. Or right after Christmas."

"Okay, and I just need to have a wee chat with my travel buddy first, to make sure her expectations are the same as mine." Alarm bells went off in Tess's head.

"Your travel buddy is a *her*?"

"Yes, her."

"Oh, listen Aiden, I can't do – I don't want to tread on anyone's toes and all that. That's a tough situation for me," Tess said, fumbling her way through, annoyed with herself for assuming that Aiden didn't already have a woman waiting for him. She found herself oddly disappointed in him, that he would try to arrange something like this when he already had a woman.

"No, no, no. It's not like that. She was here on an internship for diving and we dated for a couple weeks, then she left about eight months ago. We've stayed in touch, but just as friends. She's been dating someone else and I've also dated other people. But when she told me she was taking a job in the Philippines and looking for a travel buddy, it was easy to say yes to. We get along well and it would be easy to travel with her, that's all. But I want to make sure she completely understands and is fine with the fact that we are not traveling as a couple before you came to visit. It's the right thing to do."

"Okay, that's fair, though the thought of another woman makes me stabby," Tess warned.

Aiden laughed. "Trust me, it's not like that. But I'll feel better having a chat with her, before anything else happens. It's out of respect for her as well." Tess had to give him credit for being honest.

Plus, she reminded herself as she looked at flights later that day, this was only going to be a fling. A one-week fling on a beautiful island. Diving, dancing, and drinking with a very delicious Scotsman. It sounded like the perfect prescription to start a brand-new chapter in her dating life.

CHAPTER THIRTY-ONE

"Yaaaas, bitch!" Daniel all but squealed in excitement when she'd told him about her plans to leave for Cozumel the upcoming weekend. "Go get you some hot scuba instructor ass."

"Oh my god, what am I doing?"

"Getting your swagger back, that's what. None of these nonsense twenty-five-year-young pups. Go on, get with a real man. And a Scottish one at that. Swoooon." Daniel pretended to faint dramatically. "It'll be amazing. You'll go diving every day, which you love, and diving all night too, if you get what I'm saying."

"I get what you're saying," Tess groaned.

"There are so many jokes I can make about getting wet right now." Tess smacked him. "What? I'm talking about scuba diving, Ms. Bitch, don't you know the lingo?"

"Ms. Bitch, he says." Tess rolled her eyes, but laughed despite herself. She'd been on edge all week, picking what dresses she wanted to wear, finding cute swimming suits, and getting her dive gear in order.

"That's right, *Ms.* Bitch. You gotta give credit where credit is due. And when my friend travels down to another country to get her swag on…well, she's earned the title of Ms. Bitch, that's all I'm saying," Daniel said, handing her a glass of wine.

"I just keep thinking, what, exactly, am I doing traveling to a whole different country to meet up with a man I've only met in person for two days?" Tess said. "Am I out of my mind?"

Daniel sobered quickly. "Look, if it turns out to be horrible, you can just go diving and do your own thing at your apartment each night. Nothing says you have to spend the whole week with a sexy Scot. I mean, I'd like you to, because *stories*. But if it's not right, just do your thing. You can call us every night and we'll check in on you."

"That's true, I'll be just fine one way or the other," Tess mused. She thought about the way Aiden had responded to Micah, and how he'd insisted that she stand up for herself and make her own choices. She did feel comfortable going on this trip, she realized.

BEFORE SHE KNEW IT, Saturday arrived. She dropped the dogs next door, and headed to the airport.

It wasn't until she was waiting at her layover in Atlanta and she saw her second flight delayed that Tess felt the nerves return. An engineer was shouting into the phone about how many times that particular plane had already flown with code errors. Turning over his shoulder, he'd looked at her and whispered, "I wouldn't get on this plane if I were you."

Luckily, she hadn't had to make that decision when they canceled the flight and found a new plane. Tess sat at the airport bar, nursing a mimosa and wondering if she was ignoring the signs right in front of her face. She'd often asked the universe for signs, and what could be a more obvious one than someone straight out telling her not to get on the plane? And yet, here she was, still waiting to board the next flight.

What's the worst that could happen? Tess sipped her drink while her very imaginative brain went quickly down a storyline where she was kidnapped, sold to drug cartels, her organs harvested on the black market. She supposed, if she had to go out that way, it would certainly not be a boring ending to her story. Cursing her writer's brain, she drained her drink and then got in line to board the plane. Because who was she kidding? Sign or no sign, she was getting her ass on that plane and going to Cozumel for the week.

The plane landed without incident in a surprisingly nice airport, and Tess found herself sharing a taxi with a sweet couple from Kansas.

"Now, where are you going?" the woman asked, her face crinkling in concern. "It's not a hotel. Is that safe? I hear you need to only stay at all-inclusives here."

"I think it will be fine." Tess smiled at her. "Cozumel needs tourism to thrive. It's probably not much more dangerous than the city I live in."

"Still, I don't know how we feel about dropping you at some apartment," her husband said, his eyes narrowing as the taxi rolled up to a row of stone duplexes that, from the outside, admittedly looked the worse for wear. A man leaned against the door of one with his arms crossed. He straightened when the taxi arrived and smiled.

"It'll be fine. Really, I promise. Plus, you guys are staying at the hotel where I'm diving through," Tess said, getting out of the taxi while the driver unloaded her bag. "If I don't see you at the dive shop tomorrow, you can worry."

"I'll hold you to that," the husband said. Tess waved the taxi away, then turned to greet the apartment manager who ushered her in, showed her where the lights and air conditioning were, and handed off the keys. In moments, Tess stood alone, sweating in the humidity, taking in the apartment. It was a two-story duplex, and the first floor had a sunny yellow kitchen with a small dining table, sitting area with stone benches in front of a small television, and a beautiful red hacienda-style tiled floor that ran through the house into the master bedroom and out into the shaded private courtyard. The courtyard pictures had been what had sold her online, and Tess was pleased to see it lived up to the photographs. With two-story-high walls, two swing chairs, a small grill, and a tiny wading pool, it hit all the right notes for a secluded, relaxing area in paradise. A few lush plants were tucked into pots around the pool and by the grill area, and Tess was delighted to see a hummingbird hover over a flower. Checking the time, Tess realized she would be cutting it close if she wanted to get to the market in time so she'd have food for lunches this week. She wanted to be back home to shower and beautify herself before Aiden arrived. Rushing, she dumped her suitcase in the bedroom, grabbed her purse, and quickly Google-mapped the nearest market.

She ran to the market and raced back, carrying two overloaded bags of food and drinks, then immediately jumped in the shower.

Why was it so damn humid here? Tess all but screamed, when she stood in front of the bathroom mirror, wrapped in nothing but a towel, looking at her already frizzing hair in dismay. Her phone was buzzing with a message from Aiden, she hadn't even picked an outfit to greet him in yet, and she could not stop sweating.

"Lovely, just lovely," Tess bit out and glanced at the message.

Hey, I think I'm outside. I still need to go home, but can you come out so I can see which door it is?

It's the blue one.

There's three blue ones.

The middle blue one.

Seriously? Can you just come outside? I'm with my work mates and they all want to get home.

Grrrr, Tess grit out, and stomped out the front door, still wrapped in her towel, and waved to the truck full of grinning men outside. A wolf whistle greeted her and Tess slammed her way back inside.

"See you soon!" she heard Aiden call cheerfully after her.

This was not exactly the way she'd planned to greet him, Tess groused. She pulled a dress over her head, taking a quick photo, and then repeating it with two others. Sending the pictures to her friend, Mae, she waited for a response.

Wear the floral one with the lace cutouts and the flowers.

Tess shimmied into her sexy underwear, dashing baby powder on her thighs – anyone who'd spent time in true humidity knew that trick – and put on one of her prettiest bras. Dashing into the kitchen, she dropped an ice cube into a glass and poured some tequila over it, downing it and hoping to ease her nerves. Seriously, could she just stop sweating? Tess wondered, dabbing a dish cloth on her face. The knock came at her door, and Tess drew in a breath, her stomach turning over in knots.

"He thinks you're pretty," Tess reminded herself, and pulling her shoulders back, head held high, she opened the door.

CHAPTER THIRTY-TWO

"Hey," Tess said, smiling shyly at Aiden as he stood in the doorway.

"Wow, you look incredible," Aiden said immediately.

Tess beamed at him, loving that his default was to compliment her. It was something so simple, but she had actively craved it in her relationship with Gabe. Missing out on compliments in the past allowed her to appreciate Aiden's words that much more in the now.

"Thank you," Tess said, as he came inside. "You look quite handsome yourself."

"I brought you a gift." Aiden held up a candy cane full of chocolate kisses and a bottle of tequila. "Christmas kisses, and since we're in Mexico, a good bottle of tequila."

"That's so nice of you." Charmed, Tess took the bottle from him as he checked out the place.

"This is a nice place," Aiden said, not moving far from her.

"Yeah, I think so, too. The courtyard is really lovely." Tess stood at the counter, unsure of what to do. Should she kiss him? "Would you like me to make you a drink? I ran to the market quickly before you got in."

"We could have a drink..." Aiden moved closer, nudging Tess until her back was against the counter. "But I've been thirsty for something else all day."

"Oh?" Tess breathed, looking up into his smiling eyes, her pulse picking up at his nearness.

"Just a taste, Tess." Aiden dipped his lips to hers, brushing them softly.

A tingle of excitement shot through Tess and she leaned into him, his arms coming around her and settling at her waist. "Yum," Tess said, breaking away and laughing up at him when he chuckled.

"I'm really happy you're here." Aiden dipped his head once more to steal a kiss.

"I am too. I'll admit, I was pretty nervous on the plane," Tess said against his mouth, their kisses growing longer as he tasted more, deepening his exploration.

"I was a bit nervous today too," Aiden admitted, pulling back to run his hands up and down her arms. "But that went away as soon as I saw you."

"Really?" Tess drank in his blue eyes.

"Really. It feels good to have you here." She could feel the truth of his words. She knew she should probably play it cool, let him take her out to dinner, have a few drinks or something to loosen up, but strangely she wanted him now – just like this – without the buffer of alcohol to numb any of her nervousness. If anything, the nerves heightened her excitement, and everywhere his hands touched, a trail of heat seemed to follow. Offering him a smile and looking up at him from beneath her lashes, she grabbed his hands in hers.

Turning, Tess pulled him toward the bedroom. Aiden followed, neither of them speaking, both of them knowing exactly what it was they wanted. They'd spent the last two months flirting toward this, building anticipation, and now that they were actually together, Tess didn't want to waste a second of it. Standing in front of the bed, she tugged her dress over her head.

"You're gorgeous," Aiden breathed, his hands coming to her hips and slowly trailing up her sides. He gently nudged her back on the bed, crawling after her so that he kneeled over her.

"Really?" Tess asked, and then mentally kicked herself for coming across as needy. She was supposed to be this confident romance-novel writer, not an insecure divorcee. Though there was truth to both, she supposed, being a true Gemini at heart.

"So beautiful," Aiden said, bending to capture her lips once more before trailing a kiss down the side of her neck to nibble at her throat, sending little thrills of lust through her. "Here... and here." His lips followed a downward path until he found her breasts, and reaching around with one hand, he freed her easily from her bra. Tess arched an eyebrow at him.

"Done that a few times?"

"Practice makes perfect, darling." Aiden returned his attention, and his mouth, to her breasts. Tess reveled in his touch, and his murmured words of approval, as he roundly complimented every inch of her his mouth could find. When he dipped lower, Tess clenched her hands into the sheets, everything falling away but for the ball of pleasure he was building in her, which threatened to overtake her at any moment. Arching into him, she cried out as he skillfully pushed her over the edge, tumbling her into a well of need. Desperate for him, Tess sat up and tugged at his arms, pulling him so he covered her body.

"I need you," Tess gasped against his mouth. Aiden

nodded, his lips barely leaving hers as he discarded his jeans, taking a moment to protect them both, before hovering over her on his arms.

"You're amazing," Aiden said, quite simply, and she read the truth in his eyes. And what a wonder it was, to see herself reflected there – the woman she wanted to be – admired, adored, and wanted. He made her want to be the woman she saw there, a bold, fearless world traveler, who lived life on her terms, and embraced all the challenges that came her way. She'd done that, partially she knew, by coming here. It was like she was stepping into an upgraded version of herself – one that she loved.

Smiling, Tess pressed a kiss to his lips. "I think you're pretty damn amazing, too, Aiden. Thank you for seeing me." Then Tess gasped as he slid into her, filling her in a way she'd never felt before. Tess lost herself to the moment.

After, Aiden patted his shoulder, indicating she should curl into him. "Cuddles," Aiden demanded, and Tess laughed.

"I'm so sweaty," Tess protested.

"I don't care. Cuddles," Aiden ordered and Tess cuddled up to him, tracing her hand down his chest and the long scar she found there.

"What's this?"

"My zipper." Aiden automatically pulled her hand with his so it covered his heart.

"You had heart surgery?"

"As a baby. It's all mended now, but I think it pushed me to live the life I have."

"How so?"

"Well, every year until I was about sixteen I had to go to Edinburgh Children's Hospital for a check-up, which in itself was an annual reminder that I was different, fragile, I guess.

Once a year, they would organize a holiday party for all the kids that I would see in the waiting rooms. Each year there would be new faces starting their journey but also a missing smile where another journey had ended. It made me realize how delicate life can be, and thinking about mortality at that age made me afraid. For years, I worried about every little thing. Until one day, I decided that I would go out and do all the things that made me afraid, and if I did them, then I'd no longer need to be scared."

"Oh," Tess said, her voice catching, "And did you do all the things on your list?"

"Most of them." Aiden turned so his eyes met hers. "There's still a few things that I haven't gotten to yet."

Tess desperately wanted to ask what those things were, but by the way he looked at her, she had a feeling she could guess at least one.

"I really admire that." Tess ran her hand over his chest. "Not everyone would have tackled their fears the same way you have. Many would just drown their sorrows or hide from them."

"Oh, lass, alcohol helps, for sure." Aiden laughed. "But I needed to do more with my time here."

"Not everyone is capable of taking risks like that."

"You've done the same," Aiden traced a finger over her cheekbone, and then over her lips. "Starting a career as an author, leaving what should have been the safe haven of your husband, starting over. All of it. That's incredible and you should be proud of yourself. It's not easy, nor is it normal. I can't tell you how many women I know who play it safe and stay with assholes because they are afraid to be alone."

"I don't mind being alone," Tess admitted, cuddling into him. "I mean, I do get lonely, but I've never minded being alone. I think if you can't spend time with yourself, how do you really know who you are?"

"And do you know who you are?"

"I think I'm finally finding out."

"We all have our own paths. It's okay to take your time figuring things out. That's what I do. Except...I don't know. I'd like a better idea for my future, I suppose."

"What do you see for your future? Aside from your trip, of course."

"I guess I'll go back to the dive industry once I'm in Indonesia. I've saved enough money that I can live like a king there for a few years while I figure things out. You know what I always kind of thought I'd end up doing?"

"What's that?" Tess turned to meet his eyes.

"I always thought I'd have a cool place on the water that I could run as my own little bed and breakfast."

"Really? You'd cook breakfast for people?"

"Well, I don't want to poison them," Aiden quirked a smile at her, "But I like being in customer service. I like seeing how happy people are after they dive with me. There's something special about being an integral part of making happy memories for guests. I think that matters. People save all year to go on a holiday and you can be the one to bring a smile to their face."

"It's true, it does matter. People don't talk about their desk job – they remember that time in Ecuador when they stayed at a cool little hostel on the beach where they had a happy hour with the owner."

"Exactly."

Aiden's phone buzzed repeatedly in his jeans and he sighed, pulling her closer, clearly determined to ignore it.

"Shouldn't you get that?" Tess leaned back to look up at him.

"It's my buddy's birthday tonight."

"Oh no!" Tess exclaimed. "You should go."

"I can stay right here. With you. All night. Much better way to celebrate. Trust me, he won't care," Aiden said, already kissing his way down her throat again.

"No, I don't want to be the girl who stops a guy from hanging with his friends," Tess protested.

Aiden sighed, pulling back. "Fine, we'll go for a drink and a bite to eat, then we're coming back here."

"We?"

"Of course, *we*. Come meet my friends," Aiden tugged her off the bed.

We, Tess thought, and smiled to herself. It felt good that he called them a *we*, and then she shoved the thought down. The expectations of this trip had been defined, she reminded herself as they dressed.

Just fun, no attachments – that's just the way it had to be.

CHAPTER THIRTY-THREE

His friends welcomed her with barely a raised brow, and Tess wondered if they were used to Aiden showing up with different women on his arm, or if they were accepting of new faces because of the nature of their industry. Dive instructors made friends all over the world, and people would pass through for a week or two at a time before moving on. Either way, Tess was quickly welcomed by everyone at the table, and had settled in with a margarita, striking up a conversation with a slim Venezuelan beauty who worked with Aiden.

"I'm Elli," the woman introduced herself in her thick accent, wild curls tumbling everywhere, a tangle of beaded necklaces at her throat. "How long have you been on the island?"

"Just today. I'll be here all week."

"Wonderful. Maybe we'll dive together?"

"That would be nice. I have no idea how they plan out the boats though."

"Knowing Aiden, he'll have you on most of his trips. He plans the board for the day." Elli slanted him a glance.

"I love your necklaces," Tess said, sipping her margarita and enjoying the bite of tequila. "They're so unusual."

"Thank you! I make them. I try to make many of my own clothes too. It's more sustainable," Elli said. Tess just nodded, trying to wrap her head around creating clothes for herself. Though she was a creative, that sort of artistry eluded her.

"I see you've met Elli," Aiden said, leaning over, casually putting his arm around her shoulder and signaling to the table the nature of their relationship.

"I have. Everyone's been so nice tonight," Tess looked around at the table, a veritable United Nations as there were so many accents and cultures represented in one spot. She wondered what it would be like to have such a diverse group of friends, and briefly envied Aiden's life.

"It's a good team we have here. I'll miss it when I go," Aiden admitted, and despite herself, Tess felt her stomach twist at his words. How could he leave this group of friends and a great job? *And her*, her heart whispered, but Tess ignored it, reminding herself again that this was a "get her confidence back and just for fun" type trip.

"We're going to miss him," Elli agreed. Tess couldn't help but wonder why Aiden hadn't dated the beauty, but reminded herself that he had already told her he didn't mix business and pleasure. Maybe at some point, she'd stop looking for lies and hidden meanings in the words men told her. For now, she still questioned everything. Pulled from her thoughts by a rousing cheers that went around the table for the birthday boy, Tess raised her glass. She laughed as a cake was passed down the table and the birthday boy had his head pushed face-first into the cake.

"*Feliz cumpleaños!*"

Diving with Aiden was incredible, and Tess quickly realized why people were so drawn to him. Not only was he excellent at his job, but he took his time with people, answering their questions, alleviating their fears, and helped people of all ages to explore the gifts the ocean had to give. And what gifts they were, Tess thought as they geared up for another dive. She'd seen everything from a splendid toadfish to black-tip reef sharks on one of the deeper dives. They swam through craggy underwater tunnels cutting through the reefs, hovered along expansive coral walls, and stopped to say hello to a pretty yellow seahorse that had taken up residence in between two coral heads.

Underwater, she and Aiden had developed their own little language, often communicating with just their eyes or signaling inside jokes to each other with their hands. More than once, Tess found her mask flooding as she laughed too hard at Aiden doing something silly to impress her. He was charming, kind, and funny – it was almost impossible not to fall under his spell. Tess loved watching him on the boats as he answered questions from divers, gave out instructions to his team, and fended off more than one woman who made advances at him. She couldn't fuss too much about women hitting on him, Tess thought, as she was guilty of doing the same. Either way, he was coming home with her – at least for this week.

It felt like a dream – and maybe it was, for even though everything was very much real, it would never be Tess's reality. Understanding that she'd walked into this with her eyes wide open, Tess decided to embrace the moments they did have and bury thoughts of the future and what feelings it might bring.

Or so she tried to tell herself.

One morning, he took her on a dive – just the two of them.

"It's a slow week, so I was able to sneak away to take you on a dive," Aiden said, as he sat next to her on the boat, the wind blowing his blonde curls back from his face.

"How exciting." Tess smiled up at him, enjoying his easy confidence as the boat bounced across the waves. "My very own private dive guide."

"Let's find some cool swim-throughs and I'll show you some odd critters."

"You've already shown me so much."

Aiden's grin widened and he lowered his sunglasses to shoot her a cheeky wink.

"It has been nothing but my pleasure."

True to his word, Aiden led her on a beautiful dive. She followed him through narrow tunnels in the reef that led out to a deep blue drop off into the depths. He spent time finding macro life for her, showing her small nudibranchs and tiny cleaner shrimp. His eye for detail was phenomenal, and Tess learned just from watching him dive. Half the time she was too distracted to even look at the sea life, as she was so busy mooning after Aiden. She wondered if she could have a life like that someday, where she could enjoy a passion like this with her partner, and explore hidden depths together. Could life ever really be that simple?

***

"I THINK that Australian mom had quite the thing for you," Tess mused, lounging in the hammock swing in their private courtyard, the small wading pool glowing softly blue. It was their last evening together, the week having passed much too quickly in a blur of diving, eating leisurely dinners out, and losing sleep each night as they explored each other's bodies.

"Yeah, I know." Aiden leaned back and crossed his arms behind his head, winking at her to let her know he was kidding. Though she supposed there was some truth to it, it had to be good for his self-confidence to work a cool job that had more than one woman fantasizing about him. It was a wonder Aiden's ego wasn't any larger than it was.

"Must be nice," Tess saluted him with her glass full of watered-down margarita, "having all these women throw themselves at you."

"I certainly have no complaints." Aiden quirked a smile. "But sometimes it's really awkward or uncomfortable for everyone, especially if they are doing it to make their man jealous and you have to dive with them. I've learned to keep my eyes on people's faces, never check women out – well, at least when I'm speaking with them – and to keep a fairly respectful distance. And don't get me started about wearing a kilt to a pub. Women think they can reach right under without asking."

"Shut up," Tess said, momentarily distracted as she thought about Aiden in a kilt.

"Aye, it's a real thing. Not too pleasant being assaulted when you're just out for a wee pint with your mates. Though I can't say there weren't a few times I didn't mind."

"I'm sure," Tess said, laughing. "What about dating your co-workers?" He definitely worked with some beautiful women.

"Nope. I learned that lesson years ago." Aiden laughed, leaning back in his chair. "Don't shit where you eat, I believe is the saying."

"I suppose it's best not to muddy the waters." Tess kicked her foot out to set the little swing moving. "I remember the bar I worked at in college. Man, it was a mess of hormones and hook-ups. I did my best to stay out of it, which thankfully let me keep that job most of college. There was way too much drama when people crossed those lines or even switched up their sexual choices."

"Hmmm, sounds spicy. Do tell."

"I just remember one of our waitresses was a lesbian. Never once had she ever hinted at or discussed wanting to be with a man, and yet on our big Halloween party one year, I went downstairs to change a keg and there she was, legs wrapped around one of our bartenders."

"I'm assuming this was a male bartender." Aiden asked, shifting closer so he could run a hand up her leg.

"That it was. Imagine our surprise! She denied it after, which I kind of think is a shame – there's nothing wrong with being bisexual."

"Was the guy upset?"

"I think he had certainly hoped for more after that night, but she never hooked up with him again."

"Alcohol can do that," Aiden said, crouching in front of Tess. "But I prefer my women to happily choose to be with me."

"I happily choose to be with you." Tess gasped a little as his hands roamed their way up her legs beneath her skirt.

"Good, I would hate to think you were having a miserable time." He cocked an eyebrow at her as he knelt between her legs, nudging her knees open, and pressing a kiss to her inner thigh. Tess felt her insides go liquid as he controlled her movement on the swing, bringing her forward while his mouth trailed a path up her sensitive skin.

"Nope, definitely not having a miserable time," Tess said, groaning as his mouth found where she wanted him most. She leaned back into the hammock, closing her eyes as all of her focus centered on the sensations he was lavishing upon her. "I'd say, really, this is one of the better times I've had in ages."

"Tess?" Aiden stopped to look up at her.

"Yes?"

"Be quiet."

"Yes, sir," Tess said, and relaxed into the hammock, letting Aiden take over. She certainly couldn't complain, as the nerves in her body all but danced in joy, and he skillfully took her over the edge once more. Gasping, Tess met his eyes when he filled her, controlling her movements with the swing, leaving nothing for her to do but lay back while he rocked them deeply together. A drop of sweat trickled down her back as the night air kissed her heated skin, and Tess lost herself in the moment. It was decadent, having no control over their sex, and pleasure singed its way through her core as Aiden masterfully swung them home.

"Come with me," Aiden demanded, while Tess tried to sit up in the swing, bleary-eyed. Tugging her hand, he pulled her up and led her to the full hammock that hung between two walls on the other side of the courtyard. Piling in, he pulled her so that her head nestled into the crook of his shoulder, and she could just make out the blue of his eyes searing into hers as he curled into her body.

"That was..." Tess began.

"Incredible?" Aiden asked, and Tess leaned up to kiss him, her lips lingering on his as her emotions bounced around inside, threatening to boil over.

"Incredible," Tess agreed, smiling up at him. She tried to tamp down all the thoughts that roiled in her mind, but he must have seen it on her face.

"Don't fall for me, Tess," Aiden whispered, his eyes on hers as he stroked a hand down her cheek.

Annoyed that he could read her mind and that he had been the one to say it, Tess arched an eyebrow at him, giving her best no-nonsense glare.

"*You* don't fall for *me*, Aiden," Tess said.

"I'm sorry, that sounded arrogant," Aiden admitted, snuggling into her.

"It did, but I get it. The same goes for you, buddy," Tess said, lightly tugging a curl of his hair, though her heart felt bruised at his words.

She didn't want to think about anything else on their last night together but the way she felt wrapped in his arms, the stars blinking out in the velvet darkness above them, the faint sound of the ocean in the distance. Aiden made a little noise as he pulled her closer and they cuddled in, luxuriating in the moments they did have together.

They spent much of the night holding each other, both trying to fight off sleep, before they'd finally succumbed in the early morning hours. Sunrise came, waking them. All too soon, his ride to work was honking outside the door.

"I'll speak to you soon," Aiden said, his arms wrapped around her as he kissed her once more. "Thank you for an unforgettable week. You're amazing, Tess, you really are."

"So are you, Aiden. I can't believe the week is over already." Tess her eyes puffy with lack of sleep, snuggled into the nook of his arm. "It just flew by."

"I know. I've gotten used to watching people leave." Aiden looked down at her expectantly.

"I remember you telling me you prefer not saying goodbye." Tess brought her hand to his cheek. "Until our paths cross again, Aiden." She leaned up for one more kiss before he walked out of her life forever.

· · ·

ALONE IN THE APARTMENT, she called Mae. For a brief moment, she'd considered calling Vicki, but since it had been months now with no contact, a phone call from Mexico wasn't exactly going to improve their relationship.

"Mae... what am I doing?" Tess whispered, sitting on the edge of the small pool in the courtyard, watching a hummingbird hover over a plant. It was still outside, as Sundays often are, and nothing but the occasional car driving by marred the peace of the day.

"You're living your life," Mae responded.

"I like him. I really like him..." Tess whispered, as a tear rolled down her face and plopped loudly into the pool, disrupting the peace. She watched the ripples push across the water and thought about how every choice she made these days seemed to have a massive impact on the life tapestry she was weaving.

"You don't know what the future holds, Tess. No matter what, though, you're strong enough to handle it. And I'm always here to listen, sister-friend," Mae said, her voice a comfort through the phone.

"No, I'm pretty sure I know what it holds. Life doesn't work out like it does in my romance novels."

"You don't know that. But, if anything, I really admire your willingness to put yourself out there again. I know it's scary to feel all the things you're feeling right now, but I'd be more scared if you numb yourself for the rest of your life."

"Numb would be good right now." Tess swiped a palm across her eyes.

"Go back to bed, Tess. Things always look better after sleep."

CHAPTER THIRTY-FOUR

He called her.

Every day, in fact. Tess found herself falling into a pattern of checking her watch, knowing when he'd be done with work, and that she'd be getting a phone call sometime in the next few hours. It hadn't been what she'd expected, not with Aiden's "live each day in the moment" attitude, and yet she eagerly looked forward to his every call.

Winter had finally arrived in Denver, and snow came down in thick chunky sheets, burying her yard. Tess had to shovel long tracks around the house so the dogs could race around the yard – Ringo ready to play, and Red hightailing it back to the house as soon as he'd taken care of his business. She'd spent Christmas at Daniel and Teddy's house – her first Christmas in years away from her family.

She tried to reach out to Vicki. Chad answered the phone, and with a sheepish apology, stated that Vicki was just too busy to chat. He handed the phone off to David. It was nice to hear all about her nephew's latest endeavors with different science experiments he was doing at school. She made him promise to reach out to her whenever he needed to talk – the last thing she wanted was to lose her nephew.

When Chad returned to the phone, Tess asked, "Everything good with you guys?"

"Yes, for the most part. Work's been a killer for us both, but we're good. Dealing with Chicago winter and all," Chad trailed off. Tess knew she was putting him in an awkward position.

"Well, things are good here. I've made some great friends with my neighbors, and have been traveling – diving and whatnot." Tess filled Chad in a bit, as she was certain Vicki would press him for details.

"Sounds like you're doing great, Tess, that's nice to hear," Chad said.

Tess almost asked if Vicki was still too busy for a quick hello. Her sister had her faults, but she was the closest family member she had left. Maybe the holidays were getting to her, but despite everything, Tess missed her. However, if Vicki wanted to know what was going on in her life, then she'd have to pick up the phone. Tess ended the call by wishing them both a happy New Year.

Over the next week, Tess found herself stuck in that awkward time between Christmas and New Year's Eve, when everyone had plans galore and she had nothing on her agenda. She got a Happy Holidays e-mail from Gabe's sister. They hadn't been close, but had always been cordial. She thought it was a kind gesture until she got to the part where she conveniently mentioned Gabe had gone up to the cabin in northern Wisconsin to spend the holidays with his Babers. So they were still together.

And she was alone. But she realized she was still happier that way than when she was with Gabe.

"Come to the New Year's Eve concert with us," Elizabeth

insisted when Tess called to tell her about the message. "It's so much fun – we go every year."

"I might. Do I need to decide now? I'm kind of blah this year. I may just want to stay home." Tess dreaded the whole "kissing at midnight" part.

"Nope, you can get tickets day of. Just let me know. I really want you to come, it's seriously a ton of fun, and I'll feel better knowing you aren't moping at home alone."

"I mean, I don't see anything wrong with watching a *Real Housewives* marathon and quietly getting sauced by myself."

"That's for New Year's Day," Elizabeth insisted, and Tess laughed.

"Guess who reached out to me?"

"Who? Gabe?"

"Nope, Owen. He's coming here for New Year's with a girl he's hooking up with. Says he has a bunch of friends in the area and we should all go out."

"Interesting. Would you go? Would it be weird?"

"Nah, Owen and I are cool. He was exactly what he needed to be for me at the right time. We've been in touch a bit since then, but always just friends."

"Then go. Just don't sit at home, alone. Please?"

"Okay, I'll do something. I promise."

Despite her misgivings, Tess found herself agreeing to host a New Year's Eve party for Owen and his friends, with the promise they would clean up. She spent the day before cleaning and buying some extra party supplies. She really didn't care about the fact that Owen was dating someone; her mind was on Aiden.

Aiden who called daily to tell her a joke. Aiden who had messaged and asked for her address; Tess waking one morning to a package of toys for the dogs on her doorstep. Red had broken a tooth and had to have it removed, and all the toys were soft-chew for his recovery. It was Aiden who invaded her dreams each night. She wanted more time with him, Tess *knew* that, but she wasn't sure how or when she would ever see him again.

What are you doing tonight?

Having a small party here. Then maybe just walk to a bar on the corner. Keeping it easy.

That sounds nice. Some customers want to go out, but I'm exhausted. We'll see if I even make it that late. I'll try to stay up and wish you a happy New Year.

Aww, thanks. If you can't, no worries. I know how it is.

Tess smiled at her phone and tried calling Owen again, wanting to know what time he and his friends would be arriving. He had been texting her constantly the last week making plans, and now that it was the day of the party, he was suddenly silent. Again, his phone went to voicemail. Annoyed, she checked his Instagram to see he'd arrived in Denver. It was almost mid-afternoon. Tess looked around her clean house and thought about all the party supplies she'd bought. Irrespective of whether he wanted to be around her or not, common courtesy would have been to either not plan a party with her or at least let her know if it was canceled. Sending him a message that said as much, she finally got a response.

They weren't coming.

She was annoyed, partly because she'd gone and bought fancy cheese, but also because he'd made her feel the same way Gabe had – like she was the second-best choice. She didn't even want to date the guy, but regardless he should treat his friends better. Shoving away the feeling of rejection, which she knew she was particularly sensitive to at the moment, Tess made another call.

"Elizabeth, what time are you going to the concert?"

"We leave at seven for a friend's house. Can I pick you up?"

"You absolutely can."

"Yes! What happened with Owen?"

"He bailed. Can you believe that? Spent all week messaging me about getting his friends together, my address, planning what people were going to bring and then… nothing. He said he and his girl are just going to do something alone."

"That's rude. Who does that?"

"Right? I should've expected that of him. He's a nice guy usually, but a total flake," Tess said, rolling her eyes.

"Forget it, come have fun with us. It'll be a blast," Elizabeth insisted.

"See you soon," Tess said. While she got ready, she texted Aiden to tell him what happened. His outrage on her behalf made her feel better, along with his decidedly naughty suggestions on what they would be doing if they were spending the night together, and by the time Elizabeth arrived, she was in good spirits again.

As PROMISED, the concert was a blast. The band had gone all out and there were women dancing in flaming balls suspended from the ceiling, explosions of confetti, and a crowd more than raring to go. Tess watched Elizabeth with her boyfriend, and was once again struck by how well they fit together. She wanted that someday. To have someone look at her as though she brought light into their world. In time, Tess thought, she'd probably be able to bring her walls down enough to love like that.

Her phone buzzed in her purse, Aiden's name flashing

across the screen. Holding it up, she motioned she would step out into the hallway of the arena.

"Hey!" Tess shouted into the phone, holding her hand up to her ear.

"Happy New Year!" Aiden shouted back, and a warm glow rushed through Tess.

"I'm sorry, the concert's so loud. It's a ton of fun though. I'm really glad I came."

"I'm sorry about your party," Aiden said.

"No worries, that's the way it goes. This was the better choice anyway." Tess turned away from a guy who tried to smile and catch her eye.

"I don't want to keep you; you should be spending time with your friends. I just wanted to hear your voice." His own voice was thick with sleep.

"I'm glad you called. Sleep well, Aiden. Happy New Year."

Tess clicked her phone off, feeling the warm glow fill her once more. All but skipping back into the concert, she reminded herself not to look too deeply into anything. If she had to explain to anyone what was going on, she wouldn't know where to begin. For now, Aiden would remain a friend... and just that.

AT HOME THAT NIGHT, more than pleasantly buzzed and smiling to herself, Tess poured herself a whiskey and pulled out a barstool at her kitchen counter. It had been a fun night, which was rare for New Year's. In her opinion, it was the most over-hyped holiday of the year. Still, it felt nice to just sit in her quiet house. She didn't have to worry about whether she'd get into a drunken argument with Gabe, or if his phone would be lighting up late into the night. She didn't have to be anywhere but exactly where she was. When her phone buzzed, she picked it up and squinted at it through a haze of alcohol.

"Oh," Tess breathed, opening the message from Gabe.

I went outside just now and saw a shooting star. It made me think of you and how I know we'll always be bonded. We'll always have a spiritual connection, you and I. Nothing can take that away from us, Tess. I'm missing you tonight, that's for sure. I know this New Year may not be what you want it to be, but just know I'll always feel connected to you.

"You lying piece of..." Tess growled and almost threw her phone across the room. Instead, she forced herself to put it gently back on the counter. He was texting her, at four in the morning while his girl slept by his side. "Shooting star, my ass," Tess said, knowing how cloudy and snowy Wisconsin was.

She was the other woman now, the woman who could light up Gabe's phone in the middle of the night and keep his Babers wondering just who he was contacting. A petty side of her desperately wanted to do that, just to string him along a bit, to rile them both up. Minutes drew out as she stared at the message, processing her feelings. She froze as her phone buzzed again. Leaning over without touching it, as though the phone could see her, she beamed when she saw a message from Aiden.

Getting up for work. Hope you got home safely.

Home now. Should drag my butt to bed.

It must have been some party! Glad you are safe.

Me too, Aiden. Thanks for checking in with me.

No problem, I'll blow some bubbles for you today.

Diving sounds amazing, but I'll be honest, right now my bed sounds even better.

I'd love being in your bed with you today. Call you later.

Tess hummed the whole way to her room, and when she woke later that day, a smile still on her lips, she realized she never did respond to Gabe's text message.

Nor did she ever have to again.

CHAPTER THIRTY-FIVE

"I want to see you."

Tess's hand stilled on Red's head. They'd curled up on the couch together, and she was enjoying another snowy day in her comfy pants. She'd been taking advantage of the gloomy weather to stay inside and write, and was happy to be making progress on her next book. Between spending time with her neighbors, meeting up with Elizabeth, and working on her writing, Tess was beginning to hit her stride again. Her new normal was turning out to be a nice one, and she'd felt like the struggle of months past was finally beginning to ease a bit. Aside from her yearning for Aiden, that was, which seemed an unsolvable problem.

"I'd like to see you again, too, Aiden." Tess closed her eyes, thinking about being close to him again, diving into the depths together, or taking long strolls at night with no particular destination in mind.

"Do you think you'd come down again? You know… before I go? Or am I crazy to even ask that?"

"Oh." Tess sat straighter on the couch.

"I can't leave work – they're slammed, and I need to accrue all my extra pay and overtime for the trip. Otherwise, I'd come to see you," Aiden rushed out. Tess squeezed her eyes shut, her heart pounding as she thought about what another trip down would mean. Days under water, diving into her happy place. Nights with Aiden, wrapped around him – also a place she was quite fond of.

"Um, gosh, Aiden, I haven't really thought about it. When do you leave again?"

"The end of February," Aiden said, his voice sounding tight.

"So, sometime in the next two months then." Tess felt a little shaky at the thought.

"If flights aren't too expensive. I'm sure I can swing you another deal on dive packages," Aiden said. "I'm sure you're probably busy with your writing. I totally understand if it would be too much."

Too much for her heart, Tess thought, but pressed her lips closed before she spoke it.

"I'll look into it and if it works, I'll shoot you some dates?"

"That'd be amazing, Tess. But, again, no worries if you can't. I was just thinking about you all day today," Aiden said.

"I mean, it's not exactly a hardship to leave winter and go diving."

"And?"

"Oh, and to see you too, I suppose." Tess laughed.

"Sassy woman."

After they ended the call, Tess just sat for a moment, staring out the window at the snow-covered trees on the front lawn. Could she go back to see him again? Anxiety snuck through her at the thought, at what she could expose her heart to, and if she could be strong enough to handle the aftermath of what she could already see coming a mile away.

She called Mae, who was on her way to drop her son at a playdate, and filled her in.

"What should I do?" Tess asked.

"What do you want to do?" Mae asked.

"I want to go."

"But?"

"I'm scared. I really like him. Like… *really* like him. But what am I doing? I know he's leaving – he's moving across the world. Why put myself in this position? I don't know if my heart can handle it," Tess admitted. "This is all probably too soon. I mean, I just got divorced, what am I doing?"

"You're following your heart?"

"Yeah, but what does it know? It seems to just throw me into situations that I'm going to get hurt in." Tess pulled a thread from the throw blanket on the couch through her fingers. Idly, she tied it in a knot, and then untied it, and then tied it once more.

"Do you want to live your life with your walls up?"

"It's safer that way."

"Do you want to live your life playing it safe?" Mae amended.

"No," Tess grumbled.

"Do you want to become bitter and jaded and refuse to believe in love again?"

"No, but admittedly this situation does not have a good outcome for me. It's already spelled out."

"You never know. Why don't you take it a day at a time?"

"Because I need to know I'm not going to get hurt. I need to see the future. I have to protect myself."

"But why, Tess? You've already done the hard stuff. You know you're strong enough to stand on your own. Look at all you handled, all by yourself – well, with us there, but you know what I mean. Do you want to spend your life questioning if you should have gone to Cozumel to meet this man but didn't because you were scared it was too soon? Or that you'd get hurt? Life is full of hurt, you *know* that. Do you want it to be filled with regrets too?"

"Do you think I'd regret not going?"

"Do *you* think you'll regret not going?" Mae parried the question back at her.

"Yes, I do," Tess admitted.

"So, go. Being vulnerable is one of the strongest things you can do. It's easy to put walls up and to protect yourself from getting hurt. It's much harder to open yourself and let love in again."

"True...."

"You know, I'm beyond ecstatic to see that you'd be willing to try. I've been worried for you."

"Why?"

"Between Vicki cutting you out, the divorce, and then you hunkering down in Colorado, I just worried you'd lose yourself. That too much hurt, losing too many people – well, I guess I just mean some of the main people in your life – would turn you cold. And that's not who you are," Mae said.

"I'm scared," Tess admitted.

"So be scared. But do it anyway."

CHAPTER THIRTY-SIX

Go big or go home, Tess thought, and her stomach did a weird little flip as the plane bumped down onto the runway. She'd found an Airbnb to rent just down the road from Aiden's place, and had boldly agreed to stay for two and a half weeks. Aiden hadn't invited her to stay at his apartment, and she hadn't bothered to ask. There was something comforting about having the buffer zone of her own place, in case she needed to be alone, or if everything fell apart – her own space to lick her wounds. Space was important to Tess, and having just recently claimed her own space in her life again, she wasn't quite willing to surrender it again.

The taxi dropped her in front of the apartment, and Tess pressed the buzzer, leaning against the faded red cement wall that surrounded the courtyard. Kids raced by in the streets, and people casually honked their horns at each other and waved a hand in greeting as they drove past. Though many of the houses in the neighborhood were not pristine by United

States standards, the trade-off seemed to be a thriving community of neighbors and family. She watched as another group of children ran past, chattering away, a soccer ball clutched gleefully in the ringleader's hands. At home, kids wouldn't be allowed to run down the street together. Instead, they'd have supervised playdates in protected backyards, and everyone would be buttoned up in front of the television by dark. The warm sense of family – of community – was palpable here.

"*Hola, senorita, bienvenido,*" the owner of the apartment greeted her and let her into the courtyard, showing her around the space. Unfortunately, it was not remotely as nice as it had been portrayed in the photos online. Unsure of how to handle it, but knowing Aiden would arrive soon, Tess just smiled and thanked the man before ushering him out of the door. She wanted a quick shower to freshen up before seeing Aiden.

If she could call the trickle of water that came from the rusty spout on the wall a shower, that is. Sighing, Tess made do and wondered about the windows in the back of the apartment. Ultimately, she'd stayed in worse accommodations, so it wasn't a big deal – but there were no bug screens, and it looked like the windows had a hard time latching. Safety would be a concern. Not finding a safe for her passport or money, Tess did what she normally did in situations like this – hid it in a tampon box in the bathroom.

The buzzer sounded for the front gate, and Tess's heart fluttered in her chest. This was Aiden, she reminded herself as she scurried around looking for the gate key; she'd been with him before. It wasn't a big deal.

Liar, liar, her heart whispered as she went outside and found him leaning into the gate, his hands on the bars, a mile-wide smile on his face. Did the sun just follow this man? His blonde curls were a halo of light, and suddenly everything in her world seemed much brighter.

"Hey," Tess said, smiling at him and he leaned forward to kiss her through the gate, not even waiting until she unlocked it. The taste of him imprinted on her lips, and a frisson of excitement whispered through her.

"Hey yourself," Aiden said, and Tess unlocked the gate. It slid open achingly slowly, the metal rollers squeaking in protest.

"How was your flight?" Aiden asked, and then Tess found herself buried against him as he pulled her in for a long hug. She let herself be held there for a moment, enjoying his arm around her, loving how they fit together.

"Good, all good. It's nice to see you again." Tess pulled back to meet his dancing blue eyes. Then she turned and tugged him along, winding through the shared courtyard back to the first-floor apartment she'd rented. She unlocked the frayed metal door and, pushing it open, said, "Welcome. It's not as nice as the last place."

"I'm not looking at the apartment right now." Aiden whirled and pinned Tess to a wall, taking her under with a kiss so searing she felt herself go liquid.

"Oh, well, in that case –" Tess gasped against his mouth, his hands everywhere "– the bedroom's…" But Aiden was already leading her there, his mouth covering hers. They fumbled their way down the hallway and toppled onto the bed. Losing themselves in each other, in being together again, Tess no longer noticed the haphazard room or the broken bug screens. She only saw Aiden.

"I've missed you," Aiden said, when they lay spent, sweaty and sticky, the fan in the corner lazily blowing the humid air at them in little puffs.

"I missed you, too." Tess turned her head on the pillow to smile at him.

"Tess," Aiden said, reaching out to brush a curl from where it stuck to her face, "remember when I told you not to fall for me?"

"That I do," Tess said, mock-glaring at him. "It was not your finest moment."

"I realize that I meant it as a warning for myself." His eyes searched hers.

Tess just nodded, unable to speak. Her heart felt the same, but the words were too dangerous. She leaned forward to brush her lips against his. He held her there, forehead to forehead, and they both breathed together, silently acknowledging what was. In agreement, they moved apart, the moment passing them by, and Aiden turned and looked around the room for a moment.

"The bugs are going to eat you alive." He motioned to the screen. "I know how much the mosquitos love you."

"I know. I'll have to coat myself in bug spray each night." Tess shrugged.

"Should we get some food? Or can I take you to dinner?"

"Let's get some food and a bottle of wine and check out the yard in the back. Maybe we could play a card game," Tess suggested. "I brought cribbage."

"What's cribbage?"

"You don't know cribbage? Oh, man, it's a great game!"

An hour later, they sat in two rickety folding chairs in the quiet backyard, a few scraggly trees lining the wall and providing shade for them. Tess had brought a portable speaker, and propping her iPod against it, they'd settled on the Black Keys for their music choice. Slowly, she taught him the rules of cribbage as they drank wine and nibbled on snacks they'd picked up in the store.

It was an easy afternoon, with no expectations, no rushing about, no reason to try and impress each other. Instead, they relaxed, playing the game, chatting idly about life, while the shadows grew long around them. When night finally came, and the bottle of wine was empty, Aiden drew her to his side once more.

In this perfect moment in time, snapshotted in her mind, there was only him. Only *us*, Tess thought, and held onto that through the long night as mosquitos refused to let her sleep, lest she dream the impossible.

CHAPTER THIRTY-SEVEN

"Come stay at my place," Aiden insisted in the morning.

"I don't want to impose on you," Tess said, her eyes puffy from lack of sleep. Bug bites dotted her body and Aiden rubbed one of her legs absently.

"It's fine. I have bug screens. We're going to be together anyway, just stay with me. It will save you money, too."

"I'm not sure I can get a refund on the place."

"It's obviously not portrayed accurately online; this looks nothing like the pictures. I'll talk to the owner." Aiden leaned over to bump his forehead against hers.

"You sure about this?" Tess asked, not wanting to intrude on his space, but also not sure if she would want her own space at some point on this trip.

"I'm sure. It'll be fine. And if you need time to write, you can work from there – just don't come with me to the dive shop one day."

"Then I'll accept your offer," Tess said, leaning over to kiss him. "I doubt I'd get much sleep here unless I purchased a mosquito net."

"I'll go take care of it. You pack."

Tess beamed after him, hearing him trudge upstairs and knock on the owner's door. While she gathered her things, which didn't take long as she'd barely spent any time unpacking, her mind wandered to their easy day yesterday. Could her life be like that? Relaxing with a card game, making love at night, going for dives in the morning? It had been something she'd been aspiring toward for years – she'd even started a book series with a diver as a main character so she could research on dive trips. When she'd first started writing, she'd always asked herself, What am I working toward? It wasn't just financial success or freedom, because anyone who only works for money is left feeling empty inside. She only had to look to Vicki for confirmation of that.

Instead, she'd decided to work toward her perfect day. She'd even outlined it in her journal, though it hadn't taken much to outline. It quite simply read: wake up, go diving, grab an iced coffee, write in the afternoons. It had seemed so unattainable at the time, what with Gabe not even wanting to be near the ocean, that it was just a pipe dream she could work toward. The carrot at the end of the proverbial stick, so to speak, and yet here she was, looking dead-on at a different way of life. It was shocking, really, to stare her dream in the face and see how it could all work, to almost tangibly feel all the puzzle pieces dropping into place, and have to walk away. Which, ultimately, Tess knew she would have to do.

"All set?" Aiden asked, popping his head in the door. Tess glanced up at him, her cheeks flushing, and nodded.

"Yup, all set. Thanks for taking care of that for me. Was he mad?"

"No, it's fine. He knows the place is a bit shit. He'll refund you today, he said." Aiden hefted her bag. "Anything else?"

"I'll just grab my backpack and check the place through,"

Tess said. Moments later they were walking down the sidewalk, on their way to Aiden's place.

"What do you want to do today?" Aiden asked, and just like that they were over any potential weirdness of her staying with him.

"Do you have anything you have to get done on your day off?" Tess knew that days off were few and far between for dive instructors during high season.

"I just need to drop my laundry off and pick up a new five-gallon jug of water. Otherwise, I'm all yours."

"Let's just go walk around and explore then? I don't really want to do anything else but dive and hang out with you." Tess followed him up the stairs to his third-floor apartment. She hadn't seen it last time she was here, and was curious about where he lived.

"Your wish is my command, my lady." Aiden unlocked his door, opening it to a small apartment with a neat living room, tiny kitchen, and bedroom in the back. "Let me clear some space for you."

Tess followed him, checking out the various pieces of art and collectibles tucked on his bookshelf. She smiled at the picture of him sitting next to an impressively large black bear, a huge grin stretching his face.

"There you go," Aiden said, gesturing to two drawers and several hangers he'd cleaned out. "Is that okay for you?"

"Perfect, thanks. Let me just put a few things away and I'm all yours."

"I'm counting on it," Aiden said, his tone husky as he came up behind her and wrapped his arms around her waist.

"Or... you know... now works, too," Tess laughed as they tumbled onto his bed.

"Is this your local pub?"

They'd stopped in front of a large building, almost designed like a house, with a wide front porch and a courtyard with trees in the back, well lit, with a variety of bar games. They had been wandering their way around town with no particular agenda, simply walking and talking, Aiden pointing out favorite restaurants, or advising places to stay away from.

"Yup, we have a tendency to meet here a few times after work when we're not exhausted." Aiden pulled her inside.

"I completely understand why you're so wiped out all the time, now that I'm diving as much as you do every day. It takes a lot out of you," Tess said, nodding her agreement as she scanned the large open bar. "Today was fun though. I met a girl named Janie on the boat. She seems cool and has already asked if I'd go on any dive trips in the future with her. Not sure I would... but hey, it's always nice to expand my community of dive friends."

"Be careful who you pick for dive trips down the road though. You want to make sure you're at the same level of dive skill," Aiden cautioned, motioning for her to follow him around the side of the bar to where several dart boards were affixed to the wall. "Do you play darts?"

"Not well, but I always enjoy playing."

The bartender greeted Aiden by name, and he waved at a few people on the other side of the pub. A Bob Marley song ended and the music switched to Led Zeppelin. Tess relaxed into the moment.

"Tequila?"

"Sure," Tess said, taking the darts from him and deciding she wanted to be red. "What are we playing for?" Tess shot Aiden a saucy look.

"Hmm, I'd say winner is in charge tonight..." Aiden's

blue eyes seared into hers and a shot of lust tingled through Tess's core.

"Done and done. You're in trouble." Tess tugged the bodice of her sundress a little lower to expose more cleavage.

"Not fair." Aiden's eyes were focused, but most definitely not on the dart board.

"All is fair, my dear," Tess purred, as she stepped up and shot what she considered to be a fairly reasonable round. Pleased with herself, she twirled her skirt as she turned to Aiden and winked.

"Not bad." Aiden stepped to the line. He immediately closed out three twenties and Tess felt her heart drop.

"Play much?"

"Here and there, darling." Aiden smiled as he took a sip of his tequila and Tess glared at him. When he next stood to shoot, she leaned over and whispered in his ear.

"What if I like it when you take charge?"

His dart bounced off the board, missing its mark, and Tess beamed, slipping back to the bar to demurely sip her drink.

"You're playing dirty, lass," Aiden said, raking his hand through his curls and leveling a fake stern look at her.

"Me? Never," Tess smiled, standing to take her turn. She squeaked when he trailed a finger lightly over her bum just as she tried to make her shot.

Tess whirled and glared at him. "Did I give you permission to do that?"

"I'm pretty sure you granted me an all-access pass," Aiden said, raising an eyebrow at her.

"I don't recall doing so." Tess crossed her arms over her chest.

"You just did," Aiden said at the same time his dart hit the bullseye, lighting the board up for his win. Pleased with himself, he sauntered back to Tess, standing so close she had to lift her chin to meet his gaze.

"I'll take a congratulatory kiss." Aiden's lips twitched in a smile.

"Nope," Tess pouted, pushing her lower lip out.

"I believe the winner was in charge tonight?" Aiden asked. "Or do we need to revisit the rules."

"It was for tonight, not like, right now."

"You should have clarified that, lass, before playing the game, eh?"

Caught, Tess grinned and pulled his head down to her, lavishing a kiss on him that had his face tingeing pink. He signaled for the check from the bartender. His friends whistled from the back and he raised a hand to acknowledge them, all while keeping his eyes on Tess.

"I'll be collecting the rest of my prize immediately."

CHAPTER THIRTY-EIGHT

Tess fell into a routine that brought her great joy. Each morning, she'd get the coffee perking, haul Aiden from bed, and they'd ride in to the dive shop with his co-workers, nobody saying much, everyone lost in their own thoughts, sipping to-go coffees. After a morning of exploring the reefs, she would generally sun herself on the beach for a while, before diving right back into the ocean in the afternoon. A few days, when the winds were too high for the boats to go out, Tess stayed in town at the coffeeshop, spending hours working on her next book while gazing out dreamily at the sea. Everything felt more intense for her – it was like the ocean was even more vibrant and alive, the jokes told at dinner even funnier, and the touch of Aiden at night that much more electrifying.

If she allowed herself to examine those feelings too closely, she'd probably freak out all over Aiden, Tess thought, so she shoved them deep inside, closing them firmly in a box in her mind. A part of her wanted an answer from him, a guarantee of a future together, but despite her ability to control where her characters in her books went, she couldn't neatly arrange things that way in real life.

One night, they wandered along the sea wall and sat, their legs dangling over the rough edges, the waves lapping below them, and watched as the sun said goodbye to the day.

"You don't talk much about your family," Aiden said, bumping his shoulder to hers.

"No, I suppose I don't," Tess agreed. "It's a bit of a tough area for me. I lost my parents in college, and my sister and I aren't all that close, I suppose."

"Ah, Tess, I'm sorry." Aiden wrapped an arm around her shoulders and squeezed her into him.

"It is what it is. I had a tough time growing up with my parents, and our relationship was strained when I lost them. I went through a lot of guilt in that time, wondering if I could have been a better daughter, or one they accepted more."

"Why do you feel like they didn't accept you?"

"They were just incredibly controlling. And very conservative. The daughter they wanted was basically the daughter that everyone in small midwestern suburbs wants. Clean-cut, follows the rules, caters to the men in her life, and studies an approved field."

"Your soul is much more wild than that, Tess." Aiden twirled a curl of her hair around his finger.

"It is, and I constantly chafed at all the rules. I hated feeling trapped. I was always grounded, always in trouble. I looked forward to college just so I had some breathing room. And then, suddenly, they were gone. I wonder what I would have thought of them as an adult now. Or what they would think of me."

"I suspect they'd be proud of you and the wonderful life

you've created for yourself. I'm proud of you and I've only known you for a few months."

"Thank you," Tess squeezed Aiden's hand, "I also wonder if they'd be like Vicki and shut me out because I've made my own decisions without consulting them."

"Is she really like that?"

"Yes, unfortunately, she is. She's incredibly overbearing. It's a toss-up whether she's in competition with me or wants to control my every move."

"And yet, here you are."

"Here I am." Tess turned and smiled up at him. "Exactly where I want to be."

"I'm glad you didn't let them trim your thorns, Tess. A rose bush still needs them to thrive."

"Thank you, Aiden." Tess leaned up and brushed a kiss across his lips, sinking into him, as she did with every kiss, trying to cement this moment into her mind. "No such drama with your family then?"

"No, not really. I think when I first went off traveling, they worried. Though it was supposed to be just a six-month thing, it's turned into twelve years and counting. Now, I think they've just accepted that part of me and are glad that I'm following what makes me happy."

"That's nice. I wonder how different I'd be if I hadn't had the pressure to make certain choices in my life."

"Pressure's not always a bad thing. At least you know what you do and don't want now, right?"

"I think I'm still trying to figure that out," Tess admitted, watching as a pelican swooped low to dive for a fish.

"I'd say you're doing a damn fine job of it, lass."

. . .

IT WAS two weeks after Tess arrived when Aiden finally got another day off. Two, actually. Late last night they'd decided to spend their precious time away from Cozumel and away from his group of friends, so they could really have some alone time together. First stop was Isla Mujeres for a night at a hotel.

"Tell me about Isla Mujeres?" Tess asked.

"It's a tiny little island off the coast of Cancun. I used to take tourists up there to snorkel with the whale sharks," Aiden said, turning to look at her from where he sat next to her on the bus.

"That's amazing. I've always wanted to swim with them."

"They're incredible," Aiden said, tugging a hand through his blonde curls. "In Madagascar they are called *marokintana,* meaning many stars, because of their markings. I wish we could leave them in peace but so long as they bring in tourist dollars they'll be protected. Because above all else, sadly money wins out. If people pay to see them in the wild, they'll stay safer than they otherwise would be. Can you imagine the mentality of someone looking at these amazing creatures, the largest fish in the ocean and them thinking their fin would make a nice sign to advertise their shark fin soup?"

"It's sad to think those gentle giants could be hunted." Tess shook her head.

"Everything has a price." Aiden pulled out a tattered book and put it on his lap. "How do you feel about shark diving?"

"I'd love it," Tess said.

"Great, because that's on the agenda for tomorrow." Aiden squeezed her hand, digging into his book. Tess did a little butt dance in her seat, and then tucked into her own book, loving that they didn't feel the need to fill every silence with chatter.

• • •

As PROMISED, Isla Mujeres was a tiny little island, packed to the brim with boutique hotels and restaurants, and it was easy to walk around while they decided where to stay for the night. Coming up to one hotel at the tip of the island, they walked inside and negotiated a lower same-day rate, along with an all-inclusive pass.

"Let's get our money's worth," Aiden said, blinding Tess with a smile before pouncing on her as soon as they entered their swanky room in a little bungalow right on the water.

They ate and drank their way through the resort, returning to the room when they just couldn't keep their hands off each other anymore. Tess felt as excitable as a honeymooner, and she wondered if people would think they were. Cocooned away together, in a haze of lust, the outside world fell away once more and it was only them. Together.

"I can't believe I go home soon," Tess said, curled into Aiden the next morning, her hand tracing the scar on his chest. "It doesn't feel real."

"I know. Time flies so fast. I haven't even begun to think about packing yet, or selling all my stuff." Aiden shifted, turning a bit to pull her closer to him.

"Will that be weird for you?"

"I'm used to it. Though this is the longest I've stayed somewhere. I think I'm ready to go, but it will be tough to say goodbye – both having to say goodbye to friends as well the island I love so much. It's a bit of a transient lifestyle, being a dive instructor, and you get used to the impermanence of things. I always remind myself of the Dr. Seuss quote where he says, 'Don't cry because it's over, smile because it happened.'"

"Is that hard for you?"

"I do my best to keep a smile on my face. I love this life. I think there's a lot to see and do in this world, and if I'm meant to see a person again, I will. Plus, with social media, it's super easy to stay in touch with people if I want to."

"I suppose," Tess said, turning to stretch. "We need to get going if we want to make the ferry. I heard talk of shark diving?"

"Let's do it, pretty lady."

"Hey," Tess said, pausing while they packed what little they'd brought with them, "I could stay longer, you know."

"Here? Now?" Aiden met her eyes from across the room.

"I, uh, checked with my dogsitter and they can watch the dogs longer." Tess felt unaccountably nervous.

"Like how long? What about your flights?"

"It would just be a small change fee. They can watch the dogs for another week and a half but then they have commitments."

"Hmm," Aiden said, and Tess bit back the need to push him on this. Didn't he see that they needed more time together?

"Anywho, just thought I'd let you know that I asked. We should go – that ferry is coming in fifteen minutes." Tess pasted a smile on her face. What did she expect? The man was moving across the world in three weeks, he hadn't even packed or made any of his goodbyes yet, and she was going to monopolize the rest of his time? She needed a very quick reality check, Tess reminded herself.

"Let's do it!" Aiden said. Tess looked up at him, beaming. "The bull sharks are waiting to take a bite out of us." Aiden mocked biting her throat.

Oh.

She had thought he meant she should stay longer.

She forced a laugh, shutting her eyes on the longing she was sure could be seen there. There was nothing else she could do but enjoy their last few days together. She'd have all the time in the world to cry over him when she returned to Denver.

CHAPTER THIRTY-NINE

"You've been diving with sharks before, right?"

"Yes," Tess said, smiling as Aiden hefted two tanks, one over each shoulder, and trotted confidently ahead of her on the sand. "Though not ones of this caliber. Primarily reef sharks and nurse sharks."

They were on a long stretch of sandy beach in one of the most populated areas of Playa del Carmen. A small boat was hooked to a buoy, and a few other divers waited to wade into the water and board the boat. They weren't traveling far, just out past the swim markers, and Tess wondered if all the tourists sunning themselves had any idea just how many bull sharks patrolled the shores in front of them. Luckily, the sharks had learned to be wary of tourists and rarely came closer to shore, or Tess feared they'd be in danger. The sharks, that is, not the tourists. Millions of sharks died every year at the hands of humans, incomparably more than ever harmed people – in fact, more people died each year from riding horses than from shark attacks. It made her sad, but people feared what they didn't understand.

"You are in for a treat then," Aiden said, and she admired the way the wetsuit hugged his bum as he walked in front of her. "These ladies are beauties – many of them pregnant. I love seeing them, they're so graceful, and larger than you think. It's humbling to be able to dive with them. They have quite the reputation, as they can be dangerous, but in reality, we owe our thriving oceans to them."

"People are so fearful of them, yet without sharks as the apex predator, our reefs would suffer as other fish would take over and kill the smaller stuff we need."

"Exactly, and without the reefs – well, our oceans collapse and there goes our oxygen. You know, no big deal." Aiden pretended a nonchalant shrug.

"Right? Minor detail. Just another reason to love on sharks. I can't wait to see them," Tess said, following him into the water where he handed the tanks up to the captain, "I'm always in awe around sharks. I want to spend more time around them. I'm just entranced by how they move, their sheer presence." They boarded quickly, eager to get on with the dive, and lapsed into companionable silence as the instructor briefed them on the safety protocols, time, and depth of their upcoming dive. Excited nerves kicked up, and she couldn't wait to get in the water. There was nothing like a full-on shark encounter to keep her mind distracted. Some might suggest there were other, less dramatic ways to avoid thinking about the future, but as Tess's adrenaline surged, she couldn't think of anywhere else she'd rather be.

"Let's dive," the captain ordered, and they all rolled off the side of the boat, slowly sinking to the ocean's floor, coming to rest in the sand on their knees as instructed. It wasn't typical to kneel on the ocean floor, as divers learn to maintain neutral buoyancy, but for this dive the instructor wanted everyone in a line, on the sand, and they would wait as a group for the sharks to approach of their own curiosity and accord.

As the minutes passed, Tess let her mind wander as she swayed gently in the water next to Aiden, her shoulder bumping his. People did this for a living, she thought, instead of going into corporate desk jobs every day – *Aiden* did this for a living. He was a man who craved new experiences, loved to explore, and enjoyed the tactile side of life. Never would he be the man to put on a suit and attend a monotonous job every day. Nor would he look for that in a relationship, she realized. He might not be the man who would look for the next best thing when it came to women, but he'd need a woman who could match his thirst for life, who could get up and go at a moment's notice. While she could offer him some of that, Tess wasn't without responsibilities. She loved her dogs and they were family. There was no way she'd hand them over to someone for six months and take off across the world. In the long run, would a relationship with Aiden even work?

Aiden's hand clenched Tess's arm and she looked up, laser-focused on the shadows making their way slowly across the ocean floor, like graceful ships, gliding effortlessly closer. Tess gulped into her regulator. At over eight feet long and several hundred pounds in weight, the sheer size of the sharks put her life immediately into perspective. Before she could even register fear, her heart tumbled over into love. Quite simply, these pregnant bull sharks were stunning. A glossy sheen coated their skin, and they moved with grace, coming as close as they pleased, passing by them repeatedly to determine if the divers were friend or foe. Tess craned her head over her shoulder to see more circling them, and laughed into her regulator, almost made giddy by the experience.

The group drifted across the floor, spreading out a bit, as photographers got their shots, and nervous divers held tight to each other. Tess was filled with joy, she was so delighted with the nearness and beauty of these magnificent animals. Turning, she saw Aiden wave hello to a shark that passed right by his face, causing her laugh of delight to get caught in her throat. She wanted to be with a man who would wave nonchalantly to a shark, like they were best friends passing each other on the street. Aiden turned and their eyes met across the sand.

He held his hands together, forming a heart shape, and lifted them out to her. A considerably curious shark nudged between them and Tess kicked lightly so she could see over the passing dorsal fin to where Aiden's hands still formed a heart. Mirroring him, she gave him her heart back.

CHAPTER FORTY

"I just have to run to the immigration office to get a few papers. Will you be fine on your own for a bit?" Aiden asked after they'd come back from one of the best dives of her life. Neither of them mentioned the heart gesture Aiden made. Some things were best left unsaid.

"Yes, I'd like to do a little shopping. I'll meet you back here in an hour." Tess already knew what she wanted to find. Aiden kissed her and sent her on her way.

She wandered the streets of Playa del Carmen, pushing among the booths that crowded the streets, the vendors all calling out for her attention. She was looking for something she could give Aiden to carry on his travels that would remind him of her. A talisman of sorts, she supposed, as she picked up a bracelet and discarded it, and continued walking. The gift needed to be small, something he could tuck into his pack, but she also wanted it to be meaningful. An amber shop caught her eye, and she stopped to look in. It was one of the few shops where someone hadn't yelled at her to approach, which already raised her estimation of it.

Walking inside, she peered into glass cases, marveling over all the beautiful amber carvings, the lights above making them seem to glow from within. A small, round woman, dripping in amber jewelry and with feathers knotted into her hair, smiled at her over the counter.

"*Buenas tardes,*" the lady said.

"*Hola,* hello," Tess replied. "*Tu hablas ingles?*"

"Yes, I do. How may I be of help to you today?"

"I'm looking for a gift for someone, I need it to be… meaningful. For protection while traveling."

"This is a man?" The woman leveled a look at her over her glasses.

"Yes, a man."

"Let's see then. We have some more masculine pieces over here." The woman drew her to the back of the shop. "These turtles are quite lovely."

But Tess had already seen her piece – a small, intricately carved skull that seemed to beckon to her from the glass shelf.

"This one. The skull," Tess said, pointing to it.

"Ah, that's a lovely piece." The woman nodded her approval and took it out to hand over to Tess. About the size of a quarter, the details on it were stunning. She was amazed to see flecks of brown and leaves inside the amber. It seemed warm in her hand, as though it pulsed with a power of its own, and she put it gently down on the counter.

"Yes, I think this will be nice."

"This man has your love?" The woman cast a shrewd eye on her as Tess nosed around the shop, picking up a bracelet for herself.

"I mean… it's hard to say. It's a tough situation," Tess admitted.

"He's going traveling, you say?"

"Yes, he is. Across the world, for a very long time."

"You care for him."

"I do." Tess smiled ruefully at the woman, who surprised her by reaching across the counter to grasp both of Tess's hands in her own.

"He'll come back to you."

"I don't think he will," Tess said, pressing her lips together. "And I have to learn to live with that."

"He'll come back," she insisted, releasing Tess's hands and touching her hand to the middle of her forehead. "I see it."

"Oh, well, that's very nice of you to say."

"You must open your heart."

"It is open." Tess sighed a little as she tucked her hair behind her ear, picking up the amber bracelet to hold it to the light. "More than it should be at this stage in my life, to be honest."

"A heart should always be open. Living with it closed, well, what's the point? You will hurt, yes, but you will always hurt. How do you know good without the bad? Life isn't meant to shield you from pain, but to help you feel – all of the emotions. You must feel them here." The woman brought a fist to her chest. "Otherwise, why live at all? It's our human experience to feel these things, to learn, to grow. To turn your back on love, well, it leaves you cold inside, you understand?"

"I'm not turning my back on it, I just don't see how it could work out," Tess said, sliding the bracelet next to the skull.

"You don't see the air you breathe, but you still trust it is there," the woman argued. "Have a little faith. Now, let me pray on these."

Tess took a deep breath as the woman chanted over her gifts, trying to push down the hope that wanted to bubble to the surface. Sure, it was easy for some woman in a shop in Mexico to tell her it would all work out, but at the end of the day, the only person she could trust was herself. Either way, she appreciated the kindness and smiled when the woman came around the counter to hug her, passing her the gift wrapped nicely.

"Trust," the woman whispered.

Tess walked out, then turned around quickly, having a surreal feeling that the store would vanish behind her and that the last hour was nothing but a mirage. But the shop still stood, the owner waving to her with a smile. Tess waved back, tucking the gift in her purse, and went to find Aiden.

"I HAVE A SURPRISE FOR YOU," Aiden said when she met him moments later at the doorstep of a coffee shop. His smile was infectious, and the seriousness of the hour before drifted away as she beamed back at him. "I want to take you to one of my favorite spots here." Aiden looped his arm through hers and then looked down at her dress. "No shopping bags?"

"Nothing major, no," Tess said, and let him lead her through town, laughing at the story of his confusion at Immigration and how he might have told them he had four children instead of living for four years in Mexico.

"Here we are," Aiden said. He pulled Tess through a bamboo doorway surrounded by lush plants and down a darkened staircase, going lower into the ground.

"What is this place?"

"Just look," Aiden said. Tess gasped when they finally wove their way through a tunnel that opened into a bar and a restaurant.

"Is this a cave? Like an actual cavern?" Tess exclaimed.

"It is. And there's loads of rooms. Let me buy you a fancy drink and we'll wander through to see all the different spots." Aiden pulled her to the bar. They ordered some ridiculous drinks, and Tess laughed as they bounced their way through the tunnels, stopping in rooms with massive stalactites, or stars projected onto the ceiling. It was a beautiful idea, and Tess loved how each tunnel led them deeper into the ground, until Aiden found a small room that was empty. In it sat a large throne with several comfy chairs staggered around it, and warm red lights were tucked behind the stalagmites, creating an ethereal glow around the damp stones.

"Your throne?" Aiden asked, gesturing for her to sit, while he took a chair next to her.

"This is wonderful, Aiden. Thank you for bringing me."

"I think you're amazing, Tess. I..." Aiden turned and reached for her hand, his eyes meeting hers.

"Yes?" Tess asked, holding her breath.

"I'd like for you to stay. If you are certain you can swing it and it's not too expensive to change your flights. Will you stay longer?"

"Yes, Aiden, I'd love to," Tess said, her cheeks flushing in excitement. "Oh! I got you something."

"Oh yeah?" Aiden laughed, and they quickly moved past the weight of the moment, the words left unsaid.

"Here, a gift for you, for your travels." Tess handed him the wrapped box.

"Oh, you got me a proper gift?" Aiden looked at her in surprise.

"I did."

She watched as he unwrapped it, and when his face lit with delight, she knew she'd picked the right thing.

"Tess! This is amazing! I've been meaning to pick something up that would remind me of Mexico. I like to take a keepsake from all the countries I've been to. What with the amber here, the sugar skulls, and it coming from you? It's the perfect gift." Aiden leaned over and Tess met him halfway. As he kissed her on her throne in the underground cave, the words of the shop owner moved through her heart.

"It's to protect you in your travels."

"I'll keep it with me always," Aiden promised.

CHAPTER FORTY-ONE

"Ah, shite, my phone's basically broken," Aiden sighed later that week, as he shook the offending object at her.

"Oh no! We'll have to go out and get you a new one," Tess said, snuggling into him on his couch. The extra time had felt like a nanosecond, and she wondered if she would ever have enough time with this man. For the last week and a half, the tension had built inside her while their goodbye loomed over their heads.

It didn't help that she had seen him answering the messages on his phone and computer from his "travel buddy." Logically, Tess knew he needed to communicate with this girl – they were traveling with each other across the world – but knowing their past history still made her a bit queasy. A man she cared deeply for was about to travel with a twenty-five-year-old he used to hook up with. It struck a little too close to home, and while Tess had done her best to play it cool, the jealousy had begun to gnaw at her gut, like a snail slowly eating a rosebush.

"Nah, I don't need to get a phone." Aiden shrugged dismissively.

Tess straightened, pulling back to look at him. "What do you mean you don't need a phone? Of course you need a phone."

"Why? It just costs extra money. I have a camera and my laptop. What's the point?"

"But how will you call me? How will we stay in touch?"

"I can Skype you from my computer." Aiden's forehead creased in concern.

"Yeah, but that's not as easy as calling from a phone. You'll have to go find a private place. You won't be able to call or message at whim. It's just that much harder," Tess pressed, already feeling like she was losing him.

"Tess, I'm not spending money on a new phone that I don't need," Aiden said, his eyes never leaving hers.

"But you have to! You can't just not have a phone." Tess got up from the couch, slamming the door to the bedroom behind her as she tried to calm the tears that threatened to spill over.

"Tess." Aiden knocked politely on the door. "Can we talk about this?"

"No, we can't," Tess said, fuming. What was she going to say, 'You'll be doing all these amazing things with some young chick around the world and won't even be able to call me'? It was the truth, and even though she'd known it all along, denial was a beautiful drug when taken properly.

"Tess." Aiden opened the door and crossed the room, wrapping his arms around her. "I'll still be able to talk to you. It will be okay."

"All I know is that I'm leaving tomorrow and you won't have a phone." She swallowed over the lump that had formed in her throat.

"I promise I'll be able to get in touch with you. Can't you trust in me?" Aiden asked.

Tess stilled, not sure what she could or couldn't trust anymore. "I don't know, Aiden. It's all a lot."

He tugged her until they sat on the bed, cross-legged, facing each other. "I know it's a lot. Listen, what will make you feel better about this? What if I promise to call you... well, it will be hard to call every day. I'll be traveling in some pretty remote places. But what if I promise that someway, somehow, I'll be in touch every forty-eight hours. Will that make you feel better?"

"But...why? What's the point? What are we, Aiden?"

There, she'd finally said it.

"I... I don't know," Aiden said slowly. "I want to be with you, I want to see you again. But I am not ready for us to be a couple." Aiden's words burned through her.

"Right," Tess said, tugging at his bedspread.

"It's just... listen, I know I'll be away a long time and I don't want to make any promises that I can't fulfill. I'm a man of my word, and if I tell you I'll do something, I hold to that. I think if we were exclusive right now, it would put too much unnecessary pressure on a relationship that's still so new."

The man was absolutely right, Tess knew that, and yet it still felt like a rejection.

"It's because of her, this girl," Tess said.

"It's not that, really. I can't promise nothing will happen there, and I know you hate hearing that, but I have told you I will always be one hundred percent honest with you. And I want to see you again, Tess. I'm willing to shorten my trip so we can meet up again down the road and see where this goes."

"But what does that mean? We go off and live our lives

and date other people?" Tess looked up at him, her heart trembling in her chest.

"I... I guess so," Aiden said, his face a mess of emotions. "I truly believe if it's meant to be, we'll find each other again."

"But I'm right here, Aiden. You already found me." It was the closest she would get to expressing her feelings.

"I know that, Tess. And the timing of this all is totally shite. It's tearing me up inside. I swear, if I'd met you a month earlier, I never would have signed on for this trip. But I have, and I have a responsibility to her as well. I'm essentially her chaperone, and her family feels more comfortable that I'm going with her. I committed to this; you can't just up and leave someone like that. Not on that big of a trip. It would be wrong of me, especially at this late of a date. We've both quit our jobs, sold our things, and we are going. That's the reality of the situation. One which you knew about, as I was totally honest with you." Aiden reached out to squeeze her hand.

"You were, I know you were," Tess said, sighing. "But when I knew about it, you were supposed to be a fling. I was fine with it then. But now? The reality of all this... it's just a lot for me."

"I hate this, I really do. But I believe we'll be together if we're meant to," Aiden said, and Tess knew in her core that there was no budging him. He was going to go on this trip, no matter what, and she'd known it all along. It was time to accept the truth that was staring her in the face.

"Okay, Aiden. I hate this, and I wish you didn't have to go. Or... travel with this girl. But I get it. You're right, you were up front about this all along. I appreciate your offer of reaching out to me every forty-eight hours or so. That would be nice," Tess said, doing her best to be an adult.

"I'll shorten my trip. I don't have to go to Indonesia. I

could come visit you in Colorado after the Philippines," Aiden said, a hopeful look on his face.

"And what would that timeline look like exactly?" Tess wondered.

"Um, I'd say roughly six months or so. Maybe sooner, if I shave a few stops off," Aiden squinted his handsome face as he considered it.

Six months, Tess thought as her heart dropped to her stomach. A lot could change in six months – like going from being married to divorced.

"Why don't we just see how this all goes," Tess suggested, and leaned forward to kiss him. "As you said, if it's meant to be, it will be."

"I promise I will be in contact. Phone or no phone. You can't get rid of me that easily." Aiden's eyes searched hers.

"I hope so, Aiden."

"I have something for you," Aiden said, turning to dig in his drawer, and handing her a package wrapped in rustic paper and pretty twine.

"What's this?"

"Just something I had made for you." Aiden leaned toward her. "Open it."

Tess unwrapped the twine and unfolded the paper to find an artisan-style necklace and earrings lying in the paper. Pulling out the necklace, she held it up to the light.

"It's beautiful – so funky and different."

"I had Elli make them. I asked her to make something that would fit your style," Aiden said shyly. "I asked her to make something that would look good on you."

"That's really sweet, Aiden." Tess put the necklace on, smiling at him. "How does it look?"

"Amazing. You're amazing, Tess." Sadness crossed his handsome face. "I don't want to lose you," he said, his voice catching. He leaned over to brush his lips over hers. Tess closed her eyes and let the kiss take her away, for there was nothing left to be said. Even though he didn't want to lose her, it seemed like he was the one holding their future in his hands. It was a feeling that made Tess decidedly uncomfortable, something for her to take out and examine at a later date. For now, she opened her heart like the woman in the shop had instructed and let Aiden love her, in the only way he could allow himself to in that moment.

CHAPTER FORTY-TWO

S he gave herself a week to cry.

Daniel and Teddy dutifully listened while she moped, saying all the right things, concerned for her angst. Elizabeth came over for pizza to talk it out. But they all circled back to the same thing: Aiden was gone, and she'd known all along it would end like this. Her heart an open void, Tess was once more on her own.

"I promise, I'll be better soon," Tess cried to Daniel. "I know I'm obsessing over it right now, but I'm just giving myself this week to mope."

"That's fair. But if you go too far down that hole, I'm pulling you out, girl." Daniel poured her another glass of wine. "In the meantime, hand over your phone. Tinder time!"

"Ugh, like that's what I need right now. Listen, I'm more than okay not dating for a while." Tess sipped her wine and wiped her eyes. The thought of being with someone else, faking niceties over dinner, made her stomach turn.

"Doesn't mean it won't feel good to know there are others

out there who want you, honey," Daniel said, digging into her phone.

True to his word, Aiden had messaged her when he could from across the world, though his messages were short and they lost the immediacy of having a conversation back and forth. She was happy he was exploring and living his life, but she longed for how they'd walk everywhere with no direction in mind, stopping to dangle their feet over a wall and look at the water, talking about everything and nothing at all. She wanted his nearness, his scent, his arms holding her.

"I don't know if I need to feel wanted." Tess burrowed into the couch. "It's more about missing Aiden than needing a man to complete me."

"I so get that, but isn't it nice to be in a partnership? Aren't you happier when you have someone?"

"Honestly, I don't know the answer to that anymore," Tess admitted, sipping more of her wine, the red crisp on her tongue. "I'd say my default answer would be, of course I'm happier in a relationship, but then I've never been a relationship person. Which sounds weird, I know, since I was married. But before Gabe, I didn't date for a long time. I always moved on around the three-month mark. And if nobody was in my life, I was actually just fine. In fact, I quite liked it. I could sleep in the bed how I wanted, I could travel where I wanted, spend my money how I wanted... frankly, being alone is quite liberating."

"So, what's stopping you from finding that liberation again?" Daniel asked, stretching his long legs out in front of him. "You're single now. Why let Aiden steal your happiness?"

Tess thought about his words all week as she moped her way through what felt like another bad breakup. At the end of the week, fed up with her mood, she decided it was time to start refocusing on the things that made her happy. To start with, she had a book to work on. Sliding out her laptop, she dove into edits, losing herself in her words, letting the pleasure of productivity overtake her sadness.

Several hours later, she looked up when a Facebook message buzzed through. Taking a break from work, Tess stood and stretched, walking to the kitchen to put on water for tea while she scrolled her messages.

Hey, it's Janie from Cozumel. Remember how we talked about doing a dive trip in the future? I'm going on a live-aboard in the Bahamas. Want to go with?

Taking off for a week on a boat full of people she didn't know, even though they'd be diving all day long, just hadn't appealed when Janie had first mentioned it to her. But now, the idea took root. Being single meant making choices for herself – and doing the things she loved.

When is it again?

Over Easter. I have the week off work. Come meet me! It will be fun.

Send me the details.

Easter was another holiday that she'd typically spent with Vicki and family. Now, since Vicki still refused to speak to her – though Chad still surreptitiously asked questions to funnel information back to her – Tess thought getting away sounded like the perfect thing to do. Apparently, being single also meant forming new traditions. Her family had totally failed her, so Tess could either mope her way through another holiday, or spend it creating new memories. Before she knew it, Tess had filled out the request form Janie had sent over, and on a whim, started looking at other diving trips in the area. She'd been following an Instagram account with the most beautiful shark photos, and if she was going to be in the Bahamas anyway, maybe she could get in a few dives with this shark group. Looking up their website, she found they had no availability.

Tess leaned against the counter, sipping her tea, her eyes on the backyard where snow slowly melted into the grass. While she was glad she'd taken the week to cry over Aiden, it didn't feel good to mope about a situation she couldn't change. Ultimately, it was going to be on her to ensure her own happiness – that wouldn't come from Aiden, from Vicki, or from some random guy on Tinder. It would be through standing up for herself, following through on her creative drive, and throwing herself into exploring her own passions and hobbies. If the well was empty, it wasn't the villagers who would fill it up, Tess mused, if she was the only one who knew where the stream was.

Her phone began to ring, and Tess realized it was a Facebook call, which only meant one thing – Aiden! Despite herself, she smiled and answered.

"Hey," Tess said, walking across the room to cuddle into the couch and tuck her feet under the blanket. Red automatically assumed his spot next to her, while Ringo rustled up a toy and dropped it in her lap.

"Hi, Tess – can you hear me?" Aiden asked, his words breaking up, the internet connection clearly poor where he was.

"Barely, but yeah," Tess said. "How are you? Where are you?"

"We just got to this tiny island... checked into... hotel... and has wifi."

Tess closed her eyes as she heard the voice of a woman in the background talking, knowing he must be sharing a room with that girl. It sounded like she was making her own call to someone.

"That's great, Aiden. I'm glad you made it okay." Tess patted Red's head, trying to ignore the pit of anger that roiled in her stomach.

"It's frustrating. I want to be… to contact you better. Hear your voice. I just wanted to check in… you and see how you are. How are… dogs? Is the book… okay?"

"All's good here. Working on my book, dogs are happy I'm home." Tess rolled her eyes as she heard the faint sound of the woman's laugh through the phone. "I think I'm going to go on a live-aboard in the Bahamas with that girl Janie I met in Cozumel."

"Oh yeah? When? …will be nice. Be careful." The phone abruptly cut out and Tess, for once, was glad to no longer be speaking to him. Closing her eyes, she took several deep breaths.

She knew the score with Aiden. *Knew* it. She had walked into it eyes wide open and he'd been completely honest with her. But at the end of the day, hearing the girl's laughter in the background, and knowing they were sometimes sharing accommodations while traveling, was like a kick to her gut. There were too many parallels between Gabe having an affair with a young college intern and Aiden off traveling the world with a twenty-five-year-old. Aiden had even said he couldn't promise that nothing would happen with this girl, a girl he'd dated in the past.

Tess just couldn't move forward with this situation. It was only going to mess with her head. Jealousy wasn't a flattering color for her, and she'd rather bow out than continue in a situation that was only going to be damaging to the fragile self-confidence she was finally beginning to reclaim.

Knowing what she had to do, Tess turned off her phone

and hugged Red to her, mentally kicking herself for jumping from one sinking ship to another.

Trust, the woman at the amber shop had said. But now Tess wondered if the words were really meant for her, because the only person she could trust anymore was herself.

CHAPTER FORTY-THREE

Aiden,

I don't really know how to say this, other than to be completely honest with you – this is too hard for me. I hate saying that, because I know I'm a strong person and I can handle most things, but this situation is not good for me. I miss you so much, and I'm hurting. I'm truly hurting. I know that isn't your fault, and you were honest with me. I know you aren't playing games, and you're doing your best to attend to my needs from across the world. However, I just see this as a losing situation. I have to put my walls up with you. I've already kind of lived this, and I know how this story ends. I'm sorry, but I'm moving forward with my life.

She'd written it the night before, but hadn't sent it, instead preferring to sleep on it and see how she felt in the morning. The morning came, and the words felt right, though it tore her apart to send them. Tess knew, though, that she had to stand for herself – nobody could do it for her. Satisfied she was making the right choice, Tess clicked send.

I understand, Tess, I really do. But I'll be back soon with a hammer to break down your walls. I promise.

Tess hadn't expected Aiden to be online. She wondered where he was now, and what he was doing with his travel buddy.

I'm sorry, Aiden. I just don't believe you.

I'll do everything I can to make this easier for you.

My walls are up, Aiden. I'm moving on.

I'll still message you, if that's okay? I promised I would, and I'm sticking to that. It's okay if you can't believe right now, I can do it for both of us.

Tess covered her face with her hands, aching for this man who was so incredibly sweet and patient with her feelings.

You can still message me, but just know that I mean it when I say I'm moving forward. You're my friend, Aiden, and that won't change. But that's all this is for me now.

I know there's more between us. I feel it deep down. If it's meant to be… it will be. I have your amber skull with me, I carry it everywhere. I think about you constantly. I'm seeing some of the most beautiful things while diving, and yet all I want to do is have you with me to share this experience. What can I do to make this better? To prove to you that I'll come back to you?

I don't think there's anything you can do.

Well, there was, but that would mean he'd have to leave his trip and travel across the world to be with her. While she often saw those grand gestures in movies, the likelihood of it happening in real life was slim to none. Gabe couldn't be bothered to do anything to try and save their relationship after five years of marriage. Her own sister wouldn't speak to her for the sin of refusing to tolerate her husband's infidelity. So why would she expect that Aiden would suddenly realize his true feelings for her and leave a dream trip to come be with her in landlocked Denver? Maybe he was more of an optimist than she was, but Tess only had her own personal experience to go on. Life had shown her repeatedly that the people she expected to stand for her often did not.

I'm going to stick to what I promised you, Tess. I'm a man of my word. I miss you all the time. I will keep messaging you, and you can keep building your walls, and I'll keep breaking them down. I'm not going anywhere.

You already did, Tess thought, but refused to type the words. She knew he wasn't one to break his commitments. They were just going to continue this cycle of her obsessing over the fact that he'd left, and there was nothing she could do about it.

Have a nice day, Aiden. I hope you see some great things on your dives. I'm signing off.

Speak to you soon, sweet Tess.

Tess pressed her lips together and signed off, not knowing what else there was to say. She'd stood for herself, and the man didn't seem to want to accept it. The best she could do at this point was to follow through on her words, and move on. Opening her Tinder app, she idly read through her messages and matches, thanks to Daniel's continued scrolling, but then put her phone down. Filling the hole that Aiden's presence left in her heart with another man wasn't the answer either. It wouldn't be fair to the new man, and it wasn't fair to her. Ultimately, Tess was responsible for her own happiness.

She checked the shark-diving group she followed on Instagram. They still showed no availability, but she e-mailed them anyway. Who knew, maybe a spot would open up. Then she got back to work on her novel.

A few hours later, she checked her in-box, and found a reply.

Hi Tess,

Thanks so much for contacting us. As it turns out, we had a cancellation just a day ago and have one spot open for our trip to

Cat Island to dive with the oceanic whitetip sharks. I've attached all
the information. If you'd like to join us, please let us know as soon
as possible; otherwise, we'll post the opening on our social media.

"Yes!" Tess exclaimed, fist-pumping the air. Two weeks diving in the Bahamas to forget about family troubles and Aiden? Sign her up. Sending in her information, Tess confirmed her spot and then pulled out her calendar to begin mapping out the next six weeks of her time. If she had a plan, an agenda she could stick to, maybe, just maybe, Tess could begin to get over Aiden and move forward with her life like she'd promised herself she would.

An hour later, she had dates with her editors, plane tickets secured, and the beginning of a new outline for the next book in her series.

"There," Tess said. "I'm taking care of my own happiness. See, universe? I can handle my shit."

CHAPTER FORTY-FOUR

"Oh, Vicki, hi," Tess swallowed nervously, surprised that Vicki had answered the call. She moved to her office, and sat in her desk chair, leaning forward to pull a pack of Post-it notes to her.

"Hi. David's not here right now."

"That's okay, maybe we can talk?" Tess asked. "I was hoping we could move forward?"

"Doubtful," Vicki bit out and Tess ripped a Post-it note from the pad.

"Really, Vicki? Is that tone necessary?"

"You're the one who created this situation, so you're the one who has to deal with my mood. What did you expect? Me to sit here and be cheerful with you?"

"I didn't create this situation, Vicki. If you recall, you're the one who told me to have a nice life," Tess said, ripping the square of paper to shreds on her desk.

"Well? You always refuse to see things my way. It always has to be what Tess wants, even if it's the wrong choice. And now you're off doing god knows what in Colorado, all 'I am woman, hear me roar' and you can't even take time for your family anymore."

"How am I supposed to take time for my family if you won't answer my calls?" Tess asked, pulling a second piece of paper out and beginning to shred it.

"Oh, please. You've barely called. You've been too busy hanging out with those homos next door."

Tess froze. "You don't get to use those words with me," she hissed.

"And you don't get to tell me what to do! Nobody tells me what to do, let alone you, Tess."

"I don't give a shit what you believe, but don't use your hate speech with me. You have no idea about me, my friends, or my life."

"I would know about your life if you had stayed here instead of galivanting all over the world. And to think – you kept so many secrets from me. How was I supposed to know about all the troubles in your marriage? You never told me any of it."

"That's because it was private, Vicki. That's what happens with a husband and wife. Certain things are meant to be private, between the two of them. I am under no obligation to share my personal marital issues with you."

"Well, don't expect me to be crying in your corner for you then," Vicki huffed.

"I expected you to be there for me." The pile of ripped paper was growing rapidly.

"Maybe if you were less combative, I would have been."

"Combative? Are you kidding me? I'm so sick of you saying that. *You're* the one who is bullying me to try and fall in line with what you want and what you think – shit, you can't even respect my wishes to not call my good friends names."

"Bully!" Vicki all but shrieked. "I am not a bully."

"Um, yes, you really are. You are so controlling you can't even see it. When I didn't agree with how you wanted me to handle my problems, you told me to have a nice life and then stopped talking to me. Don't you know that is what a bully does? They manipulate you through silence, or through full-on attack to get what they want. You expect me to kneel to you, to kowtow to what you want, and when I don't? You withhold your love. Emotional bullying," Tess said.

"A bully! As if," Vicki seethed. "Listen, you do what you want – if you need to slut all over the place on those dating apps, even though it's obviously too soon for you to be dating, and hang out with all the liberals out in Denver smoking pot, then so be it. I don't even know you anymore."

"I don't think you ever really did." Tess clenched her fist around a ball of paper.

"Whatever, Tess. I'm sorry I don't meet your expectations as a sister. I think it's best that I just keep you at arm's length from now on, and protect my family from you." Tess's mouth dropped open.

"Protect... your family... are you actually kidding me with this?"

"This is just the way it needs to be, Tess," Vicki said, her voice smug, happy to be taking control of the situation again, holding Tess's nephew as leverage. "I don't think I want your influence in our lives."

"My influence? What? Free-thinking? Non-conformist? I'm sorry you can't support a fellow woman who is starting her life over, Vicki, not even your own sister."

"Combative, lying, hiding, sneaky," Vicki ticked off.

"Seriously, standing up for myself is not combative. I'm not picking fights with you, Vicki, I'm just not letting you dictate my life. There's a huge difference," Tess all but shouted. "And just because I don't tell you everything about my life doesn't mean I'm a liar! There's a damn good reason I keep things from you – you have an opinion on everything. Everything has to be done your way, or you have to give your two cents on what I should be doing. Look at you, you're the first person to tell me 'I told you so' or that I should have just done things your way in the first place. But what if your way doesn't make me happy? If I don't share things in my life with you it's because I know you'll try to tell me what to do, and be upset if I don't follow your advice. Just for once, could you trust me to make my own choices?"

"You do what you want, Tess, you always have."

"Why is it on me to change, Vicki? Why do I always have to be the one to come make amends, or bow down to what you want? When will you say you're sorry or look at your behavior for once and realize what you're doing is wrong?"

"I'm not the one with a broken marriage who is running from her problems."

"I'm not running from my problems, Vicki. I'm in therapy. I'm writing my books. I'm dating again. I'm just learning to be me again. Me without someone by my side. Me who follows her own passions and dreams. Why is that so scary to you?"

"It's not scary, it's just ridiculous. Traveling around the world alone? Shouldn't you be at home, keeping that so-called career of yours on track?"

"My career is fine. Newsflash, I can work from anywhere. I just need my laptop," Tess said, pinching her nose, her frustration with her sister's inability to ever look at her own actions with any objectivity making her want to throw something – namely her sister.

"Shouldn't you be a better sister? One who supports my

path instead of blocking it? One who stops trying to control my every move and instead accepts me for who I am?"

"Oh, please, Tess. I've been there for you for everything – everything! And you continue with this same shit that I control you, when I'm the one who knows what's best for you. Shit, I practically raised you after Mom and Dad –"

"I was an adult then. I *am* an adult now. I don't need you to raise me, Victoria."

"Why is it always about you, Tess? Everyone always talks about Tess and her writing, Tess and her travels... Tess this, Tess that. When I've worked my ass off for the life I have and am very proud of," Vicki spat out.

Tess sat back, stunned. "Nobody has ever said it's all about me. I don't know where you're getting that from. But for the last time, this is not a competition on who is doing better at life. It can't be a competition because we aren't playing the same game. We both want different prizes. Can't you accept that and love me nonetheless?"

"You and this competition crap again. I'm not competing with you, Tess. As if."

"And you continue to not listen, just like you always have."

There was a moment of silence while both sisters recognized the impasse before them. "I won't be coming to Easter this year; I'm going scuba diving."

"I didn't invite you to Easter."

"I know you didn't, Vicki," Tess said, sadness washing through her. They would never come to an agreement. At least not anytime soon. But if the door was to be closed, at the very least, she could close it with kindness. Sometimes standing up for herself royally sucked, Tess thought, so tired her body ached. "But I'll say this, Vicki. You're family, and I love you. Even if we don't agree on many things, my love for you is there no matter what. I hope someday you'll realize that."

"Honestly, Tess? I love you, too, but your actions have consequences. You've created this situation, now you have to live with it."

"I…" Tess looked at the phone to see her sister had hung up. She put it gently down on the desk beside a mound of Post-it notes, once whole, that now lay in shreds, mirroring her relationship with Vicki.

She realized love alone was not enough to put the pieces back together. She'd been questioning love a lot this year, and though everyone often spoke of unconditional love, she just wasn't certain it existed. Relationships didn't come with guarantees, but they did come with a hell of a lot of conditions.

Tess wondered if she was doing the right thing. Was standing up for herself worth losing her sister? Was there a way she could live her life on her own terms, and still have her family in it? She didn't want this. For all the challenges in their relationship, she still needed her sister. Vicki had always been there for her, even if it came with a side of judgment. She'd been bossy since they were little, but Tess knew it was her way of showing she cared. The problem was Vicki couldn't accept that as adults they were equals. She had to be the older, wiser sister who was in charge no matter what. Tess did want to mend what was broken between them. She just didn't know how.

CHAPTER FORTY-FIVE

I f only moving on with her life was as easy as it looked in the movies, Tess thought. In theory, she'd stood up for herself, put her boundaries up with Aiden, refused to be bullied by her sister, and had stayed true to following through on her creative endeavors and exploring her passions.

So, why did she still feel so numb?

Perhaps it was because the last year had been an emotional rollercoaster, as her therapist had pointed out repeatedly. This time last year she'd been talking about moving to Colorado with Gabe. Healing doesn't have a time-frame, and if anything, Tess needed to be kinder to herself. As much as she wanted to fast-forward through the process, she couldn't deny that she was hurting.

Nobody said change would be easy.

Tess sighed as she chose a beach cover-up from her dresser, rolled it into a small ball, and tucked it next to her fins. It hadn't been easy, she thought, kneeling back on her feet. In fact, next to losing her parents, it had been the toughest year of her life, with so many highs and lows. She'd gained her freedom, a chance at a new beginning, and a strong understanding of the type of behavior she would and would not accept in her life. But it had cost her her family. She wondered if this was why people stayed in bad relationships and shitty jobs, because change meant having to examine all those icky feelings that were easier ignored than dealt with. Comfort zones were a trap.

"Eyes forward," Tess reminded herself, zipping her bag closed. Her flight was early in the morning, and she needed to rest, but her brain refused to allow her to do so. Instead she zipped about, going over checklists repeatedly, as she had a tendency to do before any trip. Finally, she settled her mind on the one thing that had stayed steady for her through the last six weeks.

Aiden.

True to his word, he continued messaging her, plodding steadily along toward his goal of breaking down her walls. Tess found herself incapable of shutting him from her life. She did let more time lapse now in responding to his messages, sometimes not answering for days, yet every day or so he'd send her a message about what he was seeing and how much he missed her. It was like the man stubbornly refused to hear her. She'd told Aiden he was just a friend. Of course, they both knew she was lying.

He had called her again last week.

"I just want to know if there's anything else I can do to make this easier for you," Aiden asked. She could hear the waves of the ocean behind him.

"Aiden, no. Not really. I just... you're traveling with another woman across the world. What else am I supposed to say?"

"It's really not like that. We stay in hostels most nights,

which is separate quarters for men and women. I'm trying to speed up my travel plan, and cut more from it so I can come to you sooner. I think about you all the time, Tess. I wish you were here with me."

Tess squeezed her eyes shut, imagining him on the beach, wishing she was walking next to him. "Aiden..." she trailed off. "I just don't see how this will work."

"What can I do to make you believe it will?"

She paused, took a breath. "Let's be honest here – I have a hard time trusting. I've been through a lot this year, Aiden. A lot of people have let me down. I think you're asking quite a bit of me to believe that you won't be one of them."

"Then I guess I'll just have to show you," Aiden said, his tone stubborn.

"It's just that...you're there. I'm here. I have to deal with the reality of the situation."

"The reality is that I committed to this trip before I knew we would ever be together. I'd booked my flights, paid my way, and I had to come. And...frankly, I'm miserable." Aiden's frustrated tone carried through the phone.

"I highly doubt that," Tess said, even though a tiny sliver of glee worked through her at those words. "I see your pictures and your videos. You're exploring all these amazing places. It hardly looks like you're struggling."

"It *is* amazing here. But it would be more amazing with you. I think about you all the time. The only thing that brings me joy is being underwater and even when I am there, I wish you were diving next to me. I thought traveling like this was what I wanted...but it's not. I hate packing up my backpack every day. I want to settle in a spot for a bit and explore. This just isn't what I thought it would be."

"So? Leave the trip then."

"I'm trying to shorten it. I've already cut out several

months. I want to get back to you sooner. I'm…this is really hard for me," Aiden's voice caught, and Tess's heart tripped at his obvious distress.

"It's hard for me as well, Aiden. I'm trying to move on with my life. You know I really care about you, but I have to put what's best for myself first. And playing this 'if it's meant to be it will be' game just doesn't cut it for me. I've had an incredibly difficult year. I can't live my life in the gray area anymore. I can only deal in absolutes. What I know is I care about you, you're across the world, and I don't trust that you're going to come home to me, and that we'll be together. I'm sorry, I wish that I could be more believing in the happy ending…but I just have to protect myself right now." Tess squeezed her eyes shut, knowing her words were hurting him as much as they were hurting her.

He continued to message her every day, trying to prove he would be there for her. She could have unfriended him and blocked him, if she really didn't want him in her life, but Tess must be a glutton for punishment, because she craved his emails. She'd examine each message for meanings, trying to see the words she wanted to hear from him woven between the snippets about the dives he was doing or the towns he was visiting. In time, the ache would ease, Tess told herself. She just needed more time.

Time was delivered to her the next morning, in the form of canceled flights due to tornadoes at the Atlanta airport. When she realized she wouldn't get into the Bahamas until Tuesday, and would miss the dive boat for the live-aboard altogether, Tess called Janie.

"I'm so sorry, I don't know what else to do."

"This sucks! Now I'll be on the boat alone!"

"Hopefully, you can have dive buddies in the other guys," Tess said, unsure of how else to make the situation any better.

"Are you still coming down?"

"Yes, I will be there mid-week. On Friday, I leave for Cat Island for the shark-diving trip. I'll just spend a few days by myself on the beach or whatever and then meet you when the boat comes in."

"Seriously, I can't believe this happened."

"I can't either. There's nothing else for me to do. All the flights connect through Atlanta, and it's such a huge airport that they are backlogged for days now."

Tess spent the next three days hunkered down, writing, writing, writing. If the universe was going to force her to slow down, she might as well be productive. By Tuesday, she was more than ready for palm trees and sunny skies, and was relieved to have a seamless journey all the way from her front door to toes-in-the-sand.

Nassau teemed with life, much larger than Cozumel, and not exactly the relaxed island pace that Tess was hoping for. At least the hotel she'd booked had a nice sandy private beach, and her room had a balcony with a nice view. Checking in, she realized how many eyes were on her, traveling alone. Or perhaps she just felt that way.

Tess found an abandoned umbrella at the far end of the beach, not interested in joining the drunken crowd at the pool that was currently competing in a limbo contest. Her plan was to spend the next few days steadily working her way through her to-be-read book pile, and to do pretty much nothing else – maybe get a dive in one day, depending on her mood. Settling in, Tess sipped the mojito the waiter had brought her, wincing at the overly sweet concoction. They'd obviously tried to conceal rail rum with too much simple syrup, and she wrinkled her nose at the drink, placing it in the sand by her chair before opening her book.

"Hey mama! Bahama mama! Mmmhmm, I like my girls

thick, you know?" A man walking the beach, his accent thick with the island melody, immediately crossed to her chair and sat in the sand next to her.

"I'm not interested." Tess pulled her cover-up around her.

"Aw, come on, mama. All the ladies come here to meet men like me. They come off those cruise ships just looking to score. And you? All alone here? I know what you're looking for, sweet thing." The man reached out and traced a finger down Tess's leg. She slapped it away, glaring at him.

"I don't want you to touch me. I'm not here for that. Leave me alone."

The man just grinned, settling back into the sand, his eyes on hers. "The ladies never leave me unsatisfied. You look like you could use some satisfaction. I can see it in your face... so tense."

"I don't care what the other women come to this island for, I'm not interested. Get the hell away from me before I call security," Tess said, already looking to where the waiter was hurrying his way back, shaking his head at the man next to her.

"See? Tense." The man stood and laughed, putting his palms up. "No worries, mama, no worries." He faded away as quickly as he'd arrived, and Tess swallowed in distaste. She'd forgotten how forward men could be to a woman alone on a beach. She understood it was a cultural thing, approaching women so blatantly, but it still managed to creep her out. Back when she'd lived on the islands, she'd learned to have a strong backbone and shrug it off, which in turn led the locals to accept her as one of their own. For now though, she was fresh meat and she'd have to be careful about standing her ground with any man that approached her.

"You okay, miss?" The waiter crouched by her chair,

nodding to the man who whistled his way down the beach. "He can be a bit pushy."

"I'm fine. I'm just not here for that," Tess said.

"What *are* you here for?"

Tess gave him a sharp look, only to find his eyes curious on hers.

"Some peace," Tess murmured, "I only want some peace."

CHAPTER FORTY-SIX

A iden checked in with her even more frequently now, worried about her traveling on her own.

"Just be careful," he kept insisting and she'd smile at her phone, loving that he cared enough to worry over her.

One day, she met up with a dive group and did two dives. They fed the sharks on the first dive – something Tess didn't approve of; she wouldn't have gone if she'd known about it – and the other turned out to be a wreck dive. They descended as a group, and she was astonished to see the instructor point to the wreck and then head back toward the boat. Aiden would never have left a dive group to guide themselves, let alone on a wreck dive. When she climbed back on the boat, she couldn't believe the instructor was sitting there checking their names off a list, casually munching on an apple. Even more astonishing was when they asked for a tip when the boat returned to the dock. Despite herself, Tess turned and looked at the instructor.

"Why should I tip you? You didn't lead a dive, you just checked our names off a list. Anyone can do that." Perhaps she'd been spoiled with Aiden as a guide, but it was glaringly obvious that not everyone practiced the same high standards of guiding as he had.

Saturday arrived and Tess picked up a taxi out front of the hotel, looking forward to seeing her friend. They'd arranged for her to come to the boat, so Tess could see where Janie had stayed for the week and meet the crew. The taxi driver chatted the whole way, reminding Tess that tomorrow was Easter Sunday and it would be best to get a taxi back home early, as nobody would be working late tonight. Easter was a time of huge celebration for the island, and there would be parties lasting well past midnight and all the next day. It was good advice, and Tess promised to follow it.

The sun was just setting over the docks as Tess wandered her way down, passing all different sizes and types of boats until she saw Janie waving at her frantically from in front of a long black boat with a mock pirate skull on the side.

"Hi! How was the trip?" Tess asked, hugging her.

"Great! I ended up having a bunk to myself, which was awesome, and I did really good with my diving." Janie chattered in her raspy smoker's voice, pulling Tess onto the boat to introduce her to all the other divers. It was a mix of ages ranging from twenty- to sixty-year-olds, but they had one thing in common that Tess noticed immediately.

"I'm so sorry I stuck you on a boat of all men." Tess winked at Janie as they ate the final meal the crew had prepared for everyone.

"None of them were my type, unfortunately, but you should chat up that cute one," Janie said, nodding toward a tall guy with dark hair and defined muscles.

"Nah, I'm not looking for a man." Tess bit into a piece of cornbread.

"Still crushing on Aiden?" Janie had dived with Aiden briefly when they were together in Cozumel.

"I miss him." Tess shrugged a shoulder and looked out at the water. "But it's probably best that I'm alone for now."

"I don't blame you. I was alone for a long time after my divorce. It was good for me."

"Hey! Janie! We're going out – you ladies want to join?"

"Yes!" Janie answered for her and tugged Tess along until they found themselves chattering their way toward a bar down the road. In moments, they rolled up, and Tess knew these guys were ready to party when they ordered a tray of shots. Knowing how quickly nights like this could get away from her, Tess decided to pace herself. She laughed as they downed shot after shot, playing pool and a massive Jenga game.

When the bar was ready to close, they all tumbled outside, the guys looking for another place to party.

Two taxis sat out front. One driver in a neat suit, smiled pleasantly at them. The other driver motioned toward his car.

"You have to take a taxi to the club," he insisted, and Tess met his eyes. She didn't like the way he looked her up and down and she moved closer to Janie.

"We don't have to go to the club, we can just go home."

"No, let's go dancing!"

Tess moved to the other taxi and the group split, agreeing to meet at the club.

The taxi pulled to a stop in front of a remote bar, with a second-story open air club, and the driver got out to open the door for them, the second taxi pulling alongside them.

"Excuse me, sir?" Tess asked the pleasant driver.

"Yes, miss, what can I do for you?"

"Would you be able to come get me in an hour and take me to my hotel? I was told the taxis won't run late tonight, and I want to make sure I get home." Her hotel was on the other side of the island, and there was no way she was bunking on the boat with any of the rowdy guys in their group.

"Yes, miss, I will be back in one hour to pick you up." The taxi driver smiled at her as the other car emptied, the guys loud and happy as they joined them.

"Can you believe he calls himself Dr. Love?" The guys laughed at the creepy driver who had looked her up and down.

Tess ignored him, following them into the club.

"Why are you going after only an hour – this will be fun!" Janie slurred, having heartily embraced the shots.

"Because I have a flight out in the morning and need to get back to my hotel," Tess said, moving to talk to one of the guys in the group. "Hey, you're okay with getting her home, right?" A firefighter, he had been nice to talk to through the night.

"Yup, we've got an eye on her. Kept her from falling off the boat this week." He cheerfully hooked an arm around Janie's neck. Happy she would be taken care of, Tess found a barstool and watched in amusement as the group danced raucously to the upbeat music. Despite herself, she'd had a shot and had even joined them on the slick wooden dance floor, most likely making a fool of herself to the Bahamians who lingered at the bar and watched them.

"Your taxi's here," Janie called, what felt like mere minutes later – the hour had passed quickly.

Tess said her goodbyes and walked outside. She stopped short.

"I'll be seeing you home." Dr. Love stood by his taxi.

"No, the other guy is supposed to come get me," Tess insisted.

"He's the one dat sent me. Had an airport ride on de other side of the island, won't get 'ere in time." Dr. Love opened the front door of his taxi. "Last ride of de night, we're all closing up for de holiday."

"I can wait for him," Tess said, feeling uncomfortable.

"He not coming back 'dis way." He remained standing by the door, waiting.

Tess remembered what her earlier taxi driver had said about not getting stranded. She did have a flight to catch in the morning, she reminded herself. Despite her misgivings, she moved to get in the back seat of the car.

"No, no, in de front. I've got stuff for my party in de back," Dr. Love said.

Reluctantly, Tess got in the front, staying as close to the door as she could. She pulled out her phone. Happy to see her service working, she immediately began texting.

"Tell Dr. Love why you're here." Tess rolled her eyes at his use of the third person.

"Visiting friends, diving. My boyfriend is meeting me back at the hotel," Tess lied.

"Why your man not with you?" The man was taking his sweet time getting back to her hotel and her nerves kicked up.

"He flew in today. He's waiting for me." She held up her phone so he could see the text messages. "I can't wait to see him, it's been ages. He's such a great guy." Tess chattered on during the interminably slow ride, praying that Dr. Love would stick to the main roads. When the hotel finally loomed into sight, Tess breathed a sigh of relief. She had a twenty-dollar bill already in hand as he pulled up in front and let the engine idle. Tess all but threw the money at him as she pulled the door handle.

It wouldn't open.

Turning to him in shock, she screeched as he launched himself at her, pinning her arms to her side and shoving his slimy tongue into her mouth. A rush of adrenalin shot through Tess, and she surged forward, knocking her forehead against his, biting down on his tongue.

"Bitch," Dr. Love seethed, still holding her down as she struggled.

Tess lost it, wrenching one arm free and connecting her elbow with his chin. She released a blood-curdling scream. His hands fell from her to grab his face and she turned, scrambling with the lock on the door. Tumbling out of the car, Tess shouted at the bellman racing down the sidewalk of the hotel, "He assaulted me!"

The bellman reached her as the taxi squealed away, taillights fading into the night.

"Are you okay? What can I do?"

"He tried to…" Tess gasped, spitting the taste of him from her mouth, and wiping the back of her palm across her lips. "I need to file a report."

"With the police?" The bellman raised an eyebrow at her. She could see the disbelief on his face. As much as she hated it, Tess knew that the police would do nothing about an assault claim. It was just how it was. A small island, everyone knew someone in the police force, or somebody's cousin was the judge. If she wasn't a local, she wouldn't get much help.

"Just with your security team," she said, resigned and still shaking. "Don't let anyone hire that taxi."

The bellman nodded, looking relieved. He stayed with her while she made the report, and then walked her to her room.

"Do you need anything?" the bellman asked, and Tess just shook her head. She cringed away as he reached out and patted her arm. "I'm sorry this happened to you."

"Yeah, me too," Tess bit out.

CHAPTER FORTY-SEVEN

Tess arrived at the local airport the next day in a particularly sour mood. Being reminded of her own vulnerability was an experience she didn't wish to repeat anytime soon. However, she was traveling alone, and it had been a harsh wake-up call to the reality of what could happen if she wasn't more careful. All night, she'd lain awake wondering why she'd gotten in the damn taxi with him. She could have sucked it up and gone back to the boat with her friends. Or called his bluff and waited on the other taxi driver. But a man had told her what to do, and she'd followed, not trusting her own judgment in the matter.

What if Vicki was right? What if she was too reckless? What if the life she wanted to have only led her to harm? She felt so alone now. If she had gotten into real trouble, would her sister have helped her? If Tess had swallowed her pride and called, would Vicki refuse to answer?

She realized she was the victim in the matter and that a taxi driver should do his job and just drive her home, but the signs had been there and she'd chosen to ignore them. When had it become so hard for her to listen to her own voice? Her internal monologue was on point if she'd only have enough faith in herself to listen.

Tess stared out the window of the small plane on the short flight over to Cat Island, the sun reflecting on the blue of the ocean below piercing her eyes, until the plane bounced down the runway. A guy about her age, camera gear on his lap, turned and raised an eyebrow at Tess.

"It's the landings in these little planes that always get me."

"It's usually worth the ride though," Tess said, and laughed at him. "Shark diving?"

"Correct. Not much else on this island except for fishing."

"I bet we're sharing a taxi then," Tess said, as they walked off the plane onto a runway that housed a single small hut and three waiting vans.

"That we are. The hotel's on the other side of the island. Only a thousand people live here." The man was lugging his dive gear toward a van where a woman held a sign with their names on it.

"Should be a fun week." Tess smiled at the woman, unaccountably glad to see a female taxi driver.

"Miss Tess?" The woman smiled. "The hotel is fully booked, but we have you in a villa on the beach for the first four nights. You might want to stop and get some food though, as you won't have a car and it be a long walk to the hotel from the villa."

Tess nodded her thanks. "Is there a store on the way?"

"Only the two markets on island, miss."

"Let's stop at one." Tess turned to the guy. "If you don't mind…?"

"Taylor, and no, I don't mind."

They chatted easily on the drive to the villa, Tess stocking up on food and drink en route. The taxi driver informed her that two other women would be joining her – which, after her experience last night, was a relief. She wasn't sure she was cut out to stay alone in a villa on an all-but-deserted island. Being around people would be good for her this trip.

The driver turned the taxi off the paved road, and bumped her way down a barely discernable dirt trail, the brush scratching against the car. Finally, after what felt like quite a long distance, as most roads do when you don't know where you're going, a house loomed into view, perched on a small cliff overlooking the ocean.

"Dang, nice digs," Taylor said, and Tess nodded at him.

"A bit remote, but you can't beat the view," Tess said as the taxi driver got out to walk over and open the door.

"The other ladies should be joining you soon."

"I'll help with your bags," Taylor said, pulling her gear inside while Tess got the groceries.

"Is there wifi? Or a phone? Anything?" Tess asked, her nerves kicking up after her experience last night.

"Yeah, yeah, right there. All in the book." The woman waved to the table where a house book lay. "The tour company will call you shortly to discuss the dives in the morning."

"You okay out here?" Taylor asked as he climbed back into the car.

"I think so," Tess said, relieved to see her cell phone had a single bar of service. "Hopefully, the others will get here soon."

"Hotel's up the road about a thirty-minute walk if you need anything," the driver called as they pulled out.

Tess watched as the taxi disappeared down the lane, the bush swallowing it.

She took a deep breath. Surveying the villa, she saw it was

mainly a large kitchen and living area with three bedrooms tacked on. She left her bags in the common living space, figuring it would be rude to pick a bedroom before the other two women arrived. She slid the glass door open to stand on the wide deck that hugged the house.

There was a reason this house was in the middle of nowhere, Tess realized, and felt her heart soar. Perched above a long sand beach, there was nothing but sea, sky, and land for miles. Not another house to be seen, not a boat on the horizon, not a single person walking the beach. It was a place to tune out the outside world, to lose yourself for a bit. Tess was more than ready to embrace that.

A car door slammed and Tess jolted, shaking herself from her reverie. She peeked around the house to see a man getting out of the front seat of a van. Her heart slammed in her chest, and she darted inside. Looking wildly around for a weapon, she pulled a butcher knife from the block. She slid it into the waistband of her shorts as he rounded the house and climbed the deck.

"Hello!"

"Hi," Tess said, standing in the doorway and not moving backward into the house.

"You here on your own?" the man asked.

Tess cocked her head at him. "What can I do for you?" she said, not answering his question. Her hand hovered near her waistband.

"I bring the fruit." He gestured to his van. "How many people you have staying?"

"Three of us."

"I'm the local pastor. But I'm also the fruit man. Come, come, I sell you some fruit," the man said, a wide smile breaking out on his face.

Tess felt her adrenaline ease back a bit. Following him to

the van at a distance, she found crates of fruit piled in the back.

"Ah, I see. You do deliveries," Tess said, her tension easing a bit more.

"Yes. We heard you was out here, so I bring the fruit," he said proudly.

"That's nice of you. Um, I will definitely take some limes, the watermelon there, and some oranges. Thank you." Tess gave him the money quickly, wanting him to be on his way. Once he was, she returned inside, her arms full, and walked around the house, checking every door and window to make sure it was locked. Placing the knife on a cutting board beside her, she put the fruit in a bowl she found in the cupboard, and sat down at the kitchen counter to wait. While the pastor had been nice, he'd said one thing that had made her nervous.

We heard you was out here.

It disconcerted her, the ease of the island gossip chain. She remembered how quickly it worked from her summer job years before.

She heard the sound of another vehicle approaching, and jumped up. She watched through the window as another car pulled to a stop in the yard. Two women got out and began unloading their luggage. Relieved beyond what she'd even been willing to admit to herself, Tess went out to greet her roommates.

CHAPTER FORTY-EIGHT

It turned out that Stella and Natalie, the two women joining her, were highly-regarded underwater photographers. Tess watched in awe as they unpacked their gear, their cameras taking up the wide berth of both the kitchen counter and the table across the room.

"Wow, that's some major gear you've got there," Tess said, wandering over to look at the different lights and lenses.

"Try lifting it," Natalie grumbled, her curls wild around her head. "It's helped me define my arm muscles, that's for sure."

"Do you have any idea what you're in for today?" Stella asked, as she put her camera together.

"Shark diving?"

"Not just any shark diving. These bad boys are the big guys. We'll be about two hours from shore, hovering in the deep blue water where you can't see the bottom, and these are the sharks that pick off shipwreck survivors. We're lucky to see them, to be honest. They're amazing."

Nerves flooded low in Tess's stomach.

"You don't have a big rig, either." Natalie nodded at Tess's small hand-held camera.

"What does that have to do with it?"

"These sharks are not nervous animals. They're intensely curious, and they're going to see if they can bully you. Usually, if you have a big rig like ours" – Natalie indicated her massive camera – "you kind of just push it into their face and they'll move on, knowing you won't let them bully you."

"But I don't have a big rig." Tess crossed her arms over her chest.

Stella shrugged. "Just put your arm out then. Let them know you're in charge."

Sure, like it's that easy, Tess thought.

THE BOAT RIDE out to their dive site in the middle of the ocean took almost two hours, which was more than enough time for Tess to question her choices in life. Maybe it was foolish to go on this dive, to even come on this trip alone. Her stomach bounced about the entire ride. She curled up alone at the front of the boat, her eyes on the horizon, and forced herself to breathe slowly.

She hadn't told Aiden about the assault when he'd checked in with her this morning, not wanting to worry him. Plus, she still had some lingering embarrassment over her choice to get in the car with a man who creeped her out. She wasn't ready to hear a lecture. Anything he would say to her, she'd already said herself. Besides that, he'd seemed a bit out of sorts over Messenger today.

I don't like it here, he'd begun.

Why not? I thought you were still loving the diving.

I do, the diving is beautiful. It's the only time I'm somewhat happy.

Are the cities not beautiful?

I'm just... annoyed with it all, I guess. Nothing on land is fun for me. This isn't how I thought it would be. I'm...frustrated.

Why? What's going on?

I thought I wanted to travel this way. It's how I've always traveled.

And?

I don't think I want this anymore. I don't like living out of a backpack, or having to pack up and leave a hostel every morning. It's not as exciting as it once was. Or maybe it's just because I'm not with you.

Well, of course life is better when I'm around! Haha, but in all seriousness, it sounds like you are learning a few things about yourself.

I miss my bookshelf. I know that's weird, but I miss having a place for my stuff. I think I've settled down a bit.

There's nothing wrong with that; you can settle and still travel.

I miss you, Tess. I think about you constantly. I wish you were here with me; there's so much I want to show you. Please don't give up on me.

I miss you too, Aiden. I'd be lying if I said that I didn't. I can't talk any longer now, I have to go out on my shark dives.

Please, promise me to dive safe? Buddy up with someone smart, not someone who talks too much or brags a lot – they usually know the least.

I will, Aiden. Chat later.

It wasn't the first time Aiden had expressed some discontent with his travels, but he'd seemed particularly grumpy this morning and she wondered what was going on with him. It was tiring to travel out of a backpack – she'd done it through Australia and New Zealand for six months or so, and she knew how it could get to miss the comforts of home.

The captain slowed the boat, and Tess's head popped up, realizing that the divers were gearing up.

"Pool's open!" the instructor called, and everyone laughed, a nervous thrill of excitement shooting through the group as they all leaned over the side of the boat to see the first of the fins approaching.

"You just jump right in with them, huh?" Tess whispered to Natalie.

"Yup, you're going to love it. Promise. Just remember – don't let them bully you."

Tess gulped as she clipped her BCD on and put her regulator in her mouth. She glanced at the captain for the go-ahead. When it was her turn, she held onto her mask and reg, and jumped into the deep blue abyss, sinking softly in a cloud of bubbles, her heart in her throat.

There were twelve sharks, at least, Tess realized, her adrenaline spiking as she kicked over to where the other divers were. Now, she could see why the big camera rigs came in handy, for these oceanic white-tip sharks were no shy wallflowers. Tess jolted as one brushed right against her shoulder, surprising her from behind, his sheer size heart-stopping. Before she had a chance to react, another one brushed her left shoulder, nudging her deeper in the water. Tess's eyes widened as a third came directly at her from the front, wanting to join the fun.

Don't let them bully you.

Tess took a deep breath, calming her heart. She knew they could sense her anxiety. When the next one passed close, Tess confidently held her hand out, nudging it away when it bumped its head against her. The next one tried and Tess turned, her arm straight, and let the shark know that she wasn't going to be picked on.

No more would she let others in her life bully her, Tess

realized. She relaxed, tears springing to her eyes as she took in the haunting beauty of the sharks. They circled in the water, the grace with which they moved and their strength so proudly displayed. Maybe the people in her life hadn't necessarily bullied her, but they'd spoken over her, the loudest voice winning, until Tess had held her hand up.

Stop, Tess whispered into her regulator, her hand up as another shark approached, eyeing her up and then dismissing her as it moved on.

I am the captain of my ship, master of my destiny... I'm just me, flawed and awesome as I am. I'm more than enough on my own and I can trust myself to guide my life in the direction I want.

The power washed over her, energizing her, as Tess finally accepted what she'd been working toward all year. She was more than enough, just as she was, and life could both be beautiful and awful at the same time. There was no way to numb herself from pain, nor did she need to. Pain was a way of indicating to her the areas she needed to learn from or fix in her life. But it was her life to live, and no matter what the future would hold, Tess realized she had the power to make herself happy, just by being wonderful and weird Tess.

Blinking the tears from her eyes, Tess hovered in the water, watching as the ocean gifted her a lesson she needed to learn. When another shark drew near, swimming lazily toward her, Tess flashed back to her bull shark dive with Aiden.

Holding out her hands, she formed a heart, sending her love to the shark, to Aiden, and to all those in her life who had taught her lessons that had hurt to learn, but formed her into the woman she was today.

CHAPTER FORTY-NINE

They stayed up late that night, going over images of the sharks, laughing over the beauty of what they'd seen, swapping stories about life. Tess, after a glass of wine, confided her story about Aiden and was surprised to find both of her roommates were hopeful they would end up together.

"You never know… these things work in their own time," Stella said, patting her shoulder as she went in to sleep.

"You can't rush love," Natalie agreed, leaving Tess to sit on the deck, alone, contemplating the night sky. The beach villa at night was dark like Tess had rarely seen in her life. There were no ambient city lights, not even the light of another house, for miles. Leaning back in her lounge chair, she relaxed as the night sky unfolded above her, the stars shining like crystals flung on a bed of inky velvet. She let her mind drift, content with her day, happy to know she could handle what life would bring, even if it was a gorgeous shark swimming at her face. When her phone buzzed, she smiled.

How was diving?

Beautiful, really. I'm in awe of these sharks. I swear it was a life-changing moment for me.

That's great! I had a life-changing moment today, too.

Why? What happened? Are you okay?

Oh, I'm more than okay, I'm great. I'm leaving, Tess.

Wait, what?

I don't want to be without you anymore. I'm leaving the trip and coming to you.

Excuse me? Are YOU SERIOUS?

I wish I could call you right now, but internet is complete shite. I was reading a Steinbeck book and there was something about a line in it that made me realize that home is with you. I'm seeing all this amazing stuff and I can't get you out of my head. You're just constantly there and I realized that I don't want to be without you anymore. It doesn't matter where we go or what we do, it just matters that we are together. I want to be with you, start a life with you. Home is with you, Tess.

But... what about your travel buddy? I thought you couldn't just up and leave her?

I told her I'm leaving, but that I would stay until she has a job lined up. She submitted some applications today and should hear back tomorrow. I just want to make sure I don't dump her here all alone. Once that's sorted, I'll figure out a way back to you.

Holy shit, Aiden, I wish I could talk to you right now. My heart feels like it is exploding in my chest. I can't believe you're leaving your trip – you have so many more months planned.

None of that matters. The only thing that matters is that I don't lose you. I'm scared if I continue on this trip that you'll give up on me completely. I don't care about missing out on the rest of my travels here. I'll bring you back with me and we'll go explore the places I missed. I just can't keep going on without you, Tess.

I can't believe this is happening.

I'll be on a plane to see you soon, Tess, I promise.

. . .

A TEAR DRIPPED down her cheek and splattered on her phone, the glow the only light in the darkness. She knew her future was forever changed with a single message. Aiden had rocked her world. She took a shaky breath, her insides tingling. She suddenly felt as though she'd just sucked down eight power drinks. Tess wanted to race across the sand, or dive into the water, or something – anything. Instead, she let out a delighted squeak, knowing her roomies were sleeping, and tilted her head back to laugh at the night sky.

But – did she want this? It was a huge step to take, Tess realized, feeling a momentary frisson of panic burst through her happiness. This man was changing the course of his life to be with her. She had no idea what the future held other than that it would be defined by her relationship with Aiden and the decisions they made together. Was she ready for that? It seemed like she'd finally started getting comfortable out on her own again, finding her own happiness – filling her own well, so to speak. Would it be wise to base her future decisions on a man?

Tess checked in with her gut. Instinctively, she wanted to be with Aiden, whatever that future would look like. It felt different to her than it had with Gabe. So much of her marriage had been bowing to what Gabe wanted, but Tess knew she wouldn't have to do that with Aiden. They could build a future based on what they both wanted, and Tess wouldn't be forced to dim her light for anyone.

So this is what it felt like, she realized, to be put first. She'd been so certain they couldn't ultimately be together, that their lives were leading them toward separate paths. But, maybe, just maybe – she'd get her happy ending after all.

"IRELAND?"

"I'm sorry, lass, I just can't get to Colorado quickly enough from where I am," Aiden said, his voice sounding tinny on the phone two days later. "I'm quite literally taking train, plane, and automobile out of here, and even at that it'll be several days before I get as far as Scotland. I can see my family, and drop some things off before I come to you. But that feels too long. So maybe you'd like to meet me halfway? I thought of Ireland because I know you're researching and writing an Irish romance novel right now. What do you say? Want to have another holiday?"

Tess laughed, leaning back against the headboard of her bed, where her suitcases from the Bahamas still sat on the floor. In the last year, she'd traveled more than she had in her whole life. Being single, she'd had that freedom. But could she have that and Aiden, too? Live a constant adventure where they'd pick up and go when they got the whim?

"I...I'd have to check flights and talk to my dogsitters. How soon are you thinking? I did see that Aer Lingus was having a flight sale." Tess wondered again if she was crazy. Red cocked his head at her, and she wiggled her fingers at him so he inched his way over on his belly to lick her fingers.

"I'd say within a few weeks? The sooner the better. I'm craving you," Aiden's voice had grown husky, and she ached for him to be near.

"Oh god, Aiden. Okay, then what? Will you come back to Colorado with me?"

"I'd like to. We'll have to figure that out, hopefully when I have a better connection. Will you look into flights and let me know? I'll call once I get off these outer islands and get to Europe."

"Sounds good, travel safe," Tess said, biting back the words she wanted to say to him.

———————

"In the event of emergency, oxygen masks will drop from the ceiling. Secure yours first, before attending to anyone else who needs you."

Tess tuned back into where the flight attendant went through the emergency instructions for her flight to Ireland. Wasn't that the truth of it, though? She had to take care of herself first before she could take care of others. Realizing that she was in charge of her own happiness – hell, her own *life* – had been an incredible lesson to learn this past year. It had cost her some relationships, and that would always hurt, but gaining her own voice had been priceless. She wondered how many other people lived their lives just going through the motions, doing what they thought they were supposed to do, who would never get the memo that they could just make their own choices. Such a novel idea, and yet still so hard to learn.

Aiden had learned it early on, Tess realized, and maybe that was part of his appeal. He would never silence her. Instead, he'd embrace the person she was, and let her choose her own path – hopefully, a path with them together. It was an invaluable trait in a partner, and Tess couldn't wait to start their life together. In only six more hours…

"You really want to come live with me in Colorado?" Tess had asked, once Aiden made it to a better phone connection.

"Well, I only have a three-month tourist visa. We'll have to decide what to do from there. Are you committed to living in the States?"

"I…uh, I honestly have no idea," Tess laughed, having

never really given living outside the States much thought, let alone moving again with a new boyfriend. But...what if? The idea had taken root and it had been all she'd thought about for days. Aside from seeing Aiden again, that is.

Of course, she didn't sleep a wink. Tess stared at her tired and puffy eyes in the tiny mirror and weird lighting of the small airline bathroom. It was the best she could do, and she patted some concealer under her eyes before returning to her seat and buckling in for landing. A grey cloud cover greeted her, which was normal for Ireland, and she watched as the runway loomed below, the first light of the morning sun streaming across the green hills behind the airport.

Five o'clock in the morning had been a hell of a time to land, one which Aiden had grumbled about. She'd told him to just stay at the hotel and she would come wake him up, but he'd refused. He'd flown into Ireland the night before and was meeting her at the airport.

Time seemed to slow, as though she was trudging through molasses, as Tess impatiently collected her luggage and made it through customs. She'd waited months for this. The past three weeks had consisted of long hours of video-chatting with Aiden while he was home in Scotland, waiting for her. They talked about everything and nothing at all, and it was perfect. Now, their moment to be together had finally arrived. Nerves danced through her stomach as she approached the exit. Striding through the doors, she scanned the waiting faces until her gaze found dancing blue eyes. A smile broke across her face, and she rushed through the crowd, dragging her suitcase before she stopped, suddenly feeling shy in front of him.

"Hi," Aiden said, smiling down at her.

"Hi," Tess said, beaming. There were a million things she wanted to say, but she felt incredibly awkward with all the people milling around them. Leaning up, she wrapped her arms around him, sinking into the sweetest of kisses, loving the feel of him in her arms once more.

"Come on, let's get out of here," Aiden said, grabbing her luggage and hurrying her toward the door. Now that they were with each other again, they wasted no time in getting to the one place they wanted to be – alone together.

Once at the hotel, Aiden all but pushed her up the stairs. Tess found herself giggling, she was so delighted to be here with him. Opening the door, he swept her inside, and Tess stopped, gasping.

He'd covered the room in rose petals, and there were flameless candles lit all over the room, champagne chilling in a bucket, and a wrapped present on the table. Leading her over to the bed, Aiden sat her down and took her hands in his.

"Tess… I wanted to wait to say this in person, because it matters more this way." His hands warm on hers, her body tingled at his nearness. "I love you, Tess. I love you so much and I want a life with you – wherever that may be. Being without you was awful. I'm sorry that I left you, I'm sorry that I didn't know what I really wanted. But it's you, Tess. I'm so lucky to have met you. I've waited my whole life for you."

Tess closed her eyes for a moment, letting warmth flood through her at his words, and paused for a moment to check in with her gut – something she'd promised herself she would always do moving forward. Opening her eyes, she smiled at Aiden.

"I love you, too, Aiden. You *are* lucky to have me, and I'll be sure to remind you of that every day."

EPILOGUE

"Grab the cooler, will you?" Tess called over her shoulder as she followed Red and Ringo down to the beach, still pinching herself that they were here.

After Ireland, Aiden had joined her back in Colorado where they'd had a serious talk about what they wanted out of life. The biggest issue had been that Colorado was land-locked, and they both craved being near the ocean. After weeks of discussion, they'd finally decided to move out of the United States to tiny Flamingo Island, renowned worldwide for its diving – and most importantly, they'd been able to get the dogs there safely.

Vicki no longer took her calls, but Tess emailed her a long letter, explaining her decision and inviting her to call or visit whenever she wanted. She'd yet to hear back from her. It didn't stop her from thinking about Vicki daily, and hoping some day they'd resolve their issues. It stung, as she suspected it would for a long time, but maybe they were better off without each other. Tess's life might seem impulsive or reckless to those watching from the outside, but she knew she needed to follow her own happiness. Ultimately, Tess's career was thriving, her dogs were healthy, and she was deeply in love with someone who treated her the way she had finally realized she'd deserved. Moving to a tropical paradise was just icing on the cake.

Settling into their new routine and figuring out life on a new island, Tess still found herself in awe of the direction her life had taken. She remembered thinking about how people could actually live this life – back when she'd visited Aiden in Cozumel – and now here she was doing the same. It was exciting and challenging all in the same breath. A new country to explore, a different language to learn, and new customs to take part in. Together, they were tackling the challenges of building a new life and a new relationship together. As the ocean waves crashed nearby, Tess marveled at the perfect place she'd landed. Well, commanded from the universe, if Elizabeth had a say in it.

"Beer?"

Aiden handed Tess an icy beer, and she watched as he whistled to the dogs, bringing out a ball to toss for a delighted Ringo.

Aiden had been everything she'd wanted in a man, and when Elizabeth had pulled up the list she'd forced Tess to make a year ago – sitting in front of Aiden's dive shop – she'd been shocked to realize that Elizabeth had been right all along. Ask for what you want, Tess thought, as her phone rang in her pocket.

"Hey, Daniel!" Tess said, smiling as Ringo raced after the ball that bounced wildly across the sand.

"What are you doing right now? It's pouring rain here and supposed to freeze overnight. Don't even tell me, I bet you're at the beach."

"Um, well, if you don't want me to tell you…" Tess laughed.

"You are one lucky bitch."

It wasn't luck that had delivered her to this point, but Tess's own hard-won choices. Still, she smiled.

"That's Ms. Bitch to you."

AFTERWORD

AUTHOR'S NOTE

This was a tricky book for me to write, as I imagine it would be for many of my readers to read. Going through a divorce is traumatic. Losing family members is traumatic. Starting over when you feel like your ship is rudderless is disconcerting and deeply uncomfortable. I just want to thank you all for coming on this journey with me, and I hope that this book ultimately proved to be uplifting. For me, it was cathartic to write my way through many of the emotions that come from difficult life experiences such as Tess went through. While this isn't completely autobiographical, I can say this novel is *inspired* by my true story. I was always told that it's important to "write what you know." And, well, I know a lot about the pain of not feeling good enough, the sting of starting over, and the fear of taking risks. One thing I have learned, as Mae says in this novel, is to not let fear stop me from living *my* life on *my* terms.

So, to that, my friends, I say: "It's okay to be afraid, but go after it anyway."

A special thanks to Alan, for believing so wholeheartedly in me from the beginning. You've been my champion, my rock, and my partner through this rocky road of self-discovery and new beginnings. I can't wait for the best new beginning of all – becoming your wife!

To my friends: Jessica, Alissa, Carrie, Marla, Meghan, Kris-
tine, DeWaal, Tim, and Michelle – thank you, thank you,
thank you! You are my chosen family, my best friends, and
have held me up when I didn't always think I could keep
moving forward. I love you all!

To my author friends who have listened and helped me
through this process – Thank you! Libbie, Regina, Jayne, Lila,
Annabel, Alison, Melanie, Cynthia, Barbra, Deanna, Mindy,
Liz, Renee, and anyone else I've missed – you are the best
colleagues a girl could ask for.

To my family: You are missed. I've left a light on for you.

And last, but certainly not least, thanks to Briggs & Blue – the cutest and bestest dogs to ever dog. They have been the best snuggle buddies a girl could ask for.

To my beta-readers, thank you for your never-ending support, your attention-to-detail, and your amazing feedback. I appreciate you joining me on this crazy ride.

A note on shark-diving and respecting marine life – I am a huge advocate for shark protection as well as the overall protection of our oceans. Sharks have gotten an unnecessary bad reputation. Without sharks, we wouldn't have healthy and thriving oceans. It is an honor every time I am gifted with the chance to be around such magnificent creatures. Additionally, there are many ways to help our oceans thrive. As a certified coral restoration diver, I actively help to grow new coral for the reefs. You can donate to organizations that support the safety of our oceans. Without them, we won't have a healthy planet earth. No blue = no green.

https://www.coralrestoration.org/
https://oceanconservancy.org/
https://seashepherd.org/

Please consider leaving a review online. It means a lot to me and helps other readers to take a chance on my books.

You can sign up to my mailing list for information on new releases, free books, and fun giveaways here
http://eepurl.com/1LAiz
or through my website
www.triciaomalley.com

THE MYSTIC COVE SERIES

ALSO BY TRICIA O'MALLEY

Wild Irish Roots (Novella, Prequel)

Wild Irish Heart

Wild Irish Eyes

Wild Irish Soul

Wild Irish Rebel

Wild Irish Roots: Margaret & Sean

Wild Irish Witch

Wild Irish Grace

Wild Irish Dreamer

"I have read thousands of books and a fair percentage have been romances. Until I read Wild Irish Heart, I never had a book actually make me believe in love."- Amazon Review

Available as an e-book, paperback or audiobook!

https://www.triciaomalley.com/home-2

THE ISLE OF DESTINY SERIES

ALSO BY TRICIA O'MALLEY

Stone Song

Sword Song

Spear Song

Sphere Song

"Love this series. I will read this multiple times. Keeps you on the edge of your seat. It has action, excitement and romance all in one series."- Amazon Review

Available as an e-book, paperback or audiobook!

https://www.triciaomalley.com/home-3

THE SIREN ISLAND SERIES

ALSO BY TRICIA O'MALLEY

Good Girl

Up to No Good

A Good Chance

Good Moon Rising

"Love her books and was excited for a totally new and different one! Once again, she did NOT disappoint! Magical in multiple ways and on multiple levels. Her writing style, while similar to that of Nora Roberts, kicks it up a notch!! I want to visit that island, stay in the B&B and meet the gals who run it! The characters are THAT real!!!" - Amazon Review

Available as an e-book, paperback or audiobook!

https://www.triciaomalley.com/the-siren-island-series

THE ALTHEA ROSE SERIES

ALSO BY TRICIA O'MALLEY

"Not my usual genre but couldn't resist the Florida Keys setting. I was hooked from the first page. A fun read with just the right amount of crazy! Will definitely follow this series."- Amazon Review

Available as an e-book, paperback or audiobook!

https://www.triciaomalley.com/home-4

CONTACT DETAILS

As always, you can reach me at

info@triciaomalley.com

or feel free to visit my website at www.triciaomalley.com.